*Holding Out
for a Hero*

Holding Out for a Hero

HelenKay Dimon

KENSINGTON PUBLISHING CORP.
www.kensingtonbooks.com

BRAVA BOOKS are published by

Kensington Publishing Corp.
119 West 40th Street
New York, NY 10018

All Kensington titles, imprints, and distributed lines are available at special quantity discounts for bulk purchases for sales promotion, premiums, fund-raising, educational, or institutional use.

Special book excerpts or customized printings can also be created to fit specific needs. For details, write or phone the office of the Kensington Special Sales Manager: Kensington Publishing Corp., 119 West 40th Street, New York, NY 10018. Attn. Special Sales Department. Phone: 1-800-221-2647.

Brava and the B logo are Reg. U.S. Pat. & TM Off.

ISBN-13: 978-0-7582-2905-2
ISBN-10: 0-7582-2905-4

First Kensington Trade Paperback Printing: October 2009

10 9 8 7 6 5 4 3 2 1

Printed in the United States of America

*To Kate Duffy,
for her continued support,*

*and to my husband, James,
for making it all possible*

Chapter One

He sensed her before he saw her. The dangerous mix of high-end perfume and wealth gave her away. Josh Windsor knew some men found the combination attractive. He sniffed and smelled nothing but trouble.

Tucking his pen in his inside suit-jacket pocket, he crossed the marble courthouse hallway to meet Deana Armstrong before she materialized at his side. She would track him down anyway. Might as well take the offensive and be done with it.

"Ms. Armstrong." He nodded. "What brings you here?"

"To Honolulu?"

"To the fourth floor of the Circuit Court."

She took a step forward and put them less than two feet apart. "You."

Somehow he knew she would say that. "How'd you guess I was even on Oahu?"

"I flew over to Kauai and went to your office."

As if that was a perfectly normal thing to do. "Of course you did."

"I couldn't get near the Drug Enforcement Administration. Not even on the same floor."

"Government buildings are funny like that."

"I also checked your house while I was there."

"You . . ." Surely he heard that wrong. "Wait, what?"

"Your house."

Nope. Heard it just fine. He ignored her behavior before, wrote it off as annoying, and moved on. Not this time. "Care to explain?"

"Well, it's really a condo." She had the nerve to throw out an innocent, wide-eyed look.

To shut that down he leaned in, letting her feel the looming presence of every inch of his six feet. "You actually went to my place in Lihue?"

"Do you have another house?"

"Only one of us has a trust fund and owns multiple properties." Including a sprawling estate on one of the best beaches on Oahu. That person sure as hell wasn't him.

"What does my housing situation have to do with our conversation?" She waved her hand in front of her face. "Look, none of this matters."

"Yeah, it kind of does."

"Can we focus on the topic, please?"

Was she trying to annoy him? "Which is what?"

"I heard you were on some sort of leave from your position with the DEA—"

"Jesus, lady. Is there anything you don't know about my life?"

"—which is why I took the chance of catching you." Her voice increased in volume from cool to almost booming as she talked over him.

"Keep yelling like that and courthouse security will be all

over you in two seconds." Which, the more he thought about it, was not a bad way to get out of this conversation.

"My point is that your home address isn't exactly a secret."

"I guess not to people with detectives on their regular household payroll." When he fixed every other part of this life, Josh vowed to fix that as well. Make it so no matter how much money folks like her waved around, no one would find him unless he wanted to be found. And right now he didn't. "Did you at least water the plants while you were at the condo?"

She frowned.

He was impressed she managed to show any emotion.

"I didn't go in," she said. "That would have been inappropriate."

At last, a boundary. No sense to know when someone was flinging sarcasm right in her face, but a boundary. "Looks as if we agree on something."

Deana laced her fingers together in front of her. "I read in the newspaper that you were testifying here today as part of an old case, so I flew back home to Oahu and came downtown to find you."

Under different circumstances he might be flattered with a woman being interested enough to chase him around Hawaii, but he knew better than to get excited about this one. "So, you're stalking me now."

"Of course not."

"Harassing a federal officer is illegal." He nodded hello to the judge's clerk when she stuck her head out of an office. "Sorry. We'll keep it down out here."

Deana waited until the younger woman disappeared again before whispering. "You're overstating my actions a bit, don't you think?"

Oh, he had done a lot of thinking about Deana. The woman was a walking contradiction. Round face, high cheekbones, big green eyes and long near-black wavy hair that fell below her shoulders. Five-six and slender. An objectively beautiful woman. That part suited Josh just fine. The rest of her, not so much.

She possessed a demeanor chilly enough to freeze steel. Her serious affect and ever-present blank stare made her appear far older than the twenty-nine years he knew her to be. But that wasn't the oddest thing about her. Even now the woman hid most of her potentially impressive body under a pile of clothing. A long-sleeve navy blazer with a collar cut high enough to strangle. The only piece of skin exposed above her waist, other than her hands, was a thin slice of wrist . . . with a watch shiny enough to advertise incredible wealth.

Somehow Deana Armstrong lived her whole life in informal Hawaii and yet insisted on dressing as if it were winter at a convent in Nebraska. Few people wore full business suits in Hawaii except him and anyone else in a federal law enforcement position, most opting instead for a more casual look. Certainly no one without a job dressed anything other than casual. And the one thing Deana didn't do was work.

"Is this a good place?" she asked.

He glanced around the empty hallway leading back to a restricted corridor to the judge's private chambers. "Depends on what you want to use it for."

"Excuse me?"

He pointed to the back corner of the wall above the emergency exit and her head. "Security is watching."

"I don't care about that. I'm here because I've been trying to reach you." She rubbed her palms on her knee-length skirt.

He tried not to stare at the legs peeking out of all that buttoned-up stuffiness. "And?"

"You haven't called me back."

Clearly the woman didn't tune into not-so-subtle hints. "True."

"Are you available now?"

If she asked him two days from now the answer definitely would be no. He planned to be free of all ties by then, specifically those related to his work at the DEA. No reason not to get an early start on that. "No."

"In a few hours or tomorrow?"

"Still no."

She crossed her arms over her middle. "If I didn't know better I'd say you were ignoring me."

He thought about lifting his fists toward the ceiling in victory. "We're finally understanding each other."

Chapter Two

Deana was two seconds away from strangling him. She had hoped Josh would be reasonable. At least give her a chance to explain. Instead, he hid behind a heaping pile of attitude.

If she hadn't needed his help she would have shoveled a load or two right back on top of him. But that wasn't her style. Not in public anyway. She had a persona, a role, and she would play it even while her insides burned.

Then there was the problem with their past run-ins. Thanks to her decisions more than two years ago, she had to take hesitating steps here. Hiring every expensive lawyer she could find to fight Josh Windsor and question his credibility had seemed like a good idea at the time. Now her actions proved to be a liability.

Back then she had made sure to know about every aspect of Josh's life, down to his family history and bank account balance. With his rawness and "knows his way around a bedroom" style, she figured disgruntled men and women would line up to turn on him. That didn't happen. Seemed Josh walked all over the line but rarely crossed it to the point where someone with standing in the community had any information that could help her.

Their adversarial relationship then and her island hopping to Kauai and back to find him now made the entire courthouse scene all the more frustrating. She had better things to do than hunt down an angry man and try to talk some sense into him.

"I need your help." Getting those words out almost killed her.

"With?"

"Ryan."

Josh started shaking his head before she got to the second syllable of her nephew's name. "No way."

Not an unexpected reaction but still not helpful. "Listen to me."

"Your nephew is in jail, Ms. Armstrong."

The conversation had seemed much easier when she practiced it in her bathroom mirror. "That's true."

"He's not getting out."

She closed her eyes on a wave of paralyzing sadness. The type that kept her locked in her house curled up on a couch some days. "I am well aware of Ryan's current residence and the reason for it, thank you."

"Then you also know I'm not a defense attorney."

When Josh took a few steps back she thought he was signaling the end of their conversation and cutting out. Instead, he leaned against the wall on the opposite side of the hallway. Probably hoping to put as much space between them as possible in the six-foot-wide area.

The distance allowed her to take a quick look at her opponent. This was not the first time she indulged in a peek since meeting Josh years before. Wide shoulders and all, she hated him then. She needed him now. That made all the difference.

And whether he wanted to admit it or not, they could help each other. She read the papers, heard all about Josh's legal issues. His latest actions on the job had angered the higher-ups at the DEA and landed him in the middle of a huge mess. For a guy who lived his life as if he had nothing to lose, he was about to lose something big.

Well, she had something to offer as an alternative. He needed to fill the hours. She needed a miracle. It was as perfect as their strange relationship would ever get.

"I don't need more attorneys. Ryan has enough legal representation for four people right now." And she had the outrageous legal bills at home on her desk to prove it. All that money and still a guilty verdict. Kind of killed the theory about how juries could be swayed with purchased experts. Certainly not how it worked in the Hawaii courts from her experience.

"You're not asking me to chip in for Ryan's expenses, are you?" he asked.

"Of course not."

" 'Cause you don't strike me as a lady who needs a loan." Josh's eyes wandered with his comment.

She refused to fidget under his visual tour up and down her body because she knew his plan. He wanted to throw her off stride. Make her skittish. She could feel his eyes on her down to her shoes, and she wasn't going to flinch.

"Money is not the issue," she said in her iciest voice.

"I never could figure out why you were bothering to put all of this effort into saving a kid who is determined not to be saved."

The sharp edge of the jab slid off her midsection. "I'm an aunt who cares about her nephew."

"You know something?" Josh cocked his head to the side as the corner of his mouth tugged upward. "I just figured out what it is about you that doesn't fit."

"Pardon me?"

He pointed at her forehead. "The way you talk. It's what throws off this whole picture."

A wave of confused dizziness hit her. "I have no idea—"

"There's emotion in your voice, well, sort of, but your body never moves." He nodded his head as if warming to the subject. "Makes me wonder if there's any feeling inside there anywhere. I'm betting no."

The shaking moving through her turned to fury. Ten more seconds of his garbage and he'd be feeling her hand smack across his face. "You don't need to worry about my body."

His eyebrows rose. "If you say so."

"I need your detective skills."

The lazy grin vanished as his back snapped straight again. "No way."

"What kind of response is that for a grown man?"

"The only one you're going to get."

"Could you at least try to be civil?"

"You killed that possibility a long time ago, lady."

Okay, she deserved that. He refused to understand her position, but she couldn't exactly blame him for the anger. "I'm not asking for me; I'm asking for Ryan."

"You pay a whole team of professionals to poke around in other people's private lives for you. Get some of them to do your work. You don't need me."

Lot of good all that money did so far. "I actually do."

"Well, that's a damn shame, since I already have a job."

Time for a reality check. "Word is that might not be true soon."

"Visiting my office again, Ms. Armstrong?"

As she watched, he turned into a serious, uncompromising professional. His disdain lapped against her. He didn't say the exact words, but he didn't have to. His actions spoke for him. He hated her.

Gone was the laid-back surfer-dude laziness that hovered around him making the business suit seem all the more out of place. Blond, blue-eyed, with a scruff around his mouth and chin, he could play the lead role in any woman's bad-boy fantasies. But behind those rough good looks lurked a man serious and in charge, tense and ready for battle.

Well, he wasn't the only one in the room fighting off a deep case of dislike. He needed to know she was not one of his frequent empty-headed bedmates. She could match his intellect and anger anytime, anywhere.

"Most of the information I need about you and your current predicament is in the newspaper," she said.

"Most?"

She shrugged, letting him know he wasn't the only one who could tweak a temper.

"More snooping, Ms. Armstrong?"

"I call it investigating."

"Well, just so you know." His back came off the wall, slow and in command. "Sneaking around in my personnel file isn't the way to make me listen to you."

"Then let's try this." She reached into her purse and grabbed her checkbook. "I want to hire you."

"Don't."

She clicked the end of her pen. "Some money should get us started."

His hand shot out and grabbed her wrist before she could start writing. "Trying to buy me off isn't going to get you where you want to be."

When she dropped her hand, he let go as if touching her one more second repulsed him.

"That's not what I was doing." It was, but she figured pointing that out would only make him less receptive to her plan to help Ryan.

"Sure felt like it."

She skipped the crap and went right to her point. "Ryan didn't do it."

"Look, Ms. Armstrong. I get that this is a family issue."

She refused to blubber or beg. She'd cried enough for ten lifetimes since the whole mess started. "Call me Deana."

"We're not friends or colleagues, so Ms. Armstrong is fine." Josh took his pen out of his pocket and tapped it against his open palm. "And you may as well know I don't really care what happens to Ryan from here on."

She refused to believe Josh would be satisfied to let an innocent kid rot in prison. "You can't really mean that."

"I do. Trust me on this."

"You think it's okay to lock him away?"

"He had a trial."

"Well, I don't have the luxury of forgetting Ryan, since I'm all he has at the moment."

"I'm sorry about your brother and his wife." Josh's voice softened along with his bright aqua eyes.

She could not let her mind go there. Not now. She had to keep her focus directly on Ryan. It was either that or lose her control, and that was the one thing she could not afford to do in front of Josh. "Then help me."

"I can't."

"You mean 'won't.' " Despite her attempts to stay calm her voice increased in volume as his decreased.

"We can use whichever word you prefer."

"Why not?"

"Simple."

"I have to tell you that I've found nothing simple in dealing with you so far." And she wasn't kidding about that.

"Then try this: I'm out of the rescuing business."

"That's ridiculous."

"It's a fact."

This was one brick wall she might not be able to work around. "I hardly believe you can turn it on and off like that."

"I didn't think so, either." He shrugged. "What a surprise."

"What is that supposed to mean?"

"Basically? Find another hero, because I'm done playing the role."

Chapter Three

Two days later, Josh officially retired from the DEA. Sure, he hadn't actually told anyone that little fact yet, but leaving today's administrative hearing during the middle of testimony probably sent a message of sorts. He figured someone would get the idea when he failed to show up for the afternoon session.

"You know you're welcome here anytime." Derek Travers walked out onto the porch of his one-story fixer-upper wearing swim trunks and holding a beer in each hand.

Josh reached for a bottle without taking his eyes off the ocean in front of him. Settling back into the lounge chair, he surveyed the rocky coastline of Waimanalo. The few newer houses right on the water came with huge price tags, but the rest of this part of Oahu consisted mostly of hardworking locals who had lived there forever. Solid folks without fancy jobs, living tucked away in a quiet piece of paradise.

Most families bought long before the prices bounced past reasonable or they'd be forced to live in shacks. The downside for many was that the area lacked the tourist trade, hotels, and shopping that made Honolulu and the other side of Oahu so popular. That also qualified as Waimanalo's greatest asset in Josh's eyes.

The open land and vast quiet reminded him more of Kauai, the Hawaiian island where he lived in a condo a couple miles away from Kane Travers, Derek's uncle and Josh's best friend. Kane also happened to be the chief of police on Kauai and a character witness of sorts at Josh's hearing today. That meant Kane would pop up sooner or later, likely pissed off about the early departure from the rigged hearing.

"So"—Derek took a long drink—"why are you here again?"

"Now that I'm out of that suit my goal is to steal your liquor."

"As long as you replenish the supply, that's fine."

"Understood."

"My real question had to do with you being here instead of downtown." Derek put his bare feet up on a white paint-chipped railing in front of him and rocked back on two chair legs.

"You trying to ruin my beer?" Josh took another swig, letting the ice-cold liquid rush down the back of his throat.

"You're at my house in the middle of the day, wearing shorts and a T-shirt. Since you actually live and work elsewhere, and generally wear a suit Monday through Friday, which makes the reality of you being a government agent pretty obvious, by the way—"

"Is this a geography lesson or a fashion critique?"

Derek leaned his head back against the chair. "My only point—"

"You have one?"

"—is that you're supposed to be somewhere else right now."

"You're not making me feel welcome."

Now there was a lie. Derek was twenty-three and a graduate-school research assistant working at a place called the Oceanic Institute, which was right down the road. Josh didn't understand the finer points of this kid's job, but he knew that despite Derek's outward calm he possessed a genius-level IQ.

They'd known each other for years. Kane raised Derek. Since Josh spent most of his free time with Kane, or did until Kane got married, that meant spending a lot of time getting to know the kid.

Josh glanced over at Derek. Some time over the past nine years the kid had grown up. He stood over six feet. Athletic and part-Hawaiian with dark hair and a deep tan. Women of all ages swarmed around him. With buying the house, Derek now had an impressive place to take those young ladies.

Kane chipped in the money for the place and now they were all renovating it. That meant Josh spent a lot of time there. Oahu and Kauai were a quick commuter flight apart, and he appreciated the relatively safe work of banging nails with a hammer compared with fighting off the drug problem all over Hawaii.

"I have a deal for you," Derek said.

"The last time I bet you I had to rip down the crap metal garage on the back of your property." It was almost two months ago and Josh still had the blisters on his palms to prove it.

"Thanks for that." Derek laughed. "But be warned because this wager could turn out even better for me."

"Do tell."

"If you give me the number of that redhead I saw walking around your condo last weekend wearing nothing but a bikini you can move in here for all I care. No questions asked about this afternoon."

Josh didn't even remember the woman's name. "She's all yours."

Derek nodded his head. Even delivered one of those know-it-all grins as he picked the label off the bottle. "Hmmm."

"What?"

"Nothing."

"I'm thinking you've got something to say."

Derek shrugged. "I just think it's interesting, that's all."

"What is?" Josh swallowed a groan as he watched Kane's green pickup pull into the driveway.

"You."

"Don't do that," Josh said.

"Breathe?"

"Psychoanalyze. I get enough of that from the agency-ordered shrink provided post-shooting."

"How's that going?"

"Let's just say I prefer alcohol to therapists. But the head shrinking is over, so I'm not complaining." Josh drank back his beer, relishing the fact that quitting meant no more conversations with the idiot who wanted to talk about his childhood.

"Kane looks pissed."

Josh followed Derek's gaze. Watched Kane slam the door to his truck and stalk toward the house.

"Nothing new there," Josh mumbled.

Derek made a *tsk-tsk* sound. "I'll try again. Is there anything I should know about the hearing?"

"I testified and left." *More like told them to go to hell and walked out early.*

Kane took the three stairs to the porch in one step and stood before them in his official police-chief blues. The uniform made him look important. Despite the fancy clothes, Josh still thought of Kane as the guy who beat his ass in basketball on Sunday mornings.

"Nice outfit," Josh said with a smirk.

"Glad you think so, since I've decided to kill you while wearing it." Kane leaned against the railing facing them. "Seems fitting somehow."

"I'm not sure that wood is steady enough to hold you," Derek said.

"It's fine." Kane's attention never wavered from Josh.

With his dark eyes and black hair, Kane could be intimidating as hell. The death frown didn't help, either. But Josh knew better.

"What are you doing here?" Josh asked.

"Hunting for a self-destructive jackass." Kane grabbed the empty beer bottle out of Josh's hand and shook it. "And, look, here you are."

"Is the hearing over?" Derek asked.

Talk about a relaxation kill. "We're not discussing that part of my life today." As far as Josh was concerned they should never talk about it again.

"I am." This time Kane took Derek's bottle and drank. "It's over."

"My beer?" Derek asked.

"The hearing."

Derek let his chair drop back down to the deck. "Now what?"

Josh grew less interested in this topic by the second. "Don't want to hear the play-by-play."

Derek smiled. "Then stop listening."

"Might try a little thinking while you're at it," Kane added.

If they wanted to work off some extra energy, Josh would

oblige. "You feel like going headfirst into the ocean, warrior boy? It will get your pretty uniform all wet."

Kane snorted and walked past them into the house.

Derek waited until Kane disappeared to lean over and whisper. "He hates it when you call him that."

"Why do you think I do it?" Josh figured out early in the friendship "Kane" meant warrior in Hawaiian and had tortured his friend with the knowledge ever since.

"Kane's going to shoot you," Derek said.

"No, he won't."

"I wouldn't bet on that." On the way back out to the porch, beer in hand, Kane smacked Josh in the back of the head with the end of the bottle.

"Hey!" Josh rubbed the spot.

"See." Kane re-took his position against the railing. "I'm thinking you need something to wake your ass up. Maybe a bullet will do it."

"You were less uptight before you got married," Josh said.

"No, he wasn't." Derek laughed until he glanced at Kane's serious expression. "What? You weren't."

Kane shook off the unrelated topic. "The panel took your case under advisement pending additional testimony. Seems they had some trouble locating you this afternoon and got a little panicky."

"Why not just make a decision now?" Derek asked before sliding a look in Josh's direction. "No offense, man."

Josh nodded in understanding. "None taken."

"This is pretty high-profile. They're trying not to blow it," Kane explained.

Josh knew what that meant. It would be a few days of talking with lawyers and going over options before the government bureaucrats dropped the courthouse on his head and took his job away. Fine. He considered himself terminated anyway.

And he knew the truth behind the hearing and what really happened to put him there. His boss had set up a bad mission and illegally used a local helicopter pilot as a lure for some drug runners. The idea was to shut down a huge meth supplier who worked back and forth between Nevada and Hawaii. Would have worked except that the helicopter went down, the pilot died, and the guy's sister would not stop investigating the incident until she found the truth.

The disaster of a job blew up, leaving Josh to shoot the sister in order to free her from the bad guys. During the resulting mandatory check-in from internal affairs, Josh told the truth about the actions of his boss, Brad Nohea. Brad fought back by shifting the blame and rigging the paperwork to support his position.

All that ass-covering by the department convinced Josh he was done rescuing other people for a living. The grief just wasn't worth the effort. He could handle paperwork. The constant lying and questions about his character were different.

Kane hesitated a second. Someone who didn't know him wouldn't notice. Josh could tell his friend was waiting to drop a bombshell. "You're blocking my view, so just say whatever you have to say and then move."

Kane didn't even bother to deny it. "Deana Armstrong was there this afternoon."

The beer sloshed around in Josh's empty stomach. "What?"

"She came looking for you."

Josh swore. "That woman just doesn't give up."

"Old girlfriend?" Derek asked.

The thought killed off the rest of Josh's beer buzz. "Hell, no."

Kane shifted his weight from one foot to the other. "She's Ryan Armstrong's aunt."

Derek dropped his beer but caught it before it hit the deck. "The kid from the huge murder trial?"

Josh felt like whipping his bottle into the ocean. Now Deana was ruining his good mood without even being near him. "She thinks Ryan isn't guilty."

Kane shook his head. "Now there's a surprise."

Josh understood the skepticism. He tried to remember a time when he arrested someone who didn't claim innocence. Even with drugs in hand they'd be screaming about a frame-up.

Ryan had been the same way two years earlier when he had gotten in trouble. Drugs that time. He had insisted he was in the wrong place when a sting went down and nothing more. His family believed him until the drug tests came back positive. The family used their connections and wealth to get Ryan out of the legal system and into a rehab program. They managed to keep Ryan's name out of the paper and make sure he never took an ounce of responsibility for his actions.

Eight months later the kid's parents were dead.

Josh decided to tell Kane about Deana's plans. "She wants me to get Ryan out of jail."

This time Derek set his bottle down on the porch nice and slow. "Didn't you arrest the kid a few years ago as part of some private school drug ring?"

"Yeah."

Derek glanced at Kane and then back to Josh before trying again. "And didn't you testify against him at his recent murder trial?"

"Yeah."

"Let me skip to the end of this discussion," Kane said. "Why does Deana think you're the guy for this job?"

To Josh the real question was why they were still talking about Deana Armstrong and her ridiculous proposal. "With my connections she believes I'm the one who can fix this."

Kane whistled. "Guess she hasn't heard you're out of the hero business."

"Exactly." Josh snapped his fingers a few times, then pointed at Kane. "About time someone believed me."

"I don't. I'm just repeating the crap you told me this morning." Kane held out a small card. "But I'll let you be the one to tell Ms. Armstrong all about your new career plans."

Josh stared at the paper but did not pick it up. "What the hell is this?"

Kane's face lit up with amusement. "A social card."

"A what? Let me see." Derek grabbed it. Studied it. Flipped it over. "It has her name and phone number and that's it."

"A calling card. Unbelievable." But it wasn't. If there was something out there that reeked of money, Josh knew Deana would own it.

"She's expecting you tomorrow." Kane mumbled that important piece of information between long swallows of beer.

Josh heard him just fine. "What the hell are you talking about now?"

"Since you quit your job—yeah, I know about that, you dumbass—I figured you'd need something to do."

"You left the DEA?" Derek asked.

Josh talked over both of them. "I'm not investigating this kid's case."

Kane shrugged. "Don't tell me. Tell her."

"I did."

"Try again."

Chapter Four

Josh eased back into a chair that proved to be as uncomfortable as it looked. It was wooden, with one thin cushion against the back—he guessed the damn thing cost more than his condo. Since it shook a bit under his weight, he tried not to move as he waited for the small Asian woman who answered the door to go find Deana.

Yeah, she had a maid. With all of Deana's money, Josh didn't know why that little fact surprised him, but it did. For some reason he missed that in his background check on her. She was not the only one who liked to poke around in other people's business. He could play that game, too. Did it all the time.

From what he could tell, she left her property on rare occasions to attend charity events and a few social get-togethers. Otherwise she kept to herself and close to home. Seeing her place he understood why. Quiet and far from tourists and the hotels in Waikiki, her open-floor-plan, one-story house sat along Lanikai, long considered one of the best beaches in Hawaii. Possibly the world.

The area served as a private must-visit spot for presidents

and movie stars. The stretch of sand was located on the windward or eastern side of the island of Oahu in the town of Kailua. About fifteen minutes and *definitely* a world of wealth away from the town where Derek lived. With pure blue water clear enough to see to the sandy bottom, soft trade winds, and surrounding palm trees, the spot looked like a Hollywood creation—too good to be true.

The inside of the house was as magazine-worthy as the outside. Floor-to-ceiling windows overlooked the ocean and the two small uninhabited islands about a mile offshore. Beige couches were arranged in a large, high-ceilinged room to take advantage of the view. Glass shelves filled with expensive looking vases and various small crystal things filled the walls and kept him right where he was in the wobbly chair.

If he knocked anything over he'd be paying her back for years. And owing Deana anything was out of the question.

"Thank you for coming," Deana said from behind him.

She didn't need to speak. Even without the clicking of her heels against the koa wood floor and the sound of her deep voice, he knew she had walked in the room. Something about her set off a mental alarm in his brain. She came within ten feet and his insides switched to high alert.

He got up long enough to be polite before returning to the impractical chair. "Not as if I had much of a choice."

"You're prone to exaggeration."

"Not usually."

She sank into the only other chair in the room. It was one identical to his, but she looked completely right in the expensive seat. "Well, I find it hard to believe you felt threatened by me."

He noted she wore an outfit similar to the one from the courthouse a few days earlier. She could have walked out of a Northeastern prep school. High collar with a cardigan. The only difference was the pair of dress pants instead of the skirt, which was a damn shame because the woman had a decent pair of legs on her.

"Guess you think eighty-two degrees is chilly." As far as he was concerned, she was lucky he was wearing pants instead of shorts as he wanted to do.

"Excuse me?"

"The shrinking violet routine doesn't suit you, by the way. Don't forget, I'm the guy you tried to have fired a few years back."

She had the grace to wince. "That's in the past."

Easy for her to say. "And the command performance this afternoon is our present."

"Remember how I said you had a problem with exaggerating?"

"Nice place, by the way," he said in what likely was the biggest understatement of his life. He tried to look around and almost tipped the chair over.

A smile skimmed Deana's lips. "You don't look very comfortable."

Probably because he was folded in a pretzel and afraid of shifting an inch in any direction. "Your maid showed me in and pointed to this."

"She's not a maid, and you can sit on one of the sofas." Her gaze traveled all over him. "You look a little . . . tight there."

Before he could come up with a smart reply, and he was sure there was one kicking around his head somewhere, the elder Mrs. Armstrong came into the room. The addition to the crowd gave him a reason to get up and shift seats. Not like he had to wait for Deana's permission or anything.

"Mr. Windsor." Georgianna Armstrong approached him

with her hand held out and a smile plastered across her regal-looking face.

She appeared warm and lovely and eager to see him.

He knew that was a big fat lie.

Mrs. Georgianna Armstrong, Deana's mother, was in her early sixties. Graceful, highly respected in the community . . . and Josh didn't trust her as far as he could throw her. Since the woman probably weighed about a hundred pounds, Josh knew he could get her airborne without much of a push. Still, he had dealt with this woman and with her type his entire career at the DEA. She attended charity functions one day and plotted the demise of her enemies the next. She used money to get her way and scoffed when people—any people—failed to jump at her command.

And the woman had a crapload of money. She could trace her family back to the early Europeans who came to the islands to take advantage of the locals and pillage the land. As far as Josh could tell, her family never broke with that habit. Her grandfather and then her father bought up some of the most desired property in Oahu not already owned by the state and a few other landowners.

The family continued to own a great deal of commercial property today, stretching all along the water in Honolulu and Waikiki. Hotels, business, high-rises—if someone had built it, they probably first bought or leased the land from Mrs. Armstrong's family.

The family's ownership reached to residential streets as well. Up until twenty years ago most people in Oahu owned their homes but not the ground underneath. At some point Georgianna Armstrong, then the young heir to the real estate empire, offered the land to the leaseholders at a price. The homeowners became landowners and Mrs. Armstrong and her now-deceased husband became even richer rich people.

"It's good to see you again," the older woman said as she folded Josh's hand in both of hers.

"It is?"

"Why, of course." Mrs. Armstrong gestured toward the empty chair across from Deana, but Josh remained standing. "We are so pleased you decided to join us today."

He glanced at Deana, who looked anything but pleased. She frowned, watching her mother like she was some sort of science experiment gone wrong.

"Mother, Mr. Windsor hasn't said why he's here," Deana explained.

Probably because he had no idea why he was there. He was not the type to arrive when summoned. But there was something about Deana. He wanted to peel away all of that money and exterior chilliness and see what was underneath. He suspected it was nothing more than a second layer of ice.

Maybe it was the overabundance of sunshine and fresh air. Maybe it was his inclination to hang around Derek's house instead of going home to his own. For whatever reason, Josh remained on Oahu, and Oahu was Armstrong turf. Better to come to the mountain than have the mountain crash on top of him.

The elder Mrs. Armstrong crossed her legs in an elegant move straight out of an expensive etiquette class. "We are all friends here—"

Oh, hell no. "Not exactly."

Deana cleared her throat. "I would agree with Mr. Windsor that friendship is a little much to expect at this point."

Deana did not raise her voice, but the warning lingered in

there. One her mother obviously had no intention of heeding.

"Well, I don't see any reason we can't use first names," Mrs. Armstrong said.

He had a few things in mind, but stuck with his initial plan to get in and out fast. Didn't even bother to sit back down. "Why don't you tell me what you want so I can say no and we can all go our separate ways?"

Mrs. Armstrong's smile faltered. "I thought Deana already explained this to you."

Deana shifted, taking up a position much like her mother's. "Mr. Windsor turned me down."

The older woman waved her hand as if physically dismissing the words. "Certainly he's come to his senses by now."

"I wouldn't count on that," Deana said.

For once he agreed with Deana. "You should listen to your daughter on this."

"I am too old and this is too important to play games, Mr. Windsor."

He smothered a chuckle over the elder woman's abrupt tone. "I thought we were using first names."

Mrs. Armstrong sat up even straighter with a pile of pillows stacked behind her. "My grandson needs assistance. You are the man for the job. Furthermore, we can pay you handsomely for your time. This is a simple business transaction. One that could benefit you."

Josh pointed at Deana. "She tried that, too. I wasn't interested then. Not interested now."

Mrs. Armstrong looked to Deana as if seeking assistance before turning back to Josh. "That's nonsense. Who turns down money?"

Josh refused to back down from the older woman's staring contest. If she wanted a battle he'd give her one. Being retired from the DEA meant he no longer had to weigh his words, to the extent he ever did. "Haven't we played this game before? Is this the part where you throw your money around and start issuing threats?"

"What does that mean?" Deana asked with enough shock in her voice to suggest she didn't actually know.

Josh tried to figure out whether or not the confusion was an act. "Your mother has already engaged in bribery, blackmail, and various other illegal acts relating to me."

Deana's entire face pinched. "That's a serious accusation."

"They're actually called crimes." When Deana continued to look confused, Josh explained. "Your mother tried to pay me off so I wouldn't testify in Ryan's original drug trial. If I remember right, she offered piles of cash and made numerous promises about my future career. Something about me becoming a supervisor, as if that's anything I'd ever want."

"This is irrelevant," Mrs. Armstrong said in a haughty tone.

No, it wasn't, which was why Josh kept talking. "When that didn't work, she talked about ruining my reputation if I took the stand and said something other than what she wanted me to say. I believe getting me fired was just the start of the threats."

Deana stood up. "What?"

The older woman gestured to Deana to retake her seat. "Calm down. He turned me down on the money, and that last part was a misunderstanding."

"Oh, I understood you just fine." Drug dealers had tried to intimidate him and still hadn't been as furious or convincing in their attempts as Georgianna Armstrong had.

Deana held her ground against her mother's flippant attitude. "You actually tried to bribe him?"

Josh finally sat down again to watch the by-play between the two women. The show seemed too good to miss. Deana's usual unruffled demeanor strained around her mother. Deana had shown more emotion in the past two minutes than Josh had seen in the months since he'd met her. Being in private instead of in public could account for the change, but he figured it had more to do with the mother-daughter dynamic.

By his experience, when two strong-willed women came in contact only one could win. Looked like the older, more experienced version took this round. Josh waited for the mother to take over, start issuing orders, and flash her big wallet around. One sign of any of that behavior and he was headed for the door.

Deana regained her composure and unclenched her teeth. "Your refusal to accept my mother's offer is exactly the reason you are perfect for this job."

Deana lowered her voice to normal levels even as she dug her fingers into her pants legs as if the ground was sinking beneath her feet and the fabric was the only thing saving her from falling down. In the strain around her eyes and mouth, it was clear holding on to that cool demeanor proved to be a struggle.

Looked like he underestimated Deana. She was not about to sit there and be quiet.

Score one for the younger Armstrong.

"I'm listening," he said even though he really wasn't.

Deana did not cede the floor to her mother. "The police trust you. You have connections and respect among your peers. Your reputation is solid."

Josh wondered when they'd moved to the obvious and false flattery portion of the program. "No thanks to your family."

"People will listen to you when you say Ryan is innocent. You can cut through the years of red tape and get the prosecutor to listen." The way Deana talked over him proved she wasn't willing to turn over control to him, either.

Josh appreciated the position the family was in. The precious baby, the next generation, struggled to live up to the polish and propriety of the older generations. The story was not all that original. Ryan got in with the wrong crowd, dabbled in drugs, and believed he was entitled to everything. He traded on his family name and depended on the same people he claimed to hate to get him out of his current predicament.

Still, the boy killed his parents. Not out of fear. Out of greed. Josh didn't want any part of putting a kid like that back out in society.

"What if Ryan isn't innocent?" Josh asked.

"Do you really think your insults can deter me?" Mrs. Armstrong's brittle voice rang through the silent room. "I have lost a husband, a son, a daughter-in-law, and I am inches away from forever losing a grandson to the court system."

Deana glanced at her mother but did not go to her. Instead she focused on Josh. "And what if Ryan is innocent? What then?"

Josh didn't want to think about that possibility. Didn't want to be responsible for anyone else. Hell, he couldn't keep his own life straight. How was he supposed to undo a valid jury verdict and a mountain of evidence against a kid he didn't particularly like in the first place?

Deana stood up and walked past her mother to a table

behind the couch. Picking up a file about two inches thick, Deana returned to stand in front of Josh. "Here."

He knew what it was. Touching it would signal agreement and no way was he going there. "I don't want it."

"You're newly retired."

"Following me again? I thought we talked about that"

"Reading the newspaper." She dropped the file on his lap. More like shoved it at him. "This will give you some light reading while you're trying to figure out what to do with your life."

Somehow the chair remained upright under the extra weight. He was sure that feeling would also soon return to his upper thigh from where the rough corner jabbed him.

"How many ways can I tell you I'm not interested in your offer?" he asked.

"That's your copy. Do whatever you want with it."

What he wanted was to get the hell out of there. "If that's all . . ."

Deana nodded. "It is."

He took one last look at the tumbling waves right outside her back door, wishing he were surfing or anywhere else, and stood up.

He made a show of leaving the folder on his chair. "No thanks."

Deana grabbed his sleeve as he started to walk away. Rather than fight her, he let his body be pulled around to face her, then he exhaled as loud as possible to let her know his frustration. Nothing else seemed to work, so he thought he'd try the new tack.

She thanked him for that courtesy by sticking the folder in his gut. "Take it."

Something in her face, in those sad eyes, got to him. Instead of arguing, he grabbed the file. Fine. He could abandon it in his office at home or shred it later. Right now he just wanted out before he did something dumb.

Deana followed Josh to the door and shut it behind him. "About time."

"What an awful man." Her mother's words dripped with distaste.

Deana walked back into the family room and sat down. Inside, she seethed. "You could have told me you once tried to blackmail and bribe him."

"Oh, please. You tried to find evidence with which to ruin his credibility on the stand." Georgianna fixed the brooch on her short-sleeve sweater. "I hardly see the difference."

There was one. Deana was sure of it. The other option, that she was just like her mother in shoving people around to get her way, was not a pleasant one, so Deana pushed it right out of her mind. Her mother was a good woman, but when she was threatened the claws came out. Georgianna Armstrong knew how to use her place in society to her advantage.

Deana knew she had slipped in the past and shown signs of those traits. She vowed never to again . . . right after Ryan was freed.

"And I still don't see what's wrong with using resources if you're lucky enough to have them," her mother mumbled.

"Either way, I think we're finally moving in the right direction," Deana said.

Georgianna's head popped up, but her fingers stayed on the pin. "What on earth are you talking about? He turned us down."

"Well, that's what he said, but you're missing my point."

"Clearly."

"He came here today. He didn't have to do that. He

showed up because he's going to help." Deana felt that reality straight down to her toes.

Her mother folded her hands on her lap. "I don't mean to question your knowledge of the male mind, but—"

Deana stopped that line of thinking before her mother launched into a lecture on men. "He felt as if he was summoned. His ego rebelled and he got defensive. I put him in a position where I held the power. Under those circumstances he couldn't just say yes."

"Sure he could."

"He has to fight me a little more."

"I think you are giving this Mr. Windsor a good deal more credit for possessing depth than he actually deserves."

Deana refused to believe that was true. "He's the right man for the job. He'll realize it soon enough."

"I would remind you that he just lost his job over a scandal."

"Have you read the paper? Everyone believes he walked out of that hearing and the DEA in protest. Law enforcement all side with Josh. Public opinion is on his side. If anything, his reputation for integrity is even more solid now than it was before the hearing began."

"If you say so."

"I do." And Deana vowed to keep saying it until she won Josh over.

"Frankly, I don't see anything positive about him."

"Coming here instead of calling or just plain ignoring me proves he's going to help once he adjusts to the idea." At least that was the theory. Deana just hoped Josh would see it the same way.

"You act as if we can afford to wait around for this man to come to his senses."

They could. That was the unfortunate truth at work here. "Ryan isn't going anywhere."

Her mother's shoulders slumped. "That's a terrible thing to say."

"But it's true."

Chapter Five

Despite the rain, it felt good to be back in Kauai the next morning. Sitting at Kane and Annie's kitchen table watching Annie hover by the sink making coffee while Kane sat there reading the paper washed away some of the anxiety that had been churning inside Josh for months.

There was something comforting in the domesticity of his friends' lives. Married for less than a year, Annie and Kane clicked. Kane kept to his low-key style, saying little. Annie never stopped talking. Together, they made it work. Made it look easy.

And they always welcomed Josh. He owned a condo across town, but when he woke up this morning he threw on jeans and a shirt and landed here. Didn't go on a run as he planned. Didn't get to work finding a new career as he should. Just jumped in his vintage Mustang and headed to Kane's house.

Josh knew being jobless should have made him nervous. Instead, getting out from under the DEA bureaucracy and the politics of ass-covering freed him. He had attempted for years to fight the system from the inside, but it all ended when his incompetent boss used a civilian helicopter pilot without approval and without providing the poor guy with proper protection. Josh's boss preferred to protect his pension and sacrifice Josh rather than clear the record.

Fuck the DEA. Josh decided he didn't need the hassle. Not anymore.

"How much longer are you going to do that?" Annie asked as she sat a steaming mug in front of him.

Josh looked up. "What?"

"The tapping," she said with a smile as she slipped into the seat next to her husband and threaded her arm through his.

"What are you talking about?" Josh asked.

Kane glanced over the top of the newspaper. "The thing with the pen."

Annie nodded. "You do it all the time."

Kane folded the front page and spoke over the crumpling sound. "And it's annoying as hell."

Josh stared down at his fingers. Saw the blue scuff marks he made against the napkin.

Okay, so maybe he'd been thumping the pen against the table. He blamed the cigarettes. Almost two years without them and he still felt the itch.

"When did you two become so sensitive?" he asked.

Annie shrugged. "It was either point it out or break your fingers."

She could do it, too. Josh knew not to mess with Kane's woman. No way to do that and win.

"That's very feminine of you," Josh said.

She rapped her fist against the table. "Don't make me get up and smack the crap out of you."

"For the record, I'd like to see that," Kane said.

"And is it me or is our Josh a bit on guard this morning?" Annie's smile disappeared. "Oh, no."

"What now?" Josh asked as he eyed up the pen. Sending the message to his brain to leave it there.

"You've done something, haven't you?" She nodded. "Something that's going to piss me off."

Kane joined his wife in staring. "She means other than quitting your job."

The way they sensed something was wrong was just downright spooky. "What, a man can't stop by for breakfast without getting interrogated?"

"Hmmm." Kane winked at Annie as if they were sharing some sort of conspiracy. "Interesting, don't you think?"

"Definitely defensive." Annie's mocking tone mirrored her husband's.

"Kind of looks like he's ready to bolt for the door," Kane said.

"Picking up on that, are you?" Josh asked, matching their sarcasm with some of his own.

Annie tilted her head to the side and pretended to frown. "A little grumpier than usual, too."

Josh grabbed on to the mug in front of him to keep from picking the pen back up again. "Maybe it's the way you make coffee."

"Pissing off Annie?" Kane whistled under his breath. "Brave man."

"Don't upset the cook." Annie reached out and took the pen out of tapping range. "The drink is perfect, and you know it. Stop stalling. Tell us what has you lost in thought and looking like a moody five-year-old."

"Does your foul mood have anything to do with one Deana Armstrong?" Kane asked in a deceptively soft voice.

The delivery made Josh wonder how long his friend had been holding the question in. Probably for as long as Josh had been thinking about Deana's offer.

Going to her house had been a huge mistake. Not seeing her made saying no to her request easy. Being in that house, realizing how vulnerable she was on the issue of saving her idiot nephew, made hating her tougher. Not impossible, but definitely problematic.

Twenty-four hours of constant Deana thoughts ticked him off. "I was in a good mood until ten seconds ago."

"But deep in thought. Something's bothering that little brain of yours," Annie said.

Josh's relationship with Annie had been like this from the beginning. A series of jokes and shots as they built trust in each other. He considered her a sister. A hot redhead with a mouth that could scare a trucker and a body that kept a foolish smile on Kane's face most of the time.

It was hard to dislike a woman who saved his best friend from an emotional vacuum. That's what she did for Kane. Josh appreciated Annie for many things, but mostly for that.

"Deana gave me Ryan's file," Josh said.

Kane's eyebrow lifted. "And?"

"There were other leads. Other suspects who looked good, if not better than Ryan, for the killings." Josh cursed under his breath. "Some of the evidence didn't point to Ryan. In fact, it suggested someone else had to be responsible."

"But you knew that from the press coverage of the trial," Kane said.

"Sure, but it's different seeing it all laid out without the lawyer spin on it." It all sounded more plausible somehow, which was why Josh had wanted to shred the damn folder before he got on the commuter plane and read it on the way home.

"I feel sorry for Deana," Annie said.

Josh felt certain only another woman could listen to

everything he said and come to that conclusion. "Excuse me?"

Annie reached out and covered Josh's hand with hers. "I think it's sweet of you to look into this for her."

"Sweet? That's not a word I would use to describe Josh," Kane said.

Josh ignored Kane and aimed his argument at Annie. She was the one who would refuse to let this go, so he may as well deal with her now. "I'm not looking into anything. And you've never even met Deana Armstrong, so I don't know why you're invoking the sisterhood bond."

"So?" Annie asked.

Kane leaned over and kissed his wife on the forehead. "Who can argue with that logic?"

Annie pinched her husband's arm and earned a scowl in return.

"Isn't that sort of crucial to know her before you decide you like her?" Josh asked.

"Not really. I mean, she's lost so much." Annie threw him that sad-puppy look.

Josh knew better than to fall for Annie's act. And he fought off the urge to sympathize with Deana. "The woman hates me."

Annie patted Josh's hand one last time before letting go. "Don't be ridiculous."

Kane rolled his eyes. "Yeah, who could hate Josh?"

"She wouldn't have called if that were the case," Annie said.

Wrong conclusion. "She wants to use me."

Kane leaned back and threw an arm around Annie's shoulders. "Since when do you care if a woman wants to use you?"

That one was easy for Josh. "When she isn't doing it in a bedroom."

"You're not sleeping with her already, are you?" Annie looked appalled at the idea.

Josh didn't like the thought, either. "Hell no."

Annie's gaze flicked to Kane and then back to Josh again. "Do you want to?"

How the hell had they gotten onto this topic? "Did you miss the part where Deana hates me?"

Kane snorted. "You act as if that disqualifies her from your bed."

"I'm just happy to know he's a little discriminating when it comes to women," Annie said in a loud whisper to her husband.

"Are you two done?" Josh asked, hoping to hell they were.

Annie started to tap the pen and then slammed it against the table. "I don't see what the problem is here."

"There's more than one." Josh called up all the reasons from his mental "con" list. "I'm not a police investigator. I'm not for sale. This family tried to destroy me once."

"For heaven's sake." Annie snorted, adding enough drama to make a pre-teen proud. "Don't be an idiot and let your ego get in the way."

Josh wasn't expecting name calling. "What?"

"You know as well as we do that you're going to help this woman." Annie emphasized each word as she spoke.

Josh looked in Kane's direction for assistance.

Kane shook his head. "Don't get me involved in this losing battle. I agree with Annie."

"You went to her house, took the file she offered, and read it," Annie said as she ticked off her points on her fingers. "You did all of that knowing you were going to help her. You're just too pigheaded to admit it now."

"I was being courteous when I agreed to see her."

Kane's mouth dropped open. "Try again."

Josh leaned back in his chair. "Thanks for the support, buddy."

"What Kane is floundering to say is that you aren't *that* guy, Josh. You don't walk away from injustice or women who need you." Annie leaned forward and wrapped her hands around her coffee mug. "You are going to take up this project because you won't let a potentially innocent kid stay in jail."

Hell, right now Josh wanted to be that guy who walked away. Wanted to not give a shit. But there was an even bigger problem at work here. "I think Ryan did it."

"So? Prove it. Make Deana see that," Annie said.

"Oh, she'll love that," Kane mumbled until Annie frowned in his direction. "What?"

If possible, Annie's mouth flatlined even farther. "Don't be so negative."

"Honey, I've been a police officer for a long time. I can tell you that people hear what they want to hear and nothing else. If Josh proves the prosecution was right, Deana will be furious."

"Exactly." Josh thought it was about time Kane took the right side of this argument. "I'm supposed to take Deana's money and then tell her Ryan, her beloved nephew, killed his parents, who also happen to be Deana's only brother and sister-in-law? I can only imagine how well that will go over."

"So?" Annie asked.

Josh began to wonder why he skipped exercise and came here instead. "Again with the *so* response."

"Thanks to marriage this part of the female vocabulary I

do now understand." Kane brushed his hand over Annie's ponytail. "She is wondering why you would care about screwing Deana financially since you pretend to dislike the woman."

Annie's eyebrows lifted. "Is she pretty?"

"Very," Kane said.

Having two knowing smiles aimed right at him kicked Josh's brain into gear. "Stop."

"What?" Annie asked, even managed to sound innocent while she did it.

"Do not go off on some crazy-ass matchmaking mission."

"Wouldn't dream of it." The false innocence in Annie's voice suggested that was the exact direction she intended to go.

"Never going to happen." Josh thought about repeating the word "never" a few times but refrained.

Annie's smile was big enough to fill the room. "Of course not."

"I don't even like Deana."

"Kane said the same thing about me, and now look at us." Annie kissed her husband on the cheek.

"Must I?" Josh grumbled.

Annie reached around, picked up the phone, and waved it in Josh's face. "Call Deana and tell her you'll help."

"No way."

Kane made a *tsk-tsk* sound. "Don't fight it, man."

"Exactly." Annie treated her husband to another kiss. "You're going to pack up and get on the next plane back to Oahu. Right, Josh?"

"You doing my scheduling now?"

"Kane will drive you," Annie said as if Josh never spoke.

"I will?" Kane asked.

Annie kept right on rolling. "I'm sure you can stay with Derek on Oahu."

Josh felt the floor sink beneath his feet under the weight of Annie's gabbing. "Don't you think we should ask Derek first? Or me?"

"So long as you bring beer he'll let you in," Kane said.

Josh decided to take one last shot. "And what if I say I'm not going to do this?"

Annie shook the receiver in his face. "Then I will climb over this table and beat you with this phone."

Kane laughed. "That's one of her favorite threats."

Josh gave up. For a second he wondered if between Annie and Deana he ever really stood a chance.

"Marriage has made you soft," Josh said to his friend.

Kane's smile grew even broader. "But not stupid. Women always win. Just accept it and move on. Call Deana and pack your bag."

Chapter Six

"I don't approve of this strategy." Deana made the statement for the third time as she walked down the hallway a step behind Josh.

Thanks to a knee-length skirt and two-inch heels she had to double-time her steps to keep up at all. Even then, she nearly got knocked over by a group of lawyers coming in the opposite direction.

"We're even, because I don't remember inviting you on this trip." Josh pushed open the glass doors leading to the office of the Prosecuting Attorney without looking back at her.

He hadn't said much of anything since agreeing to take on Ryan's case. One confirming phone call and a quick stop at Deana's house to ask a few personal questions about Ryan and his lead defense attorney, and Josh was off and investigating. She only knew about this related excursion at all because a confirming text about his meeting came in while Josh was at her house an hour before.

It paid to be nosy now and then.

"What choice did I have since you refused to fill me in on your strategy?" she asked.

"How about we skip the talking and get to the part where you stay out of this investigation?"

Easy for him to say. They weren't talking about his nephew. He wasn't the one walking into a building he despised, one filled with memories better forgotten.

Josh waved to a few people milling by the door and mumbled a few hellos before walking up to the reception desk. "Hey, Mary. Is he ready for me?"

Despite her being about sixty and wearing a wedding ring, under Josh's attention the older woman giggled like a schoolgirl. After babbling something about the DEA problem, the woman picked up the phone.

The woman never even acknowledged Deana hiding behind Josh's broad shoulders, which, as far as Deana was concerned, was a very good thing. Standing there, seeing the curious stares from passing lawyers was bad enough.

Josh leaned on the desk and turned back to Deana. His eyebrows lowered. "What's wrong with you?"

Deana noticed his smile faded the second the flirting with the other woman stopped. "Is there anyone you don't know?"

"I've worked in law enforcement for a lot of years."

"In Kauai, not here, and not as an attorney."

"People like me."

"I find that hard to believe," Deana muttered under her breath.

"You did hire me for my expertise and connections, remember?"

The last thing she needed was a lecture. "I brought you on board with the hope you would be neutral."

Josh tapped his pen end-over-end against the desk. "And walking into this office somehow shows I'm not?"

"Your friendliness with the very people who prosecuted Ryan is a bit disconcerting."

Josh continued to throw her a blank stare. "Your point?"

So much for hoping he'd understand without a diagram. "There isn't a person in this building who believes Ryan is innocent."

"I hate to tell you this, but there aren't many people in Hawaii who think Ryan is innocent."

"That's not true."

"No one but you, your mother, and Ryan think he got a raw deal. Most think the life sentence was a gift or a result of his family's wealth."

"He's only sixteen." Funny how everyone forgot that little fact in their bloodlust to crucify him.

"All that proves is that there's no age minimum on stupid when it comes to killing."

"Thanks for keeping an open mind on this. I *really* appreciate it." She glanced around and was hit with awful flashbacks of her last trip here.

And then there was the Mary problem. Recognition finally dawned on the older woman's face at the mention of Ryan's name. Her eyes shot open and her mouth snapped shut on what could only be called a look of distaste.

Deana waited for Mary to say something. Anything.

"Deana." The sound of Josh using her first name stunned Deana for a second. He stepped away from the counter and crowded closer, pitching his voice low. "Talking to the prosecutor is part of my process."

"But—"

Josh's forehead hovered only a few inches from hers.

"And you know what? You're not going to be in the room when I do it."

Now there was a wrong assumption. Ten minutes with the prosecutor, hearing his skewed view of the case, and Josh would walk away from the case. "I'll remind you that I'm the one paying the money."

Josh straightened up, putting space between them again. "If that's your argument, I can leave right now and never come back."

Okay, so the money angle was the wrong way to go. Josh made it clear he hated being reminded about checks, cash, or any other form of payment. She found his sensitivity ridiculous. Talk about being touchy for no reason. There was nothing wrong with being paid a good wage for work. Surely he was smart enough to see that.

She tried a different tack. "I have a vested interest in the outcome of what you find out here today."

Josh pointed to the green couch behind her. "You can vest out here in the waiting area."

Mary did not even try to hide her laughter.

Whatever Deana might have said died on her lips when Eric Kimura, the Deputy Prosecuting Attorney, appeared behind Josh's left shoulder.

She could not possibly be this unlucky. No woman could.

Eric shook his head as if he wasn't expecting to see her, either. "Deana?"

The air sucked right out of the room. She would have screamed except the security guys stationed right next to the door probably would have shot her. She wasn't exactly in friendly territory at the moment.

"Hello, Eric." She skipped the part about it being nice to see him again, because it wasn't.

"Hey, man." Josh's welcoming smile disappeared as he

looked between Deana and Eric. "Do you two know each other?"

Eric finally broke eye contact with Deana. "You could say that."

Deana fought to keep her world from tilting. If the dizziness shaking her from head to toe were any indication, that wasn't going to be an easy task.

"Oahu is not a big place," she said, totally ignoring Josh's question. "And we can't really stay and talk to Eric because we have a meeting to get to."

Josh's eyebrow lifted in question. "I don't know about you, but my meeting is with Eric."

"Should I leave you two alone to straighten this out?" Eric asked.

Josh shot the other man a warning glance. "Don't even think of moving."

She struggled to understand what was happening. "Eric wasn't the prosecutor on Ryan's case, Josh."

"I know."

"Then what's going on?" She asked because she needed a straight answer before the pounding in her head ratcheted up and drowned out everything else.

Josh's eyes narrowed "I'm conducting the investigation as promised."

"Think of another way to get it done," Deana said.

The air around Josh crackled with awareness. He acted as if she had overstepped. As if he was somehow above being questioned.

Boy, did he have a surprise coming. The one thing Eric taught her was to not back down when you believed in something. He never intended to deliver that lesson, but she picked it up just fine when they were dating.

"Not that this isn't interesting, because it is, but I have

work to do." Eric signaled to Mary. "When is my next appointment?"

"Hold it." Josh held up a hand as if to emphasize his order. "Clearly there's something I don't know here. Someone care to fill me in on the problem?"

"There's not a problem," Deana said.

Eric turned his gaze to the floor, doing his damnedest to prove her a liar on that point. Typical. Never step up and take a hit to the reputation when you can let someone else do all the nasty work. That was Eric.

He was tall and handsome in his perfectly pressed dark gray suit and short black hair. A driven, only child of parents who came to Hawaii straight from Japan. They poured everything into him, and Eric returned their hard work with a swift rise in the Office of the Prosecutor and a possible future as *the* Prosecuting Attorney of Oahu, if the voters saw fit. He was the same man she once believed was perfect for her . . . until he proved he absolutely wasn't.

Rather than bore Josh and the eavesdropping receptionist with the details, Deana went for the brief version. "Eric and I know each other."

"Yeah, I got that much," Josh said.

The receptionist snorted, then bowed her head and pretended to read something on her desk.

Deana toyed with telling the other woman off but turned to Josh instead. "Is any of this really relevant?"

Josh hesitated for a second. "I'm thinking it might be. This reaction isn't a good thing. Might get in the way of the investigation, which is why I need details before I take one more step."

"Deana is right. We've known each other for years," Eric said.

Josh didn't move. Didn't look all that satisfied with the explanation, either. "Know each other as in biblically?"

"What does that mean?" Deana asked.

"Yes," Eric said at the same time.

Josh blew out a long and loud breath. "Okay, this is a problem."

"Why?" Deana asked. "And why meet with Eric anyway?"

"As you know, I oversee the major felonies division. Josh and I go back a few years. Hello, by the way." Eric held out his hand to Josh. "So, he called and asked if he could come in and talk about Ryan."

Josh returned the handshake. "And for some reason you forgot to fill me in on your personal connection to this matter."

"I don't have one," Eric said.

Deana felt the words more than heard them. As if she needed a reminder of why this guy was an ex and not a current boyfriend.

"Well, if this is the meeting, should we go to your office and get started?" she asked. As far as she was concerned, they'd shared enough private information with the office staff and the few attorneys who hovered nearby.

"No need." Eric handed Josh a thin envelope. "There's not much I can tell you about this case. Whatever I have that can be disclosed is already public record."

"I see," Josh said as he glared at Deana.

"You want the basics?" Eric didn't wait for a response. "Ryan killed his parents, Chace and Kalanie Armstrong, in order to get his hands on a sizable inheritance—"

"That's not true," Deana insisted, more out of habit than anything else.

Eric kept right on talking. "Like many rich kids before him—the Menendez brothers, Bart Whitaker, the Rafay kid, and hundreds, maybe thousands, of others—Ryan wanted quick cash fast. He made it happen the hard way and then set about to spend all the money he could get his hands on."

Deana longed to knock the smug expression right off Eric's face. "We all know your public position on Ryan."

"That's the only one there is, Deana."

"Eric, maybe we could schedule a meeting later." Josh shot her a blank look. "Alone."

"If you want, but that's honestly all I can give you." Eric shrugged. "There was nothing all that unusual about the case. From a prosecutorial perspective, pretty easy."

Those three weeks of trial nearly killed Deana, and her ex-boyfriend—the man who watched her grieve and held her while she cried over her brother's casket—viewed the entire scene as fun. "Happy you enjoyed yourself."

Eric frowned. "You know that's not true."

"Sounds like it."

"This was not personal, Deana. My office just played the facts as they came. Out of respect for you, I stayed out of it. It seemed like the best choice for both of us."

For him, maybe. That's what she could never make Eric understand. She wanted him in the case. She wanted him to fight for Ryan, to believe in his innocence. Instead, Eric protected his butt and his future political career and refused to help.

"I guess that's it then." Josh wrapped his fingers around her elbow.

The gesture, both intimate and a little threatening, confused her. "But I thought—"

Josh steered her toward the glass doors and called back to Eric. "I'll call you soon."

"Sounds good."

"He doesn't mean it, you know." She made the comment in a soft voice just loud enough for Josh to hear.

"Meaning?" Josh asked as he shuffled her toward the door.

"After this meeting, Eric won't let his staff put your calls through."

Josh's steps hesitated as he glanced down at her. "That what he did to you?"

No longer stalling, she picked up her pace. "We're not talking about me."

"Well, either way you're wrong. Eric will talk to me. Without you." Josh shoved the door open and gestured for her to walk through.

"You think you're so special?"

His jaw clenched. "Hell, yeah."

Chapter Seven

Josh managed to hold his temper until they reached the elevator bank. But just barely. He wanted to unleash. To
let out all of the frustration he experienced since figuring
out Deana was following him around Hawaii.

She took away his choice. She walked into his life and
forced him to do the one thing he vowed not to do—rescue
someone. And now he had to wrestle with the visual image
of Eric and Deana being in bed together, thoughts that only
infuriated him further.

Josh waited until the two lawyers standing in the quiet
hallway disappeared back into their offices. "What the hell
was that about?"

She hit the DOWN button. "You tell me. You're the one
who dragged us out of there before we could find out anything helpful on Ryan."

"I did that to keep you from insulting the one guy I need
to communicate with me during this investigation."

"Eric? You mean the same guy who basically told you to
go away so he could get to a more important meeting on his

schedule?" She stopped tapping the button and stared up at him.

"Actually, yes."

"In case you're wondering, there wasn't another meeting. That was fake. Eric wanted to get rid of you."

Josh snorted. As if he hadn't picked up on Eric's lie. Hell, Josh knew Eric blew him off. Josh also knew Eric's unhelpful reaction had to do with Deana's presence and nothing else.

"He's my best contact in that office," Josh explained.

She shook her head. "If Eric is Ryan's only chance, we may as well give up now."

Josh refused to argue. She wanted to see Eric as the enemy. Fine. Let her make this impossible. He didn't care. He could let it go.

That theory lasted all of two seconds. . . . "Eric is a good guy, you know," Josh said, because he couldn't help himself.

"You two are real close, are you?"

Josh had made a decision about Eric's character a long time ago. They weren't friends. Didn't hang out or even talk all that often. Still, Josh had worked with the man on a few drug cases and knew Eric valued justice as much as he craved the big corner office with his name engraved on the door.

"Is that a real question or are you just being insufferable to annoy me?" Josh asked even though the real question was why he kept killing himself defending Eric to her . . . and why he cared about any of this.

Even though Josh now knew the source of the Eric–Deana tension was a dating relationship, he wanted to know more. Everything about Deana intrigued him. She was an odd mix of inconsistencies and predictabilities. Hot and cold at the same time. What really pissed him off is that he hadn't seen the Eric angle coming. Whatever the two of them had, they kept it quiet. Or, at least the sordid details never reached Josh in Kauai.

"We can agree to disagree on the issue of Eric," she said.

She didn't move. Didn't even blink, but Josh could feel her turn up the chilliness factor. If Josh guessed right, the only thing keeping her from bolting for that emergency staircase to her left was a heap of pride and a refusal to be seen as weak.

He appreciated the self-preservation aspects of her position, so he tried to explain. "Eric controls most of the evidence."

She shrugged. "Doesn't matter because he won't help you."

From the choppiness of her voice Josh wondered if they had strayed off topic and were talking about something other than Ryan's case. "We need to come to an understanding."

"We already did."

"I thought so, but apparently not." He glanced around for the perfect spot. Before she could balk, he took her hand and with the other palm pushed the door to the men's bathroom open.

She leaned back, putting most of her weight behind going in the opposite direction. "What the hell are you doing?"

"Talking to you." Since the element of surprise was on his side, and because he outweighed her by a good sixty or more pounds, he got her into the white-tiled room with only a few tugs.

"This is ridiculous."

"Don't move." After a quick check of the two stalls to

make sure they were alone, he clicked the lock on the door and faced her down.

"We're going to talk in here?" Her squeal bounced off the metal stalls.

It was the most emotion he had heard from her all day. Even during a scene with a man who clearly once meant something to her, she had managed to keep her cool, to sound distant and uninterested.

That was over. Josh needed answers. Needed her to understand who was in charge and how exactly this bizarre business relationship of theirs was going to work. Getting her cooperation was key. She had backed her body into a corner, seemingly careful not to touch the wall or anything else in the small area.

Red stained her cheeks. "You can't just—"

"Yes I can."

"It smells in here."

He inhaled the antiseptic scent of bleach and urinal cakes. "I've been around worse."

"Lucky you." Her chest rose and fell.

Even under the high-buttoned blouse, he could see her fight for breath. He assumed that had more to do with the close quarters and her lack of control over the situation than her concerns about the crap on the bathroom floor.

"This is a public restroom," she said as if that would have some impact on his decision to talk to her.

"Your choices were the lobby, the elevator, or here. This is more private and more convenient."

She glanced around, making a face at the stray toilet paper rolled across the floor. "And the most disgusting."

"Sorry, your highness. Next time I'll rent out the penthouse for you."

Her hands dropped to her sides as her fidgeting stopped. "Don't do that."

"What?"

"Judge me based on my bank account."

"If the diamond tiara fits . . ."

Anger sparked in her eyes. "Dragging around that attitude of yours must get pretty damn exhausting. Good thing you don't need money like the rest of us."

"We can talk about me later." He stepped in front of her. "Right now we're discussing you and Eric."

"No, we're not."

"Look, lady." Josh slapped his hand on the tiles behind her head, crowding her against the wall until her attention focused solely on him. "Your love life is screwing up my case."

For some reason the fact she even had one ticked him off. He pictured her as hiding in her house and coming out now and then. As asexual despite that tempting long hair and beautiful face. Realizing under all that stuffiness and bossiness sat a real person made him less comfortable. Sort of itchy. Made him think of her as a woman instead of a case or a wallet, and that was not okay.

"You're out of the loop," he said.

"What?"

"It's just me from here on out. That was the plan to begin with, but you insisted on coming today. No more. This isn't a group effort. Can't be."

She lifted her chin. "I had to follow you in my own car because you refused to let me ride with you."

"Most people would take that as a hint."

"I just assumed it was part of your usual rudeness."

"I knew I should have tried a few wrong turns and lost

you." He bent his elbow and dipped in closer. "Won't make that mistake again."

"You're not funny."

"We're starting over. Under the new rules you're out of the day-to-day stuff."

She held her hands together right under her breasts and close to his chest but not quite touching him. "Absolutely not."

"You'll stay at home and wait for me to report to you. No more looking around and seeing you waiting nearby."

"You make me sound like your employee." She screwed up her mouth as if she tasted something sour. "Or a dog."

"The former description works for me."

Deana shoved against Josh's chest with the heel of her hand. "That's very evolved of you, but my answer is the same. No."

"You aren't calling the shots here." And he vowed she was not going to make him move, either. He didn't intend to pull back or go away until they had this problem worked out. The fact she smelled good, like some sort of exotic flower, didn't exactly make being this close a hardship.

From this angle he could also see the gold flecks in her green eyes. Pretty.

"We are partners in this," she said. Even nodded her head as if doing that sort of thing made the comment true.

"You are dead wrong."

"Don't make me—"

His mouth hovered a few inches from hers. "Are you going to threaten me with money again?"

She shifted her head to put a tiny bit of space between them. "Of course not. You make me sound like a—"

"Ice queen?"

"How original." She put her hands against his chest and pushed. "Can you back up, please?"

Despite dress shirt and suit jacket, Josh felt the touch right down to his bare skin.

"No."

Like that, the atmosphere in the room changed. He smelled her. Saw her. And for the first time, wanted to open that shirt and see what she hid underneath.

"You should . . ." Her breathy voice barely registered over the whirl of the room's automatic fan.

"What?"

She swallowed. Hard. "We should go."

The woman talked sense. A smart man would turn around and walk right out of the room. An even smarter man would hand back the check and the file and get on a plane to Kauai. Only a dumb man would give in to the urge to kiss her, but he was going to do it anyway. This was less about desire than about satisfying his need to know.

Just as he leaned in with his mouth close enough to feel the soft puffs of air from between her lips, she dodged to the side. Her hands shot to the very top of her shirt and that highest button right under her chin as she walked to the sink. With shaking hands she turned on the water and slipped her hands under the stream.

Fury slammed through him. Looked like being that close to the hired help was beneath her. "You suddenly feel the need for a bath?"

"Germs."

Damn her. "What did you just say?"

"I touched the wall."

Her lies made the situation even worse. "No, you didn't."

"It's time to go." She grabbed for a paper towel and yanked hard enough to pull the roll out of the container. "Damn!"

The brown paper rolled across the floor, crisscrossing the previously laid toilet paper trail. He watched her crouch down and try to clean up the mess. Saw the woman who was so terrified of kissing him be okay about running her fingers over the filthy floor.

An old rage overtook him. He had stopped letting people treat him like crap decades ago. He no longer just took it because that's what he needed to do to stay in an apartment or get food. That kid grew up, got a badge, and refused to give anyone the power to make him feel unworthy again. Then along came Deana and he morphed back into that stupid poor kid again. The sensation shook him.

She glanced up. "You could help me."

"No thanks." He unlocked the door. "Don't want to get my hands dirty."

That was the second time Josh exited a room and left her staring at a closed door. The guy knew how to get the most drama from a situation.

Deana's bigger concern centered on how in just a few seconds he had managed to make her insides puddle. When he had moved in close and she inhaled that masculine mix of sunshine and musk that clung to his skin, her resistance shattered into a million pieces. Even now her hands trembled and refused to stop. She clenched and unclenched her fingers, trying to gain control over her muscles.

In that moment of closeness she wanted him to kiss her. And like every mindless woman she had read about in that file on his past, she wanted him to want her back. She had mentally classified the others as silly and gullible. Stupid, even.

Then what the hell did that make her?

Chapter Eight

Josh could think of a thousand places he'd rather be on a sunny Thursday afternoon than at the Halawa Correctional Facility. Surfing, lounging on Derek's deck, washing his car. Hell, taking a dip in the ice-cold ocean surrounded by a school of jellyfish sounded better than this.

Every time Josh drove up the state road leading to the prison the same sense of desolation hit him. Here in the middle of paradise sat a depressing overcrowded men's prison facility: two buildings, one for medium and another for maximum security, including housing for the mentally ill; concrete slabs, a high wire fence, and a hopelessness that stretched from the mountains to the water.

Ryan's new home was in maximum security. For the time being he was housed in protective custody out of fear for retribution and concerns about his age. Trying teens as adults in homicide cases was not the norm in Hawaii. Being a felon from such a famous murder case and good-looking at that made Ryan a substantial target.

Everyone knew that except Ryan, who was busy trying to make it tough to guard him. Rather than keep his head down and mouth shut, the kid had lodged a number of complaints. He balked at the intense scrutiny and long hours of boredom that came with constant lock-up.

Having talked with the warden, Josh knew the precautions were for Ryan's protection. Josh also knew Ryan had a potentially bigger problem. Due to overcrowding, the state farmed prisoners out to Arizona, Oklahoma, and Mississippi. As a minor it was unlikely he'd be shipped out but not impossible.

Josh tapped his pen against his yellow lined legal pad as he waited for the guards to bring Ryan in. The small, stale-smelling meeting room was less than ideal, but it would work for an initial talk. Sizing up the kid was the goal.

Josh had read through the files and all of the newspaper accounts. He hadn't heard back from Eric, but Ryan's newest high-priced counsel, Elias Johns, a partner in a downtown firm, had been more than happy for the help. Johns made an associate and other legal staff available as well as all of the parts of the file not protected by attorney–client privilege.

Josh understood why Ryan got convicted. The case was solid. Problem started with the kid's past criminal record. Between troubles at school and a foul attitude, Ryan didn't exactly make a favorable impression. Pointing the finger of accusation in his direction proved relatively easy.

But doubts lingered over Ryan's guilt. Other suspects and other pieces of evidence pointed in other directions. And, as much as Josh hated to admit it, many jurors believed the Armstrong family deserved to know hardship, as evidenced by interviews the defense conducted with the jury after the trial. These jurors felt the Armstrongs should be punished for having all of that money and good fortune.

Looked like having piles of cash wasn't always a positive thing.

Josh heard the footsteps followed by the clicking and buzzing sounds of unlocking metal doors. A few seconds later Ryan walked in with two guards behind him.

Josh nodded to the officers. "Thanks, guys."

Once they were alone Ryan slouched down in the chair across from Josh. A mop of brown hair still hung over his right eye. The ever-present mopey frown continued to be his only expression. He'd grown about an inch. Sure looked as if he had filled out through the shoulders.

In the three months since the verdict and thirteen months since the murders, Ryan had aged from fifteen to sixteen. Josh did not see any evidence of increased maturity from the extra year. Ryan did possess the Armstrong attractive gene. Josh didn't have to look too hard to see similarities to Deana's mouth and eyes.

Strong features and a square jaw with too-big clothes and shuffling step. Without the prison-issued outfit, Ryan could have slipped into any high school anywhere and fit in fine. Without the drugs and with a little more focus, he could have been a popular school athlete with a designer wardrobe and expensive car to match. He chose, instead, to be a drug dealer and killer.

"She convinced you to come." Ryan traced his fingertips over the scratches in the table.

"Your aunt? Yeah, well, she's persuasive."

"Never thought she'd deliver."

"Me, either," Josh muttered.

For the first time since he walked in, Ryan glanced up. His clear blue eyes held both contempt and fear. "Why d'ya let her push you around?"

"Guys do that sometimes."

"So you're banging her."

Josh thumped his closed hand against the table with

enough force to make the kid jump. "Watch your language."

"Nobody asked her to, you know."

"Want to know the truth?" Josh decided to tweak the kid to see if his tough-guy outer shell covered up anything worth saving underneath. "I don't know why the hell your aunt keeps going out on a limb for you. As far as I can tell, you're an arrogant pissant who blew a good life and now wants to blame everyone else. You know what that makes you?"

Ryan stared down at his hands. "Don't care what you think."

"It makes you a fucking loser."

Ryan's head snapped up with his face flushed red. "You're still sore about what happened when it all went down."

Josh knew the kid was talking about the drug bust more than two years ago where one of Ryan's friends stuck a gun in Josh's face. "You could say that."

Ryan's fingers moved faster over the table's marks. "Didn't do any time for that."

"You got lucky."

"Not luck"—Ryan tapped his forehead—"brains."

Josh twirled his pen in his fingers to keep from shoving this kid against the wall and yelling some sense into him. "And now you've graduated to murder. Congratulations."

Ryan's smart-ass smirk disappeared. "No."

"Your parents are dead. You would have been rich if you hadn't gotten caught."

Tension played across Ryan's shoulders and on his face. "I didn't kill them."

"Why should I believe you?"

Instead of dissolving in tears, the kid sat up straighter. "I don't give a shit if you do."

Josh heard Ryan's sneakers hit the floor as the front of his chair returned to the ground. The tough act. It was the only play this kid had. He liked to act street, as if he had a rough upbringing instead of a life consisting of private school and a house on the beach.

"Tell me what my aunt promised you to get you here." Ryan peeked up under all that hair.

"What do you care?"

"Something good?"

Josh ignored the kid's mocking tone. "She asked me."

"I'm supposed to believe you give a rat's ass what happens to me now, after all the drug stuff?"

"I wouldn't go that far."

"Whatever. You've seen me." Ryan threw his hands out to the side. "Are we done here?"

"What I see is that you haven't changed all that much. Seem like the same kid who looked for the easy way out of a drug charge."

"I beat that fair."

"With your parents' help and money. Guess that can't happen again now that they're dead, huh?"

Ryan's face fell. Josh had seen the sudden change with juvenile offenders before. One minute they tried to play him, next came trembling lips and tears. From old souls to little boys sometimes out of real emotion and sometimes just to beat a charge. Josh couldn't get a read on where Ryan fell on the scale.

"You don't get it." Ryan's voice bobbled in the middle of the sentence.

"Explain it to me."

"They were my parents."

Josh noticed Ryan didn't talk about loving them or missing them. "And they had all of the money."

Ryan shook his head. "Didn't care about that."

"They decided how much you got and when you could have it. Problem was, you wanted it right now."

Ryan continued to look down, refusing to make eye contact. "Not true."

"They cut your access to cash when you got in trouble with drugs. Tried to tell you who you could hang out with. Who your friends should be."

"You didn't know them." Ryan slumped back in his seat and wiped a hand across his eyes. "Don't talk about them."

Ryan's voice grew deeper, as if his anger bubbled right under the surface. That's what Josh wanted. To push Ryan and see what kid came out on the other side of the questioning. It was a matter of figuring out how to break through all that teenage "I don't need anybody" crap and get a true read on the kid.

"Probably some sort of tough love thing. I'm betting a therapist told your parents to give you a boundary and set a bunch of new rules. But you didn't like that, did you?"

"I changed after rehab." Ryan rubbed at the table markings as if he could somehow erase them with his thumb.

"Sure. You got smarter. Played the game better. Would have been surprising if you hadn't."

Ryan lifted his head and stared Josh down. "I got clean."

"But they didn't forgive you."

Ryan just shrugged.

"And you resented them for that," Josh said.

"Go fuck yourself."

A guard's face appeared in the small window of the door in response to the kid's yelling. Josh waved him off. He wanted this kid talking, so he kept pushing. "Someone beat your mother's head in with a baseball bat, and that's all you've got to say to me?"

"Why should I tell you anything?"

"Because I'm here. Because I could be your only shot."

Ryan ground his finger against the table. "You think I did it. You're just like everyone else."

"I'm trying to see if you should be out of here."

"Aunt Deana thinks . . ." That sudden the anger rushed out of him, leaving behind a kid who looked far younger than his age. "She's only doing this because of guilt."

Josh gave the kid credit for being perceptive. "She cares about you and is trying to get you the help you need to prove your case while the appeals process drags out."

"She can't do anything." Ryan lowered his voice to a near whisper as he wiped his hands over his face. "It's too late. I'm stuck in here."

The kid's emotions yo-yoed from one extreme to the other. Josh chalked part of the problem up to hormones and typical teenage angst and drama. But nothing about Ryan's life qualified as normal. Before the arrests, he was privileged and spoiled. Now he was stuck in an unfathomable cycle of isolation and violence.

And then there was the part Josh kept trying to push out of his mind. He looked at Ryan and saw glimmers of Deana. Josh tried to fully separate the two but failed.

"I've read your file," Josh said.

"Uh-huh."

"I read about your dad's business partner." Josh knew he had the kid's attention now. He feigned disinterest, but his body snapped to attention, every muscle stiffening at the mention of the past. "Also know about the debts and fighting between your dad and this guy."

Ryan's head shot up, but he stayed silent.

"Then there's your old friend," Josh continued. "The one

who came looking for drug money and got mad when you turned him down."

"My dad kicked him out." Ryan's eyes glazed over as if he were lost in a memory.

"Bet that didn't go over so well."

"Dad was pissed. I'd promised not to hang out with any of the guys from the drug stuff. When Dad saw Frankie . . ."

"Did Frankie threaten your dad?"

Ryan looked up with pleading in his eyes. "It was just talk. Stupid shit we all say when we're pissed off. I didn't take it seriously."

Josh wondered whether that would turn out to be the biggest mistake the kid ever made. "What else do I need to know about your case?"

"I didn't do it." Ryan looked Josh straight in the eye. No hesitation. No stumbling. "I could never do that shit. No way."

Eye contact or not, Josh didn't trust a thing the kid said. The cloudy eyes, the anger, all of it could be part of an elaborate con. The psychologist's report talked about Ryan's propensity for lying and his acute narcissism. For whatever reason, Ryan viewed himself as a perpetual victim who deserved better. And Josh's history with this kid supported that view.

"I need to hear the story from you, Ryan. Every part of it, no matter if you've told it a hundred times and whether or not you think I know it," Josh said. "Start with the days after the drug arrest and take me to now."

"That's a lot."

"It could all be important."

Ryan traced his finger along the edge of Josh's notepad. "And if you think I'm innocent?"

"I'll turn over the evidence, cause a scene, go to the

media. Basically, I'll do whatever it takes to get your conviction overturned and you out of here."

Ryan smiled, this one genuine and not the baiting kind. "Cool."

"But let's get one thing straight." Josh waited until he was sure he had the kid's full attention. "If I think you did it, I walk away and then fight to make sure you live the rest of your life in this place. Your appeal will be meaningless and I'll be the first face you see everytime you try to leave here early."

"Aunt Deana agreed to that?"

He doubted she entertained that possibility. That was part of the problem.

Chapter Nine

Deana touched her fingertips against the blurry tile wall, then pushed off into her final turn. A bluesy tune rang out of the built-in deck speakers as her body sliced through the cool water on the return lap to the other end of the pool.

She closed her eyes and fell into a rhythm. Tried to block out the melody and focus, instead, on keeping her stroke in time with the beat. She needed a mind wiped clear of any thoughts or memories. One where the sound of Ryan's agitated voice from the other end of the phone didn't still ring in her ears.

Seemed Josh liked to spread cheer wherever he went. In the span of a short visit the day before, Josh convinced Ryan to give up hope. Even if Josh believed the prosecution's story, he didn't have to drive that point home to a scared teen locked behind bars and desperate for help.

With each stroke, each rise of her arm, her thoughts crushed in on her. Doubt, fear, anger. The dragging sense of loss that would not leave. Identifying the bodies of Chace and Kalanie at the morgue. Listening to the police investigators voice their doubts about Ryan's story and how he couldn't possibly have slept through the entire attack as he claimed.

Some days the reminders proved to be too much.

She brushed the wall and stood up. Water lapped against her hips in the shallow end of the pool. She rubbed her eyes, willing to do anything to stop the visions spinning around in her head.

Dropping her hands, she mentally assessed her options for saving Ryan. She could not come up with a single strategy that didn't include Josh. Controlling him would be the issue. She had trusted the defense attorneys, had let them do their jobs, and they failed. She needed more of a say in tactics and analysis this time around.

When the hot sun began to burn her arms, she gave up on her planning and let her mind turn to lunch. A movement by the house caught her attention. As if she had conjured him, Josh stood right there on her deck, less than twenty feet away, with a stern frown on his face.

"Josh?" She barely made a sound, but she knew he heard her when he started moving.

He took the last three steps down to the edge of the pool. "What is that?"

Her mind refused to adjust to the sight of him. One minute she thought about him, the next he appeared. She wiped her eyes one more time. "What did you say?"

He hitched his chin. "There. What the hell happened to you?"

She finally focused on his blue eyes and how his stare locked on her chest. It was not as if she wore a tiny bikini. She had grabbed her usual navy tank with the low rounded neck. Practical for exercise and not all that sexy.

Then it hit her. The marks. He saw them, couldn't take his eyes off them.

A familiar wave of dread crashed through her body. Since his focus didn't waver, she reached for her robe on the side of the pool and struggled into it with one hand while the other covered the area from her sternum to the top of her breasts.

"I wasn't expecting you," she said.

"Deana."

"I'll meet you up on the deck."

"Deana, stop."

But she couldn't. The cotton fought her, forcing her to wrestle to get the thing over her shoulders. She ended up in three feet of water with her cover floating up around her.

Josh's gaze dropped to the material bunched between her breasts and anchored in her tight fist. "Tell me how you got those scars."

She forced her shaking legs to move to the stairs and climb out. "Why are you here?"

"The scars, Deana. Where did you get them?"

The soaking-wet robe weighed a ton and stuck to her thighs, making it tough to walk without stumbling. "That's not important."

"It sure as hell is." He stepped forward, the flat line of his mouth fierce but his touch gentle as he wrapped his fingers around her elbow. "Explain."

"This is not your business."

The anger in Josh's eyes still lingered. "Did someone stab you?"

Eric had asked that question the very first time he saw her without a shirt. She couldn't even remember the answer she gave back then. She had no intention of explaining this time, either.

"No," she said this time to keep things simple.

"This is why you wear those clothes, right?"

Deana didn't understand his question. "What are you talking about?"

Josh folded his hand over her clenched fist. "There's no reason to hide. Let me see."

She tightened her death grip. "Absolutely not."

Being this close to him closed her throat. Seeing the pity in those sad blue eyes made her want to scream it back open. That was the last thing she wanted from Josh. From anyone.

"Deana, I—"

"Stop this." She pushed his hand away and walked around him, fighting for breath with each step. When she finally regained her voice she tried again. "Tell me why you're at my house."

He didn't budge. "I want an answer to my question."

She stepped up onto the deck and slid into one of the deck chairs, careful not to let the material at the top of her robe slip to reveal any more skin around her breasts. "Yeah, well. So do I."

Josh just stood there on the edge of the pool with his hands on his lean hips. "Did Eric do this?"

It was tempting to let Josh think so little of Eric. Her anger still burned hot enough to want some measure of revenge, or at least to cause Eric pain. But there had been enough false accusations in her life to last forever.

"Of course not," she said.

"You sure?"

"I think I'd know something like that."

Josh's gaze flicked to her chest and then back up again. "I'm not moving until you tell me."

"Then I hope you went to the bathroom before you came out here, because it's going to be a long stand." She crossed her legs and didn't try to grab the soggy robe as it fell down and slapped against the deck.

Josh's gaze bounced down to her legs this time. "Hadn't really thought that far ahead."

"You have any idea how tempting it is to push you in the pool?"

Josh glanced over his shoulder at the water. When he looked back, the tiny lines of stress around his eyes had disappeared. "You seem eager to drown me."

"You might want to keep that in mind." She tucked one end of the top of her robe under the other, checking to make sure everything she wanted covered stayed covered. "How did you get in?"

"Your maid."

"She's not a maid."

"I'm not familiar with proper titles for your household staff. All I know is that she keeps answering your door."

"She's Mrs. Chow."

"Do you call all of the help by name?"

"She's not *help*."

"Then what is she?"

"Not your concern."

Josh dropped into the seat across from Deana. "You're a pain in the ass."

"I could say the same about you."

"You wouldn't be the first." He fiddled with the edge of the fruit plate—remnants of Deana's breakfast—sitting between them. "You're not going to share, are you?"

At least they were finally finding a new subject. "About Mrs. Chow?"

"About what happened to your chest."

So much for moving on. "That subject is off limits. I called you because I heard from—"

He tapped his finger against his lips. "I can find out, you know."

She should have shoved him in the pool when she had the chance. "I'm paying you to investigate Ryan's case, not to poke around in my life."

"This one would be on the house."

"Rather than wasting time with that, I'd like you to tell me what you were doing at the prison yesterday."

"Mowing the grass." He flashed her a look that telegraphed "duh" without saying the word. "What the hell do you think?"

"You upset him."

"I see little Ryan called his overprotective auntie and asked her to have the big bad investigator stop picking on him," Josh said in a singsongy voice.

"Must you do that?"

"Hell, I'm surprised the kid didn't call his congressman or seek asylum from the State Department. Maybe we could have him sainted."

She was grateful Josh stopped staring at her breasts, but shutting down his mouth seemed to be impossible. "Are you done?"

He looked up at the sky as if he were considering the question. "For now."

"Ryan's reaction is why I left you the voice mail."

"The one saying you *had* to see me today? Yeah, about that . . ." Josh thrummed his fingers against the table. "I hate being ordered around."

"Ryan was upset."

Josh plucked a grape off the plate. "Your point?"

"Ryan is having a hard enough time without being bullied by you."

"You do understand he's in prison and not at summer camp, right?"

"He's upset about what you said to him."

"He'll get over it." Josh popped the grape in his mouth and chewed for a few seconds. "Eventually."

"I'm serious."

"I can see that." Josh's gaze dipped to her chest again but didn't linger this time.

"Ryan believes you think he's guilty."

Josh squeezed a second grape between his fingers. "That's not exactly news."

"You are being paid—"

He leaned back with his feet stretched out in front of him. "Do us both a favor and stop mentioning all of your money."

She checked Josh's finances at the time of the first trial and knew he did fine. Sure, he didn't earn a fortune through the government, but he didn't spend much, either. Despite the lazy air about him, there wasn't much negative to find. Not a drinker, gambler, or traveler so far as she could tell. His money obsession just didn't make any sense. Ticked her off, too.

"I was pointing out the realities of our business relationship," she explained in the calmest voice she could muster.

"Sure you were."

"What do you have against money?"

"My problem is not with having it. It's with flashing it around to avoid responsibility."

The charge stuck more than she wanted it to. "And that's what you think I'm doing?"

"Look at how your family treated the drug charges against Ryan. Look at what you're doing now about the murder convictions. Hell, look at this place. It's unbelievable." Josh swept an arm out taking in the swath of land from the glass doors to the ocean.

Sure the house was plush, but it was so much more than land value and location. The sound of the ocean at night soothed her. She chose every stick of furniture in the house, every plant in the garden, and every tile in the pool with ultimate care. This house saved her, allowed her to nest. It was the first place that was ever hers—not her family's but hers.

But he was dead wrong about how she viewed money. About who her brother was. Josh made assumptions and went flying off on tangents. An absolutely annoying trait as far as she was concerned. "You don't know anything about me or my family."

"We can share stories." He ignored the grapes and tried an apple. "Start by telling me about the scars."

She refused to get trapped in that cycle again. "My rules are simple enough to—"

"Rules about what?"

"Stop interrupting." She ran a hand over her drying hair. "You need to keep me informed about your actions. This is not an unusual request."

"I'll file a weekly report."

"I'm not kidding."

Josh smiled. "That's a problem, because I am. I'm kind of done with weekly reports. Gave that up with the steady DEA paycheck and retirement plan."

She closed her eyes on a deep sigh. It was either that or scream, and once she started that she wouldn't stop. "Could you at least agree not to upset Ryan?"

"Stop treating him like a kid. He's in prison. Being babied could get him killed."

"He is sixteen."

"He's a convicted murderer."

She had reached the point in the conversation where she had to leave or dunk Josh's head underwater. "If you're trying to convince me never to leave you another voice mail you're doing a good job."

Josh raised a fist in the air. "Mission accomplished."

"Enjoy the breakfast." She pushed back from the table and stood up.

He caught her before she could take two steps. His fingers curled around her elbows and pulled her close enough to catch the smell of peppermint on his breath.

"You don't need to hide them," Josh said as his eyes searched hers.

"Wh-what?"

"Scars or not, you're beautiful."

"This isn't appropriate." Deana fought to keep her voice steady even as her insides revved and churned.

"The high collars aren't necessary."

He didn't have any idea what he was talking about. He hadn't been there. Hadn't lived through the guilt and secrecy. Hadn't stayed up nights wishing he could take back just ten minutes of his life.

"I don't need a pep talk." She kept her hands wound around the material holding the top together.

"What do you need?"

"To change."

He brushed his nose along the side of her face in a gesture so soft and sweet a breath thumped in her chest. When he blew a puff of air against her ear, her shoulders shook on a shiver.

"You know what I mean," he whispered into her hair.

No, no, no. This couldn't be happening. The kick-up of her heartbeat. The way the air lodged in her throat and refused to break loose. She recognized the signs and tried to punch them back down before they ran wild and got her in trouble.

"I need to change out of my wet suit," she said.

His fingers traced a line along her chin. "The air is warm. You're fine. More than fine, I'd say."

"I don't—"

The kiss cut off whatever else she might have said. Her thoughts jumbled as his mouth slanted across hers and his fingers slipped into her hair. And she didn't fight it. Couldn't.

Before her brain started working again, her arms slipped around his neck and her body nestled against his from breast to thigh. When she sighed deep into his mouth, his hands slid to her back and pulled her even closer.

The kiss blocked out the sound of the crashing waves and the burn of the sun. The taste and feel of him overrode her common sense. Only the whisper of her name on his lips cracked the spell. Using every ounce of strength, Deana forced her legs to take a step back from him. Rather than break all contact, she let her hands trail down his chest to land on his stomach.

Josh moved faster, tunneling under the top of her robe and exposing her skin to the breeze. Instinctively her hands moved to cover the area. Only the reverent way he smoothed his fingertips over the jagged ridges of the scars kept her from dragging the robe's edges together again.

"You don't need to cover up any part of your body," he whispered.

This was happening all wrong. He was taking the choice away from her with his mumbled words and drugging kisses. The softness around his eyes wore her down until she lost her grip and let him see her nightmare.

Now she knew what had mesmerized all of those other women. And just how dangerous a man could be.

She grabbed the edges of her robe and closed them again. "I'm going inside."

"You're running away."

"I plan to walk." She broke away from him.

"And I plan to watch."

"Don't be here when I get back."

Chapter Ten

Josh spent most of the next day sitting at Derek's kitchen table with a laptop in front of him and boxes of files piled on the floor around his chair. After hours of leaning over and not standing up, Josh's back ached. His head pounded from a mix of too much coffee and too many potato chips.

Still, he couldn't stop. Whenever he did, he saw Deana's face. Saw the puckered lines that extended from under her collarbone in a jagged Y to the tops of her breasts. She talked tough and refused to share anything about the injury, but the sadness in her eyes told him what he needed to know. She had survived something horrible. Something that shaped her and kept her isolated.

He needed the details.

This was what he did for a living. Dug and dug until he found that one piece of information to tip the case. He wanted to hear the explanation from her, but he would settle for finding the basics somewhere else. Whatever it took to break through her reserve.

Getting her to kiss him again had also moved up on his to-do list. The memory continued to shake him. He had expected a cool reaction, one that would let him exorcise her from his thoughts and this unwanted attraction from his system. What he got, instead, was a woman on fire from the inside out. Nothing chilly under all those clothes. Just pure woman wanting him back.

And now Josh had to figure out what the hell to do about that spark. He pressed the heels of the hands to his eyes, hoping something brilliant would come to him. Being intrigued was one thing. Sleeping with a woman who helped pay his mortgage fell into a never-going-to-happen category. Or it always had until now.

"You can still move your legs, right?" Annie asked the question from her position at the kitchen sink. She leaned against the counter, snuggled up against Kane's side, drinking coffee.

Josh dropped his hands and adjusted to the bright light flooding the room. The question was when he stopped being alone. "I thought you two were going to the beach."

"We did." Annie held up three fingers and wiggled them. "Hours ago, and now we're back."

"Give the man a break, honey. He's working," Kane said. "It's nice to see he still knows how."

Josh dropped his pen long enough to hold up a finger of his own. "Kiss my—"

Annie frowned. "Josh."

"Find anything yet?" Derek walked into the small room in a T-shirt and board shorts. He didn't stop until he hit the refrigerator and threw the door open.

Josh envied the kid his day of surfing. "Do you ever go to an office?"

"First, it's Saturday. Second, I work in sustainable fisheries. My life is the water, my friend." Derek grabbed a can of soda and popped the top, saying the line like he practiced it every day.

"You sound ridiculous," Kane said.

Josh agreed with that assessment, but he also envied Derek's relaxed demeanor. The kid worked his tail off but never ruffled. One more way Derek resembled Kane.

"Kane's right, but for the record does that crap work with women?" Josh asked.

Derek broke into that huge smile. "Oh, yeah."

"Give me that." Annie took Derek's soda and poured it into a glass. "This isn't a dorm."

Derek frowned. "No, it's my kitchen."

Annie sent a group frown to all the men in the room. "Kane and Josh are bad influences on you."

"Hey, I'm a married man," Kane said. "My fun days are long over."

Her eyebrow inched up. "You plan on sleeping outside tonight?"

"As fun as this is, I'm working here." Josh pointed at the doorway to the family room. "You should all feel free to go somewhere else and then stay there for a very long time."

As expected, they all ignored him.

Derek leaned over Josh's shoulder and stared at the computer screen. "What are you doing?"

Josh clicked the minimized the window and brought up his home page. No need to get everyone poking around in Deana's business. "Just getting up to speed on Ryan's case."

Derek pointed at the tab with Deana's name on it. "Looks to me like you're investigating your new boss's background."

"Hmmm. I guess she is your boss. Never thought of it that way." Annie's smile grew. "I like it."

Deana's power position in their relationship was just

about the last thing Josh wanted to think about. "Makes one of us."

"You trying to get fired? You know . . ." Kane coughed. "Again."

Josh shut the top of the computer. "Don't worry about me. Just go do whatever the hell it is you three do on Saturday before dinner. Preferably something outside and away from here."

"You all know this is my house, right?" Derek asked.

Annie reached over and tried to pry the laptop open around Josh's fingers. "Let me see if you're looking for trouble."

Josh put his arm over the computer to keep it shut. No way was he losing this wrestling match to Annie. He outweighed her and Kane still had a hand on her back, so Josh knew he had the advantage.

"Why do you always think I'm doing something bad?" Josh asked.

"Probably from experience." Derek took a long drink.

Annie drummed her fingernails on the laptop. "Tell me why you're bothering Deana."

"I'm not."

"You're digging into her life. Why? You have ten seconds to explain yourself, Joshua Windsor."

Kane whistled. "You're in trouble now. You made Annie break out the full-name thing."

"That's never good," Derek said.

Kane pulled out a chair and sat down perpendicular to Josh at the square table. "May as well tell us what you're up to and avoid the hours of agonizing torment as Annie argues you to death."

"Sounds like my last date," Josh said as he tightened his grip on the computer. He knew Kane planned to take it at the first opportunity.

Derek shook his head. "Man, you're definitely off your game with women. No wonder you're kicking around here and coming home alone each night."

"It's a disappointing thing to see a man lose it like that." Kane stared at his wife when she made a little growling sound. "What? It is."

Annie dropped into Kane's lap. "Don't encourage the locker-room talk."

"Let's get back to the subject." Derek reached into the chip bag next to Josh and brought out crumbs. "About Deana . . ."

Josh decided life would be easier if Derek were still a kid and not too smart. Having friends less nosy would also work. "Look, it's nothing. I just wanted to get a better handle on her, so I did an Internet search."

And didn't find a damn thing new or of interest. Whatever happened to Deana happened in relative silence. Josh tapped into his office computer. Leave it to his idiot former boss at the DEA to forget not only to cut online access but also to drop the password off the system. Didn't matter anyway, since Josh couldn't find a local police record about Deana's injuries. Nothing from newspapers, either.

That left Eric as the best possible source of information. Josh tried to come up with a good way to drop that question into a conversation. Not exactly easy.

"For the record, I think you'd be smart to keep your hands off Deana." Kane leveled a man-to-man stare at Josh. "You hear me?"

Josh wanted to follow the advice, but all he could think about was getting his hands all over Deana. The image kept spinning through his head until he couldn't think of anything else.

"Good lord, you're sleeping with her." Annie said it more as an accusation than a statement.

Kane shook his head and swore. "Knew we should have taken him back to Kauai and locked him in a bathroom before he did something stupid."

"Is it too late to neuter him?" Derek asked.

How the hell did a guy get any work done in this house? "I'm not sleeping with Deana—"

Annie set her mug down against the table with a bang. "But you want to."

Josh ignored that. "I need to concentrate on getting through these police and medical files so I can make a list of alternative suspects."

Kane leaned back in his chair. "I'm police. I can help."

No way was Josh dragging Kane into this mess. One of them being dumb enough to get involved was already one too many. "I work alone on this."

From Kane's scowl, Josh knew his friend didn't like the answer. Tough shit, because Josh intended to protect Kane whether or not Kane wanted it.

Derek kept staring out the window. "Uh, hello? Guys?"

"Look, Kane," Josh said. "It's not an official investigation. You can't use office resources or personnel on this. If you do, you'll only raise a conflict-of-interest flag."

"As interesting as it is to talk about you sleeping with Deana and Kane losing his job, we have a bigger issue." Derek shoveled chip dust into his mouth as he talked.

Josh decided to ignore the older idiots and handle the youngest one first. "Derek, the computer search of Deana isn't a big deal. Let it go."

"I'm not talking about that." Derek crumpled the empty bag in his hand. "I'm talking about her."

"So was I," Annie said.

Derek shook his head. "No. I meant that she's here."

Josh glanced between Annie and Derek. "Who?"

"What exactly is in that bag, Derek?" Kane asked.

"Nothing, thanks to Josh." Derek practically pressed his nose against the window. "And the *she* is Deana, who should be knocking on the door any second now."

Annie smiled. "Good. I can finally meet her."

Josh tried to think of a worse idea. Annie with Deana—yeah, that was a combination certain to drive him to his knees. Annie would badger and Deana would sit there looking kissable. Not good at all.

"Very pretty." Derek's eyes narrowed. "But, man, that thing she's wearing looks hot as hell."

"Wait, you're not just screwing with Josh? Deana is actually here?" Kane asked.

Josh knew the answer—from the clothing description only one person could have walked up to the house. "That woman has a stalking issue."

"I can arrest her for you," Kane said.

"And miss talking with her about Josh? No way." Annie rested her head on her husband's shoulder.

The doorbell rang, but Josh hesitated. He was about to face down Deana for the first time since she kicked him out of her house. He'd hoped this follow-up conversation would take place later, when he had more information and when his friends were nowhere around.

Josh's chair screeched against the tile floor as he stood up. "This is not an opportunity for matchmaking."

"Sure it is." Annie had the nerve to look serious when she said it.

"I guess it's too much to hope that you'll leave without meeting Deana," Josh said as he tried to come up with the best strategy to deal with what was sure to be an annoying next ten minutes.

Kane cleared his throat. "Is anyone going to actually answer the door?"

Josh pointed at Annie before she could move. "You stay right there."

"That's not a very friendly thing to say to me."

"Usually not very effective, either," Kane replied with more than a little laughter in his voice.

Josh didn't wait for one of them to run ahead and open the door. "Nobody move."

"Wouldn't dream of it," Derek said.

Josh dodged the small sectional sofa in the family room and headed for the door. He glanced back into the kitchen and saw that Kane had spun the laptop around and was fiddling with the keys. Having cops for friends made keeping secrets tough, but Josh knew he would have done the same thing in Kane's position.

The doorbell rang again. When Kane yelled to "open the damn door," Josh debated strangling his friend versus letting Deana in. The third chime forced the decision.

"What are you doing here?" Josh asked the question the minute he opened the door and saw Deana on the doorstep.

Her fist froze in midair as if she were preparing to knock this time. "Is that how you greet people?"

"Uh-huh."

"Most people say hello first," she said.

"Fine." Josh balanced a hand against the door frame to try to block her view of the cavesdropping roundtable in the kitchen. "Hello. Now, what are you doing here?"

With her hair smoothed back off her tanned face in clips of some sort, Deana looked fresh and young. The white pants worked in the tropical surroundings. The slim black turtleneck and matching cardigan looked more Northeast than Hawaii. But that wasn't news.

A hand shot out under Josh's arm in Deana's general direction. "Hi. I'm Annie."

Josh didn't have a choice but to invite Deana inside the house now. He backed up to leave room, noticing for the first time that Annie, Kane, and Derek all stood directly behind him. He made a mental note to yell at the annoying welcoming party later.

Making introductions took two seconds. Everyone shook hands and traded welcomes. Josh noticed Deana appeared more relaxed with his friends than him. The strained smile gave way to a warm one and had Derek grinning back like an idiot. Josh could almost see Annie mentally planning double dates.

Time to stop all of that. "What are you doing here, Deana?"

Annie frowned at the delivery. "What kind of way is that to talk to a guest?"

Kane laughed. "Yeah, Josh."

Annie edged her way in between Josh and Deana. "Clearly she's here for dinner."

"I'm what?" Deana asked.

"*What?*" Josh said at the same time.

Annie touched her hand to Deana's elbow and steered her toward the kitchen with Derek close on their heels. Josh figured two more seconds and Derek would start drooling.

"This is perfect timing. We can sit down and chat before we eat," Annie explained to Deana.

Josh watched the women walk away as the floor collapsed beneath his feet. "What the hell just happened?"

Kane slapped Josh on the back. "Basically? You're screwed."

"I can't have Deana here." Josh needed the separation of

work and home. Needed to keep Deana on the outside and away from the parts of his life unrelated to the investigation.

"It's just lucky for you I closed your computer," Kane said. "Yeah, we'll talk about what I saw later."

Josh vowed to avoid that lecture. "Like hell."

"I'd save my energy for what's about to happen if I were you."

Josh watched as Annie laughed at something Deana said. "This is going to be bad."

"It's not going to be good." Kane coughed. "Not for you anyway. Me, well, I plan to enjoy the shit out of it."

"Thanks."

"What are friends for?"

"I was wondering that myself."

Chapter Eleven

Deana wondered for the third time how she ended up sitting at Derek's kitchen table eating pizza with three people she didn't know and one she kept trying to wipe clear from her mind.

From a scorching kiss to a cozy dinner in one day. Maybe asking for Josh's help wasn't such a great idea after all. She had spent the past hour turning down beers, dodging questions, and shifting the conversation back to the other people in the room. She now knew Kane and Annie were newlyweds. Deana pried details out of them about their fast courtship and enjoyed a much smoother back-and-forth about Annie's photojournalism assignments.

Deana tried to hang in there and follow Derek's explanation about his research project. Something through Hawaii Pacific University and an institute there. And fish. She picked up on the part about fish . . . sort of.

Nothing else made much sense. Likely because she had trouble concentrating on the topics while Josh sat there, arms crossed, wearing an unwelcome frown. The guy had brooding down to an art.

Kane wasn't all that much better. Sure, he acted friendly enough, especially when his wife elbowed him or flashed him an overly excited smile. Still, she could sense Kane watching and analyzing. It was as if Josh and Kane expected her to steal the silverware.

The heat only added to Deana's discomfort. She was sweating her butt off. She slipped her shoes off and rested her bare feet against the cool marble tile. That helped with her internal temperature, but not much.

Everyone else wore T-shirts. She had on a silk sweater set. The outfit seemed like a good choice back at her house. Her *air-conditioned* house. Derek depended on open windows and trade winds to keep his house cool. Just her luck the air wasn't moving tonight.

"Problem?" Josh asked as he reached for what she counted to be his fourth slice of pizza.

"Other than your attitude?" Kane asked with more than a touch of a warning in his tone.

Derek winked at her from his position sitting on the counter. "We apologize for Josh. He usually doesn't shut up."

"Don't bother defending me. Deana and I understand each other just fine, don't we?"

The challenge. Josh had issued one as sure as if he had stood up and suggested a round of arm wrestling. Between the lazy disinterest he showed for the table conversation and the way his gaze rarely left her face, Deana knew. He didn't want her here. Didn't appreciate her interference. Apparently kissing didn't move the man to give up his scowl.

"We're trying to reach a middle ground," she said, refusing to back away from this simmering fight.

"You can take off your top," Josh said.

Kane coughed over a swallow of beer before finally regaining his breath. "Should we leave the room?"

"Men are such idiots," Annie muttered under her breath.

"Damn, Josh." Derek shook his head as he threw another crust down on his plate. "Not the most tactful delivery ever. What's wrong with you?"

Deana appreciated the flash of support from total strangers, but she didn't even flinch at Josh's comment. He thought he had her all figured out. He categorized her as some sort of crime victim and planned to rescue her like he did with everyone else. For someone hell-bent on convincing the world he was not the sort of guy to ride in and avenge every misdeed, he sure was acting like one.

But he had her story all wrong. No one hurt her. There was only one person to blame for the scar—Deana Alyssa Armstrong. She didn't need a savior. So, Josh could just aim all that hero power somewhere else, preferably in her nephew's direction.

In the meantime a lesson in shoving back was in order. "I think I *will* get more comfortable, if no one minds."

Josh didn't move, but his big blue eyes grew even wider as she slipped the cardigan off her shoulders, revealing a sleeveless turtleneck and arms toned by daily laps in the pool. Then his stare moved lower. Over her breasts and down, as if assessing every curve.

She knew the shirt highlighted her shoulders while hiding her scar. From the way Derek grinned, she guessed it showed off her figure as well. Just as she planned.

Kane waited until his wife's mouth was full of food to break the unexpected silence. "You never said why you showed up here today."

Rather than spilling it now and running the risk of having Annie choke on a chunk of pizza, Deana went with a partial explanation. "To check Josh's progress."

Kane nodded in understanding. "Then you'll be happy to know he spent all afternoon working."

About time Josh showed some interest in the task at hand. She'd been looking for some sign of hope. Maybe it finally arrived.

Derek swallowed the last of his pizza. "Josh even took some time to do a little side job and search the Internet on another subject."

"Remind me to kill you later," Josh mumbled.

The subject of that search was not exactly a secret. Deana had expected Josh to engage in some poking around into her background. She didn't panic over the thought because she knew there was nothing there. "Find out anything interesting during all that searching?"

Josh pushed his uneaten food around on his plate. "I'm still working on it."

The man could evade and posture as well as any lawyer she had ever met. That was not a good attribute in her view. "How about you share some of your insights on Ryan?"

Josh sat back and threw his napkin on the table. "All I know so far is that your nephew is in jail and everyone who says he bashed his parents' heads in with a baseball bat appears to be correct."

The glass slipped out of Annie's hand and thunked against the table. Kane caught the beverage, letting the soda slosh over his forearm. Without missing a beat he wiped up the mess with a spare napkin, then curled the fingers of his other hand through his wife's.

Looked like Josh wasn't the only man in the room with a protective streak. Unlike Josh, Kane showed it without shouting.

In all, the scene in the cozy kitchen struck Deana as homey and comfortable. She knew Derek lived here with Josh popping up as a recent guest. She suspected Josh's friends flew over for moral support after this morning's newspaper headlines announced Josh's termination from the DEA for failure to comply with administrative warnings.

If Josh was upset, he hid it well. He stayed focused on the conversation and aimed his anger right at her. Still, it had to destroy a man's confidence to see his name connected to charges of governmental negligence, even if the reporter painted him as the innocent party in the mess.

Regardless of the reason for the Travers clan show of force, Deana envied it. She missed that sort of bone-deep loyalty. Longed for it. She had enjoyed a close relationship with Chace. He was a solid man. Funny and smart, hardworking and dedicated.

They had spent hours talking about Chace's worries over Ryan's choice of friends and problems with drugs. She tried to convince her brother that Ryan's experiences amounted to growing pains, all while fearing her nephew was traveling down a familiar and dangerous path. Even now she wondered if she had only shared a bit more about her past with Ryan, maybe she could have provided the wake-up call he needed.

As a scared kid she had basked in the momentary relief that came with her parents stepping in and making the horrible tolerable. As an adult, she knew nothing ever worked like that. Living with the daily guilt proved much harder than she ever imagined. She knew a little taste of what Ryan had experienced in that first round. If only he would have been grateful for the drug intervention and seized the opportunities his family offered two years ago.

Looking back now, his drug use seemed tame compared with being convicted of a double familial homicide. Deana refused to believe Ryan played any part in the deaths of Chace and Kalanie.

But in those horrible dark moments of uncertainty, when she spent too many hours alone with her thoughts, concern pricked at the back of Deana's mind. What if the lesson Ryan learned from that initial drug arrest was the wrong one? What if he came to expect he could do anything and get away with it?

What if he followed in Deana's footsteps but failed to heed the warning signs and, instead, veered off into the worst place imaginable?

She pushed the negative thoughts out of her head. "If you're not ready to give me a report on the investigation, we can talk about another issue."

"I just told you what I thought about Ryan," Josh said.

Josh never quit. The more reasonable she tried to be, the more defiant he became. She had wondered if the kiss would make him nicer, soften him somehow. Apparently not.

"I came over to discuss something else with you." A subject she hoped might go better with a crowd than in a one-on-one discussion.

"You have another relative in trouble?" Josh folded his arms behind his head and leaned back in his chair. "Interesting. Do tell."

"Most of my relatives are dead, but thanks." She forced those words out. It actually hurt her throat to say them. Still, she needed to knock that sarcastic snottiness right out of him.

Annie let out a little *"oh"* sound.

Derek tapped Josh on the shoulder with a bottle of beer. "That made you look like a jackass."

"Amazing how little effort it took to do that," Kane added.

While Deana liked the pile-on, she knew she had to get this out or she'd never say what she came to say. "It's a housing offer."

Josh slowly lowered his arms back to his sides. "A what?"

"I know you live on Kauai," Deana said in her most reasonable voice, even though she felt anything but at the moment.

Josh's gaze burned into her. This differed from the heated stare he shot her right before they kissed. This one looked more like he wanted to shoot her.

"Yeah, you mentioned something about visiting my place during your stalking phase," Josh said.

Derek raised his hand. "I'd like to hear more about Deana's housing plans."

Deana refused to get sidetracked by Derek's joking, Annie's smile, or Kane's assessing gaze. Keeping Josh nearby meant it would be easier to watch his progress and control any mishaps, to avoid the same mistake she made with Ryan's first set of lawyers on the homicide case.

Yesterday the idea seemed so logical. Move Josh in and keep him close. Then came that stupid kiss. Ever since then she had been rethinking the idea. She went back and forth in her head three times on the drive over. Even turned the car around once, only to remember that this was about Ryan and not her and head back in the right direction.

"Your work for me requires you to stay on Oahu," she explained.

Josh picked up his napkin and rolled it between his palms. "Uh-huh."

"Does Josh really not know where this is going?" Kane didn't bother to lower his voice when he asked the question to his wife, who just smiled in return.

Deana could not imagine this conversation going any worse. Apparently every discussion with Josh would go this way, whether they had chaperones or not. "Anyway, I think it's unfair to expect you to go back and forth."

"I'm fine."

"And, really, that is not conducive to solving the case and getting Ryan out of prison as soon as possible."

Josh's hands froze in the middle of ripping the napkin to shreds. "That's not my job."

"Yes, it is."

"I told you—"

Deana waved him off. "I'm not going to argue with you about that subject now."

"Then what are you going to do with him? Just wondering since I can never come up with a good alternative." Kane asked in a serious voice even though he wore a smile on his face.

Deana set her glass down nice and slow. Despite having practiced this speech on the way over, she didn't want to screw it up by spilling her soft drink all over herself.

"I'm not paying you enough to stay in a hotel," she said to Josh.

Annie slipped her hand into her husband's. "I'm so glad we came to Oahu today. I would have hated to miss this dinner."

Deana shut out everyone but Josh. "Expecting you to stay here is unfair to both you and Derek."

"Mostly to me," Derek said.

A line of stress etched around Josh's eyes and mouth. "What exactly are you proposing?"

Kane shook his head. "Man, he's slow today."

Deana agreed with Kane's assessment. "I have a guesthouse at my residence on Lanikai. It's yours for as long as you need it"

Josh hopped on top of her words before she got them out. "No fucking way."

"Nice language," Kane mumbled under his breath.

Unlucky for Josh, Deana was tired of being ignored and minimized. "Look, I know you hate all rich people for some demented reason, but this is a logical solution to the problem."

"What does Josh have against money?" Derek asked.

Score one for the youngest and biggest brain in the room. Deana had been wondering that same thing ever since she confronted Josh in the courthouse.

Josh stood up and went to the sink. "You can dress the offer up any way you want. The answer is no. I have a house and a place to stay on Oahu. No charity needed."

Now that it was out there, Deana grew more convinced than ever this was the right move. She could see the files and boxes stacked around Derek's kitchen. She had watched Kane clean off all Josh's notes right after she arrived. With them packed away, she stayed in the dark.

Yeah, she needed Josh on a short leash. Chipping away at his attitude would be the problem.

"Mrs. Chow will move in with me temporarily, and you can have the cottage," she suggested.

"You have a cottage on your property? That sounds lovely." Annie turned to her husband. "We should do that."

"Our *house* is barely a cottage." Kane squeezed his wife's hand before turning back to Josh. "And who is Mrs. Chow?"

"I feel like we missed a significant part of the conversation," Derek said.

"She's an old family friend." Deana knew she should ex-

plain more but didn't bother. Not until she knew how much
pushback she was going to get from Josh.

"What about your mother?" Josh asked.

An odd question, but at least he wasn't yelling. Deana
took that as a good sign. "She'll live in her own house, of
course."

Josh's eyes narrowed. "You don't live together?"

"I'm not five. I'm old enough to have my own house,
don't you think? She doesn't cook my meals, either, in case
you're wondering."

"Josh doesn't do a lot of thinking," Kane said.

"Just slows him down," Derek added.

Josh held up his hand. "Everyone shut the hell up for a
second."

Annie scowled at him. "When did your language get so
nasty?"

Poor Josh looked as if he were the animal guest of honor
at a hunting party. Every muscle in his body snapped
straight and his mouth stretched into a line flat enough to
hurt.

"Your mother was at your house the other day," he said.

"To meet you. She lives in Diamond Head in the house I
grew up in. You were there years ago. She hasn't moved.
Says it reminds her of my father."

"I figured they . . ." Josh glanced around the room as if
seeking assistance.

"I think he's referring to your father's death." Warmth
moved into Kane's dark eyes. "I'm very sorry, by the way."

Annie and Derek offered their condolences as well. No
one needed to bother. Deana viewed her dad's death as just
one more numbing memory in a long line of them. He suffered a heart attack the day after her brother's murder. For
a man who worked and played harder than anyone in

Hawaii, the news of his only son's violent death and dear grandson's possible involvement proved too much.

Deana pushed down the flash of pain and concentrated on getting Josh to do what she wanted. "The Lanikai house is all mine."

"I love that part of the island. So peaceful with very few tourists," Annie said.

"It wasn't that long ago that you were a tourist," Derek pointed out.

"We are not living together." Josh emphasized each word.

And Deana could not be more pleased with his thought process. "Of course not."

"Notice how he jumped to that conclusion?" Kane whispered the question to Annie.

"You would have your own house and complete privacy. The idea would be for you to be able to make your calls, do your work, and spread out." When Josh didn't say anything, Deana decided to talk louder. "Honestly, I can't afford to have you go back and forth to your house on Kauai."

While everyone else stood around staring, waiting for Josh to blow up or shut down or something, Derek pushed ahead. "I thought you were loaded."

Annie threw up her hands. "What is wrong with the men in this family? Has no one ever heard of being tactful?"

"I meant afford in the sense of time," Deana said. "Prison is pretty dangerous for a prep-school kid."

Kane snorted. "For everyone, actually."

Josh hadn't even glanced at his friends. He leaned against the counter, keeping his focus centered only on Deana. "You know we can't live together."

"Why does he keep saying it that way?" Kane asked.

"And why can't they live together?" Annie asked a beat later.

Derek shrugged. "There's always a room here for you, but you probably would be happier with more space."

That answer supported what Deana had expected—the kid needed his house back. Turned out he might be her best ally in getting Josh where she wanted him.

But Josh clearly was not as impressed with the young genius. "Don't help her, Derek. It would be a conflict of interest for me to live near her, let alone on her property. The goal is to have this investigation be as neutral as possible."

Deana noticed he hadn't exactly said no to her suggestion. Of course, he hadn't given in, either. "And it will be. You can be objective from my guesthouse."

Josh grabbed on to the counter behind him. "Everything I do has to be above reproach. If at some point in the future I insist Ryan is not guilty, we need someone to believe me. With your suggestion the view will be that you paid for my services and for the answer you wanted in the report."

If that was his biggest concern, she figured they were going to be fine. "That's ridiculous. People won't believe that of you."

"Did you read the paper this morning?" Josh's soft voice should have sounded like a whisper. Instead, it rang out in the quiet kitchen.

She had and discounted it almost immediately. "That was about the DEA making you a scapegoat."

A charged silence filled the room at her response. The wariness playing in Kane's eyes disappeared. It was as if with one statement she somehow earned a bit of trust from a crowd that did not surrender it easily.

Even the tension across Josh's shoulders eased. "I appreciate your faith in my reputation, but—"

"Then take the offer. Consider it part of your payment and say yes."

"What kind of idiot says no to a beachfront house?" Derek asked.

"This is not—" Josh looked at his friends' faces. Whatever he saw made him change course and point at Deana. "Can I see you outside for a second?"

"But we can't hear you from there," Kane joked.

"Figured that out, did you?" Josh slipped his hand under Deana's arm and gave her a gentle lift up and out of her seat. "We'll be back."

"We'll be here," Kane said.

Josh stopped for a second. "And you three should find something else to do other than eavesdrop on my life."

Annie frowned. "Killjoy."

Chapter Twelve

Josh waited until they hit the front porch and he closed the door tight behind them. Back inside Annie had worn a knowing expression, and Josh knew Kane wanted to let a lecture fly. No reason to provide more fodder by arguing with Deana in front of them.

Deana spun around with her chin in the air and her attitude on full display. "Is this necessary?"

Only if he wanted to keep what little was left of his sanity. "Have you lost your mind?"

"Not to my knowledge."

Deana's chilliness broke the thin reins holding his temper in check. Irrational rage exploded in huge bursts inside him. "Who talks like that? I ask you a simple question and you shoot back something a professor might say."

She crossed her arms in front of her. "You called me out here to argue about grammar and sentence structure?"

No, he brought her outside to prevent a scene. Now that he had her on the porch with the fading sun behind her and her long wavy hair blowing soft against her cheek, he wondered if his subconscious had a different plan all along. No matter how hard he tried he couldn't hold on to his fury around her for very long because his mind now wandered elsewhere. It was easier when they hated each other.

She ordered him around, pushed him away, and tried to pay for his loyalty. If a man tried any of those things, Josh would beat him senseless. With another woman, he would have walked away. But nothing worked in the normal way around Deana. She grated on his nerves, yet the image of her beautiful face refused to leave his head.

Seeing her tonight acting carefree with Derek eased the tight ball of anxiety that had been rolling around in Josh's stomach ever since his agent job began slipping away. Finding out everything about her became his new obsession. The external scars proved Deana had suffered. He worried the internal ones went even deeper.

He'd been there. Understood how bad life could be—a lesson learned long ago. Overcoming his mother's constant absence and the chronic lack of food and heat made him who he was. He had accepted everything years earlier. But Deana still dealt with her devil. He wanted to help her wrestle the beast to the ground.

"How did you know I was staying with Derek?" he asked, figuring they may as well get all the damning information in the open.

In what could only be called a tell, she glanced out at the wide-open ocean instead of at him.

"Deana?"

"I guessed."

The hesitation and lack of eye contact told Josh exactly what he needed to know. "You're having me followed again, aren't you?"

"You're paranoid."

More like flat-assed right. "You hired me to save Ryan and then hired someone to check on me. What is wrong with you?"

The realization would have knocked him right on his ass if he hadn't been leaning against the door. The fact she didn't fully trust him grated, but it wasn't a surprise. The shocking part was how she could kiss a man like that and still refuse to believe in him on any level. The situation left him frustrated and eager to do something stupid to prove her wrong. Really stupid.

"After the meeting with Eric, you refused to share any details about your whereabouts—"

Her excuses ticked Josh off even more. "Yeah, I wonder why."

"I just needed to know you were working, so I asked a friend to check in on you."

Not one ounce of apology in that explanation. Josh wondered if she ever regretted anything. "What else would I be doing? It's not as if I have another job."

And there it was. The sharp stabbing pain in his side. Informed and in control, he had made the decision to leave the DEA. It was time. Past time, probably. But going out with his actions under suspicion was never part of the plan. Hell, no matter what Brad Nohea thought, Josh knew he deserved better. He'd earned more respect than having a box of stuff from his desk delivered to his door by a nameless messenger.

"Cut the tail on me," he said. "Now."

"Fine."

"I'm serious, Deana."

Her hands tightened on the railing. "Talk to me and I won't need to go elsewhere for basic information."

He knew being in the loop was important to her and he

understood why, but he needed to set this ground rule. "We aren't saying the same thing."

"Trust has to be earned."

This woman could piss him off faster than anyone he had ever known. Every word hit him like a slight. Still the anger refused to fester. It struck, rattled around for a while, and then dissipated. He wanted to nurture it and feed off it, but it kept blowing away into nothing.

"The best way for you to earn my trust is to call off your minions. That shit may have worked with the legal team, but it doesn't fly with me," he said.

Her gaze searched his face. "What about my trust?"

"With our history, the fact I agreed to help and I'm here should tell you I've earned it." He stepped away from the door and closed in on her.

"You're doing all of this for Ryan." She shifted her weight from one high-heeled shoe to the other. "I appreciate that."

He didn't know why the hell he was helping out. He wanted to believe it had something to do with justice and a mouthy kid who deserved one last shot. He feared it had mostly to do with the woman standing in front of him.

She nodded. "Fair enough. You have my trust."

That went a little too well for his taste. "Just like that?"

"Just like that."

For some reason he thought she meant the vow. She may not like him, but she was desperate for help. No other man rode to her rescue on this. Only he was dumb enough to heed that call.

"Now that we have that settled." She folded her hands in front of her. "We were talking about the guesthouse offer."

That chilly demeanor had taken up residence again. The warmth she showed to his friends morphed back to the "all business all the time" side she seemed to save only for him.

Fine. She wanted cold and impersonal, then he would give her exactly that. "You know very well why we can't live on the same property."

"Why?"

Screw subtlety. "The kiss."

"So?"

"So?"

"I expect you to be a professional." She tightened her fingers into a tight ball. If she exerted any more pressure she'd break her wrists.

She swallowed hard enough for him to see it. Looked as if the tough-talking woman might not be so frozen after all. Whatever else she was, unaffected wasn't it. Whatever kept zinging between them went two ways. He was not alone in sensing it. They had heat, the kind that guaranteed a trip to bed at the first opportunity.

And Josh didn't plan to hold back. He knew what he should do, but that had never really been his style. His body wanted one thing from her and it wasn't intellectual conversation. Hell, he didn't even need talking. Speaking only seemed to get them in trouble anyway.

"My control is not the issue." Because he knew he didn't have any left.

"Then what's the problem?"

"This." He took one step and slipped his hands down her bare arms, giving her plenty of time to pull back as he lowered his head.

She didn't fight him. If anything, she fell deeper into the kiss. A hot mouth and soft lips. Firm high breasts pressed against his chest. A slim waist under his hands. Everywhere he touched and tasted she was there with him giving as much as she took.

The kiss raged on, each of them taking a turn at the lead

and neither backing away. His mouth slanted over hers as her fingers clutched him around the neck. The building heat between them broke open, feeding the kiss and igniting a fire just under his skin.

Touching her blocked out everything else. If his friends had their noses pressed against the window, he didn't notice. He couldn't even hear the sound of the pounding surf or the squealing tires of passing cars.

If a jeep loaded full of kids hadn't raced by cheering the kiss on and honking the horn, Josh would have scooped Deana up and headed for the nearest private area with a flat surface. Instead, he reluctantly moved. As the shouts faded in the distance, Josh rested his forehead against hers. Heavy breathing echoed in his ears. It took him a few minutes to figure out the sharp intakes of breath belonged to both of them.

The sensible thing would have been to step away, but he didn't want to let her go. He kept her wrapped in his arms tucked close to his chest. The fingers resting on his shoulders didn't show any sign of moving either.

"That's why," he whispered.

Her breath blew across his neck. "We can control this."

"If you think we can stay out of bed, you've lost your mind."

"This is a separate thing from the investigation."

Josh pulled back and stared down into Deana's eyes, looking for some sign that she understood the import of her comment. "You think you can break apart the pieces of your life like that?"

She reached into her pants pocket and pulled out a key. She dangled the chain in front of his face. "This is for you."

"Are you listening to anything I'm saying?"

"I'll take the risk."

Is that what he was? "It's going to happen, Deana. You, me, sex."

She put her fingers over his mouth. "I'm doing what's best for Ryan."

Josh kissed her open palm. "Believe it or not, he's the last thing on my mind at the moment."

"I'm doing this for you, too."

One thing he did not need was her adding him to a list of pet projects. "Because?"

"I'm thinking someone needs to rescue you for a change."

He shrugged that off. Refused to examine it or even acknowledge it. "And what about what you need, Deana?"

"I'm a big girl. I can take care of whatever I need."

That conjured up a few visual images guaranteed to keep him up and sweating tonight. "I'd rather do it for you."

"Then take the key."

"You'll find out I'm a determined man."

She hesitated for a second. "I'm counting on it."

Chapter Thirteen

Ten minutes and one lingering kiss later Josh stood with his elbows resting on the porch railing as he stared out into the black night enveloping Derek's house.

Deana's key weighed heavy in his pocket. They left everything open-ended. The way she didn't fight his not-so-subtle promise they'd soon have sex made him itch to jump in the car and get over to her house for a little demonstration.

But his conscience kicked in. Literally. The walking six-foot Hawaiian version of it stood right there on the porch. As soon as Deana pulled her car out of the driveway, Kane had stepped outside and joined in the silence.

Josh waited until he couldn't stand the quiet one more second. "Anything you want to say?"

"Good dinner."

"Not exactly what I had planned for the night, but yeah. I managed not to strangle anyone, so it was a success."

"And I hadn't counted on spending the evening listening to Annie whine about not getting the chance to say good-bye to Deana, but I bet I will now that she left." Kane moved beside Josh and mimicked his stance gazing out at the dark ocean. "Remind me to run you over with my truck tomorrow as a thank-you for that one."

"Why do you think I'm out here and not in there trying to ignore a game of twenty questions?" Josh glanced back at the window and was somewhat surprised not to see Annie's face plastered against the glass.

"It'd be a hell of a lot more than twenty."

"In that case, I might sleep out here," Josh said.

They both laughed before falling back into a comfortable silence. It had always been this way with Kane. Even back to their days in the DEA together, long before Kane traded suits in for a police uniform, they had a steady rhythm. Basketball on Sundays, weight workouts, and beers after work. They engaged in friendly competition and never let a woman come between them.

Josh didn't want secrets about Deana to be the first time. "She needed to go home."

"Before or after you wrestled her down on the porch and stuck your tongue in her mouth?"

Shit. "You're into peeping now?"

"Hey, you're the one who stood in front of the window putting on the show."

"You could have gone into another room."

"But watching you try to figure out your love life is better than anything on television." Kane smiled. "For what it's worth, Annie likes Deana. I think Annie has most of your wedding planned."

"Like hell."

"Good luck telling her that."

Josh exhaled, letting the air slowly leave his lungs. "I can't get Deana out of my head."

"Been there."

"Yeah, well, I want it to stop."

Kane shook his head as he let out a rough laugh. "Oh, man. It doesn't work that way."

"Should."

"Doesn't. Trust me."

"I want to think about something else. Anything else." Josh wanted to give a shit about a woman other than one who thought wearing turtlenecks in eighty-degree weather made sense. The whole situation was insane.

"Funny, but I would have said you were letting another part of your anatomy guide your actions lately," Kane said.

"If I remember, you were once pretty interested in a certain secretive redhead with a host of personal problems and a murder rap hanging over her head." Josh thought back to those days. Watching Kane fall stupid in love with Annie and lose most of his usual common sense had been a shock. The burden had fallen to Josh to stay rational and check Annie out, a privacy intrusion Annie rarely let him forget.

"You might want to remember the end of my story," Kane said. "I married that sexy secretive redhead. You planning on going there with Deana?"

Now there was a sobering thought. "Not interested in having a ring in my nose, but thanks."

"That might be good."

Not at all the response Josh expected from his pro-marriage friend. "Why?"

Kane shifted to the side until he faced Josh. "Look, I appreciate the fact Deana's hot and all, but the potential for trouble is pretty good here."

"When has that stopped me?"

"This is different. Personal. Deana's emotional attachment to the case colors everything. That family bond is likely to make her irrational. That could pit you as the bad guy in this scenario."

More than *could*. It would. Josh could feel it. "You think I don't know that?"

Kane went still. "Then there's the money issue."

"Thought you never worried about a person's bank account."

"You know what I'm saying, Josh."

He did. Years ago after a combination of too much liquor and a need to burn off stress, Josh came clean. He filled Kane in on his past. Talked all about his upbringing with a single mother who liked to take her clothes off for money and thought it was funny to drag her son along to hotels to watch. How he grew up worse than poor, seeing things no young kid should see.

His mother didn't have boundaries with men or alcohol. Josh had a front-row seat to it all. Watched her destroy herself and was helpless to stop it. He had set out every dirty detail for Kane, who just nursed his beer and listened. Never once did he judge. Kane accepted and moved on. This was the first time Kane ever broached the subject.

"The cash is the least interesting thing about Deana," Josh said.

"I'm more worried about her using that big checkbook to ruin you if this turns bad for her. She knows a lot. Has resources and information."

Josh appreciated the concern, but it was misplaced. "How much worse can my life get? I'm already unemployed and disgraced."

"You're out of work and it's temporary. Your integrity isn't in question." Kane dropped his head and stared at the porch floor for a second. When he lifted it again the darkness behind his eyes had turned more bleak. "Just do me a favor."

As if Kane even had to ask. "What?"

"Talk to Eric."

"About?"

"Get the scoop on Deana and know what you're getting into before you climb into bed with her."

"I'm not—"

Kane held up his hand. "Don't even try. I'm not blind or stupid. Sex is on the agenda. After that kiss and the way you two circled each other at dinner without even moving, I'm betting it's happening soon."

"Annie know you talk like that?"

"I saw you with Deana tonight. I know when two people are about to do the horizontal dance."

That was Josh's exact plan. Kane understood where they were headed and how fast. Now Josh needed to make sure Deana did. "I'll think about it."

"Since you took her house keys, stop moping around and make the call to Eric." Kane hesitated for a second. "Or I will."

Chapter Fourteen

Two days later Josh sat on the other side of Eric's desk and stared out the window behind the other man's head. From this height, Josh could see the area outside, including the State Capitol and Iolani Palace, the former residence of the last two monarchs to serve Hawaii and now a landmark.

As Josh expected, Eric welcomed the visit to his office so long as Deana didn't tag along. That was the deal. Eric spelled out the terms and Josh complied. Since Josh had spent two days avoiding Deana, going alone today suited him fine.

But there would be hell to pay later. Dropping off his bags at the guesthouse this morning and then leaving Annie there with Deana didn't go over too well. Or that's what he surmised from the numerous text messages both ladies had left on his cell. The last one from Annie promised a painful death. Josh suspected she could deliver on that.

"What can you tell me about Frankie Butler?" Josh asked.

Eric flipped through the file pages in front of him. "Just turned eighteen and has been a smart-ass for a huge part of those years."

"A typical teenager then."

"One with a long record. He's been in and out of trouble since he turned twelve. Started with petty theft and graduated to running drugs."

Josh tapped his pen against the legal pad balanced on his lap as he tried to put the information together in his head. "Then got messed up in a murder."

"He's been a busy boy."

"He ever bother to go to school, or was he too caught up with extracurricular criminal activities?"

Eric scanned through some handwritten notes. "Since the trial he started studying for his GED and insists he's going straight. At the time of the murders, he was a dropout."

Not exactly the perfect star witness to a homicide. "Any chance he's really cleaned up now?"

Eric leaned back in his oversized leather chair. "Let's say I'm not convinced. I talked with this kid before I handed Ryan's case over to an assistant."

"Not impressed?"

"Frankie knew what to say and how to say it, but I never bought the changing-my-life speech." Eric shook his head. "Always got the sense he'd be back to drug pushing as soon as everyone stopped looking at him."

"But you believed him when he said he didn't have anything to do with the murders."

"I did. The police did. The jury did." Eric counted off the strikes on his fingers. "Everyone who heard Frankie tell the story bought it. Ryan's defense tried to pin everything on Frankie, but between the two Frankie made the more believable witness."

That didn't make any sense. When confronted with conflicting stories from a smart kid at a private school and one who spent his life in the system, Josh expected Ryan to get the benefit of the doubt. Here, public opinion immediately turned against the kid.

Eric stopped talking long enough to answer the phone and ask his assistant to hold his calls before continuing with his assessment. "Look, I knew Ryan. I'd been to family functions and seen the kid in action. He had his parents, grandparents, and aunt snowed."

"Yeah, I know." Josh rubbed the back of his neck. "You're not the only one with a history with Ryan."

Eric nodded. "Right. You arrested him once. Don't know about you, but all I got was attitude and entitlement."

"And those were the good parts of his personality."

"From what I learned about the earlier drug case, Ryan had his grandparents thinking you were the bad guy," Eric said.

Not just the elder Armstrongs. Josh knew for a fact Deana saw him as the problem during that time. Now he had no idea how she viewed him. He kept his distance for now to avoid finding out just how much of a conflict of interest they could create together.

"All this is true, but there's a difference between being a teen shit and a killer," Josh pointed out.

After a brief hesitation Eric slipped a manila envelope from under one of his case folders and handed it over. "This is for you."

Josh untied the string and opened the top. The contents consisted of a DVD and a stack of papers. He held up the plastic case. "Give me a hint."

"It's a copy of Ryan's interview with the police the night of the murders. This is the part when everyone thought he was a victim lucky to have survived the massacre. He was being questioned for clues into the bloodbath."

"You're saying he didn't have an attorney present."

"He wasn't being interrogated. Not at the start. As it went on . . . well, it became problematic and eventually the police read him his rights."

"Were you in the room for all of this?"

"No. I was too close to this case on a personal level."

That was a different line of questions. One Josh intended to get to right after the present one. "Sounds like it."

"I did have the detectives tape everything while I was busy letting Deana's parents know what had happened and driving Deana in for the I.D." The strain of the memory played across Eric's face in sunken cheeks and hollowed eyes. "Here I thought I was protecting the kid. Turns out I was creating evidence against him."

Questions about Eric's relationship with Deana had swirled in Josh's head for days. He had written whatever they had off as casual dating. Now he knew better. Delivering the news and identifying bodies fell pretty deep into the serious boyfriend category.

"Why didn't I hear about your connection to Deana before now," Josh asked.

"The newspapers hinted, but if you weren't looking for it you wouldn't have noticed. A favor to me, I guess."

Josh came to Eric's office to talk about Ryan, or so he told himself. Now that the topic had switched to Deana, Josh felt every nerve ending inside him snap to life. "How serious were you two?"

"Very." That was it. No explanation. Eric dropped the topic right there and moved on. "Ryan claimed to have slept through the beatings."

Josh had seen the crime photos. Blood-drenched walls and broken people. He could barely tell Chace and Kalanie apart from their crumpled forms on the floor. "How is that possible? Was he sleeping in the same house?"

"Two doors down." Eric tapped his fingers together in a triangle under his chin. "Then there were all those other facts."

Josh knew the incriminating stuff by heart. "House alarm turned off when it never was. No forced entry. Obvious signs of a faked burglary."

"Ryan's lack of emotion troubled me the most. Deana fell apart. Actually crumbled . . ." Anger showed in Eric's clenched jaw as he swore. "Ryan didn't shed a damn tear. I know because I was there. I watched him, checking for any signs of remorse."

The circumstantial evidence stacked up to a pretty convincing case against the kid. He had motive; the past record and the pieces of the crime scene didn't fit without Ryan being implicated. Not hard to see why Eric gave up on Ryan's innocence so fast.

"People grieve differently." Josh pointed that fact out even though it didn't explain the kid's shopping spree less than a week after his parents were gone. Ryan didn't turn back to drugs. Instead, he focused on buying an expensive watch and clothes. Just one of the many reasons Josh wanted to shake the kid. Hard.

"Don't forget his parents' will that left young Ryan a very wealthy young man. Everyone who knew Chace understood he was on the verge of sending his son away to a strict private school and cutting off the allowance. Hell, I knew that from my conversations with Chace."

"He talked with you?"

Eric blew out a long breath. "Chace asked for my advice

in getting Ryan into a therapeutic high school of some sort."

When it was piled up like that, Josh could see where the circumstantial evidence looked even more compelling. "Why didn't you testify at trial?"

Eric stared at a spot on his armrest. "We had enough evidence without me, so I stayed out of it. If the defense had called me, I would have testified, but the defense team was not that dumb."

"The move probably saved your career."

Eric's head shot up, his eyes burning with intensity. "I stayed away for Deana's sake. So that she wouldn't have to deal with one more blow."

Josh couldn't hold it in anymore. He had to know. "What happened with you two?"

The anger rushed out of Eric's face. "You asking for the case or for you?"

Josh refused to directly respond because there was no way to do so without looking like a complete ass. "Just getting background."

The corner of Eric's mouth kicked up in a smile. "You didn't answer my question."

"I could say the same thing about you."

"There's nothing much to tell. She left me." Eric delivered the answer without fanfare or anger. The words came out with all the emotion of someone reading baseball scores.

For Eric the three simple words might not have meant much, but they lifted a weight off Josh's chest that he didn't even know was there. "Sorry, man. Any idea why?"

"I thought turning Ryan's case over and stepping out of it was the right thing to do. Deana disagreed."

"You still . . . ?"

"We're over." With his elbows on the desk, Eric leaned forward. "Where are you two?"

"I work for her."

"Uh-huh."

Josh knew he should drop the topic to avoid looking desperate. Still, he had to be clear. Leaving and letting Eric think this was all a fact-finding mission on Deana would not be good for anyone. "She's not the easiest woman to decipher. I'm just looking to understand her so that our work relationship can function."

Eric barked out a dry laugh, one filled more with confusion than amusement. "Sounds as if she hasn't changed much in the last nine months."

"Was she as secretive when the two of you were together?"

Eric frowned. "I'd say private. We dated for a year, but it took months before she wanted to venture in public for more than a dinner or charity event."

A year? The harsh whip of jealousy smacked against Josh. He decided to joke the moment away rather than dwell on it. "Some guys consider staying in at night a good thing."

Eric smiled. "No arguments here, but my job requires some attendance at public functions."

Josh took the final step. "What about the scars?"

Everything moved in slow motion. Eric sat back in his chair and grabbed on to the armrests with all ten fingers. Tension pulsed off him, clearing out the friendly mood and all signs of willingness to be helpful.

"You've seen them?" Eric asked in a harsh whisper.

"Yes."

Eric's faced closed up. "Then you're doing more than working with Deana."

That amounted to the one question too many. Josh saw it now. "I didn't mean—"

"The car accident isn't something she talks about. It took awhile to get her to show me." Eric glanced away for a second. "Sounds as if you didn't have to wait."

Now that he had the information he needed, part of Josh wanted to stake a claim on Deana. Josh could see from Eric's tight reaction that he still wanted her. Made Josh wonder if she returned the feelings.

"I saw her in a bathing suit at her pool." Josh slipped the pen into his jacket pocket when he realized he was tapping it fast enough to hurt his wrist. "That's it."

For a second Eric didn't move. He sat stiff and unbending. Then his shoulders fell back to normal position. "It's not my business."

The pressure eased. It was as if someone opened a valve and let air back into the room.

Josh decided to go to a safer topic. Interesting that talking about murder seemed preferable to talking about Eric's history with Deana. "There are some missing pieces. Ryan didn't have any blood on him. The murder weapon wasn't in the house."

"He got them out somehow. We could never explain it."

"The easier conclusion, at least the one the defense played, was that someone else was there and committed the crimes."

"But the other facts don't fit."

"Any chance Frankie was the one who committed the murders? Maybe he wanted revenge on Chace for kicking him out of the house. It's possible he set Ryan up to take the fall."

"Frankie isn't smart enough to steal gum, let alone pull off a double homicide and not leave a single clue behind."

"Since Ryan is sitting in jail, one could argue he wasn't all that good at homicide, either."

"Have you read the trial transcript?" Without being asked, Eric had expedited the process. He ordered the recordings transcribed and delivered to Josh's doorstep.

Josh had put off the internal battle over whether to move into Deana's house by ignoring it and reading the pages instead. The damn transcript went on forever. It filled more than one box.

"Thanks for sending the material over. It cut down on time on my end," Josh said, knowing from courthouse personnel that Eric had paid the huge bill on the transcription from his own pocket. "I'll send you a check."

"This one's on me."

Josh didn't belabor the point, since he knew Eric was doing this for Deana, not Ryan. "I have one question."

"Only one?" Eric asked.

"How does a private prep-school kid like Ryan get tied up with a dropout loser like Frankie?"

"Drugs. They both used and sold. As far as I can tell, this is a case where all the money in Hawaii couldn't keep an otherwise smart kid like Ryan from doing something stupid."

Wasted opportunities sure pissed Josh off. He guessed Deana hated her nephew's choices, as well. And people said he was the one with the savior complex.

Chapter Fifteen

Deana walked to the window in her den and glanced outside for what had to be the fiftieth time. The room faced the guesthouse and the road leading into the property. She had been on the lookout for Josh ever since he slipped away that morning.

That was nine hours ago. Not a return call or text since.

The only thing that kept her from throwing his bag into the ocean was Annie's promise to shove Josh in it first. Feeding off the other woman's anger made Deana feel better. Proved fury loved company, she guessed. Since Annie left to find Kane, Deana was left to stew on her own.

But now the wait was over. The little weasel had come home. Lights off and quiet, Josh practically coasted down the driveway. She half expected him to stick his feet out and run the car into the parking space with the engine off.

She should have taken his bag. That would have forced him to come down to the main house. Instead, he closed the car door and snuck onto the porch of the guesthouse. Sure, he wasn't actually bent over and ducking behind trees, but the move still looked like sneaking to Deana.

At least he was alone. The opposite possibility had become her new nightmare. Ever since the idea of his being out with another woman popped into her head an hour ago, it refused to leave. Redheads, blondes—she imagined them hanging off him in a bar somewhere. Josh had earned the ladies' man label through an impressive display of serial dating. She remembered that from the first time she had him investigated. She knew from the most recent background check a few days ago that he was in between bed partners.

Not a surprise knowing his pattern. He'd engage in months-long relationships at the most. Monogamy always, but then how hard was it to be faithful when the time together lasts a few weeks tops?

But none of that mattered. Josh could date any woman he wanted, when he wanted. Her interest in his social life had to do with how much quality time it would leave for the investigation. The guy liked to kiss. He'd be kissing plenty of women while he stayed in her guesthouse. That was a fact and one she could deal with . . . sort of.

After all, it wasn't as if she dreamed of being one of his conquests. They had a spark on a hormonal level, an attraction born of proximity and nothing more. She didn't—

Josh's face appeared right in front of her in the window. One minute she glanced through the screen and saw the lights in the guesthouse. The next she saw Josh's mouth, scruffy from a lack of shaving, turned up in a huge grin. He just popped up out of nowhere and broke into her daydreaming.

She screamed loud enough to rattle the walls.

Josh's eyes bugged out for the entire length of her yelling. "Jesus, Deana."

"What are you doing out there?"

He cupped a hand against his ear. "Hoping my sense of hearing will come back soon."

"You're lucky I didn't throw something."

"Like?"

"The sofa." Her heart hammered inside her chest begging to get out. "Why are you in my bushes?"

"Not to scare the shit out of you, believe it or not. Man, I'm surprised the neighbors didn't hear that and come running."

"You have some need to see the police tonight? Was that your idiotic plan?"

"Since I just lost twenty percent of my hearing, no."

Her hand shook so hard that she had to press it against the windowsill to steady it. "I have a phone, you know. And a doorbell."

"And a problem with stalking."

"Excuse me?"

He glanced over his shoulder at the guesthouse. "See anything interesting?"

How in the world did he know? "I'm just standing in my house."

"You were waiting for me to get home."

"That's quite an ego you have there."

"I bet you waited all day."

She realized for the first time how pathetic that made her. "That's ridiculous."

"My thought exactly." He hitched a thumb in the direction of his car. "You suck at this, by the way. I saw you the minute I pulled in. Figured I'd double back and see why you were hanging out of the window."

"I was standing." She pushed off the ledge and moved away from the window. "Now I need to sit."

"I could use a drink."

She shrugged her shoulders, trying to ignore being blown off. "Go ahead."

"Good. I'll be right in."

"I didn't mean here."

But it was too late. He had left the window with the same flourish as he appeared. She expected the bell to ring any second . . . unless he just broke the door down. If he wanted to complete the terrorfest he started that would be the way to go.

She started down the hall and gave a quick look in the mirror by the front door. She didn't run. She refused to run to please Josh. He could wait. Of course, he hadn't actually rang the doorbell as she expected. This guy rarely did the same thing anyone else would do.

She held her hand over the doorknob and listened for signs of life on the other side. Nothing. If this was some game, she was not a fan.

"Josh?"

"Open the damn door." His angry voice carried right through the wood and echoed in her open entry.

Without thinking she obeyed. "What is wrong with you now?"

"Why were you just standing there and not letting me in?"

Good question. "Maybe I'm trying to restart my heart after that scare."

He frowned, walked past her, then kept on going. "Now who's being dramatic?"

"Where were you all day?" The question slipped out before Deana could muster up the common sense to stop it.

His stupid grin when he turned around to face her proved he liked the attention. "Miss me?"

"Hardly."

"Sounds like someone needs some company. Good thing

I'm here." He slumped back into the sofa with an arm stretched over the top of the cushions.

She wondered if she should have just forgotten about him hours ago and gone to a movie.

"I have an investment in you and an interest in your time. My fear is that you're wasting it," she said.

His smile fell. "You know how to kill a moment."

Better to kill it than feed it. She joined him on the couch. A good three feet separated them across the cushions, but she could smell his scent from there on the edge. A mix of musk and Earl Grey. Masculine and intoxicating.

Yeah, she needed the female antidote to this guy. He was downright dangerous. On him the sexy whiskers worked. And the way he looked at her, at times as if he wanted to shake her and others as if he wanted to strip her, didn't do much for her internal promises to maintain control.

"What did you do today?" And if he said a woman's name she vowed to smash a lamp over his head.

"Tried to track down Tommy Olive."

At the sound of the man's name her mouth turned to a sneer. It was a visceral reaction. Homicidal rage flooded through her just thinking about the man and his collection of silk Hawaiian shirts and his shiny convertible Bentley. She knew if Olive walked into her house right now he could rip him to pieces with her bare hands. Actually tear the skin right off him.

And she wouldn't feel a minute's guilt. Not over this. Not this time.

Her brother had such amazing business sense. Probably inherited it from their parents. Everything Chace touched increased in value. Everything worked except his dealings with Olive. Starting a commercial real estate business on the side with Olive led to Chace's and Kalanie's deaths. Deana felt as certain of that as anything else in the world.

"He's been missing since before the murder trial," she explained, even though she sensed Josh knew the details.

"He popped up in Arizona."

"What?" A mix of relief and excitement bubbled up inside Deana. She had waited months for a break like this. "This is fabulous news."

"It is?"

"He's the one." She grabbed Josh's hand, willing him to understand. "Do you know how big this news is?"

"I think—"

She leaned over and kissed him. A short peck on the lips—enough to wipe the blank look off Josh's face and quick enough to ensure it wouldn't go deeper. "How did you get Olive? The police tried and couldn't locate him. You must have used some inside contacts."

Josh squeezed her fingers and didn't let go. Instead, he rubbed his thumb over her knuckles. "Let's back up a second."

"There's no reason to wait." She slipped her hand out of his. This was not the time for soothing. They needed to move to action.

"Deana—"

"We need to call the lead detective and have him reopen the case. Olive can't squirm out of this now." She stood up and went for the phone. Her fingertips touched one end right as Josh stood up in front of her, blocking her path.

"Hold up a sec."

When he tried to slide the receiver back in the cradle, she pulled it out of his hand and held it tight against her chest. "I can't, Josh."

Her words cut off the second his hands touched her

shoulders. With a light touch, he massaged circles into her shoulder sockets. The tension drained from her muscles as fast as if he had pulled a plug. She would have dropped the phone if her brain didn't kick in right as her death grip eased.

"I need you to listen to me," he said.

She tightened her hold on the receiver as if it were a lifeline. In many ways, it was. "There's nothing else to say."

"You know that's not true." Something that looked awful close to pity filled his eyes.

No no, noooooo. She refused to let anyone stop her from moving forward. Even him. She had to make the call. "We need to catch Olive before he runs again."

"Here." Josh pried the phone out of her fingers without applying any pressure. "Sit."

"Why?" Bad news was coming. That familiar anxiety welled up and clogged her throat. The muscles in her knees gave way and she sat down hard on the couch cushions. "What is it?"

"Olive's not going anywhere."

That was inexperience talking. If Josh only understood how long it took to reach this breakthrough.

"You don't know Olive like I do," she said, willing him with every ounce of strength inside her to get the picture.

"He's dead, Deana."

She heard him, but the words refused to compute. "What?"

"Car accident."

She didn't know she was rocking back and forth until Josh wrapped an arm around her and pulled her close to his side. She couldn't feel or hear any of it. The touch. The sounds of his voice. The soft mumbling of words of encouragement. She knew it was happening, but none of it registered in any real way.

"I don't understand," she said in soft whisper, unable to raise her voice any louder.

"Some of the information Eric gave me this morning—"

She glanced at Josh, and from the resulting headache immediately regretted moving her head that fast. "You saw Eric without me?"

Josh smoothed his fingers through her hair. "The files mentioned Olive having business interests on the West Coast. I did some digging and confirmed the police reports that he hadn't used a credit card or popped up anywhere."

"You can check stuff like that?"

Josh nodded as his blue eyes grew softer. "I also asked a friend at the Doe Network, this group that helps to pair unidentified and missing people around the country with photos of John Does from the morgue. She found a preliminary match. It's not a definite, but Eric and the police are pretty sure it's Olive."

"You did all of this today?"

"Yeah."

She didn't want cuddling or comfort. Not now when everything else felt so messy and uncertain. Breaking from the warmth, she stood up and paced a few steps in front of Josh before stopping to face him. "How did the police miss this?"

"It would have been damn hard to find."

She held up a finger. "It took you one day. That's it."

"The death was posttrial and Olive was staying off the grid when you needed to locate him, so tracking him down then proved impossible. With Olive's death, I got lucky and had an in at the Doe Network, otherwise I never would have put it together."

"A *she*."

"What?"

Figures his little helper was a she. "Nothing."

Deana closed her eyes and tried to pull her scrambled thoughts together. She wanted nothing more than to bring Olive back to life so she could kill him again. But there was something more important at work now. Ryan's best shot at any sort of normal life outside prison just disappeared.

"Now what?" she asked, even though she dreaded the answer.

"You aren't in any worse position today than you were yesterday."

"How can you say that? Tommy Olive killed my brother and his wife and any evidence of that fact died with Olive." She massaged her temples to lessen the pounding in her brain.

"You *think* he did it."

"Clearly Eric's files left out some facts." She dropped her hands to her sides. Even had to ball her fingers into fists to keep from gesturing and flailing and otherwise losing what was left of her composure. "What a surprise."

"Meaning?"

"Olive stole money from my brother's business and Chace figured it out. Chace confronted Olive, tried to collect, and Olive ran."

"I know. That's all public record. It's in the trial transcript," Josh said.

She didn't need to see the typed pages, since she lived through the live nightmare version. "Then you also know that criminal charges were filed against Olive the month before Chace was murdered."

Josh folded his arm across his chest. "Which you view as motive."

She could tell from Josh's body language that he was cutting off his mind from any possibility other than one that kept Ryan in jail. "You don't?"

"I'm still listening, aren't I?"

But he was pushing her away. All clench with his arms wrapped around his middle like that. Not very receptive. That's what scared the hell out of her.

"You don't have to be a math genius to do the addition here, Josh. Olive had the motive. He was a grown man with access and resources. Blaming a kid would not exactly be a hardship for a businessman of his caliber."

"Your evidence of homicide is that the guy was an adult and ran?"

She was two seconds from screaming the house down to get Josh's full attention. "Of course."

"He had an alibi for the night."

That word made her crazy. "All that means is some lying bitch of a girlfriend gave Olive cover. And not a good one. Besides, he could have hired someone to carry out the killings."

The words flowed out without any thought from her brain. She had perfected the skill of staying calm while she described every atrocity her brother suffered. She had learned to talk about the murders as if they were part of some disjointed event unrelated to her. But for a second there, she spewed. The words and hatred spilled out.

Just as fast she clamped down her emotions. If she gave life to her true feelings she would relive the horror of that night over and over. The blood, the bodies. She couldn't go there.

Josh must have sensed the internal battle. For a second all of the steam blew right out of him. In its place was a gentleness, in his voice and touch, that nearly broke her will.

"You okay?" He whispered the question.

"Obviously not."

"We can stop—"

"I can't just walk away from this." She grabbed Josh's arm, unleashing the fierceness rising inside her on the bare skin of his arm. "Olive is guilty and I'm the only one left to fight for that fact."

Josh glanced down to where her nails pierced his skin, but he didn't try to pull away. Didn't even flinch.

"If your scenario is right, Olive still had to disarm the alarm, get into the house without alerting Chace and Kalanie, and murder them without making enough noise to wake Ryan," Josh explained.

Every defensive fiber in her stood on end. "It's as plausible as the story against Ryan."

"And Olive had to do all of that without leaving one speck of forensic evidence. Not a fingerprint. No DNA."

She forced her fingers to unclench from his arm. "Whose side are you on?"

"Yours."

Before she could pull back or come up with a new argument, Josh pulled her into his arms. With her head tucked under his chin and her body snuggled close to his chest, she tried to stay strong.

"I don't want you to touch me," she said even as she relaxed into his chest.

"Then you're about to be very unhappy because I plan on touching you a lot from now on."

She stared up at him, searching his face for something. She wasn't sure what, but she expected some sort of sign. "I need a few minutes."

"For what?" His voice strained at the question.

"To think about all of this. To process the information about Olive and Ryan and how—"

"Think about me instead."

His fingers massaged her neck while his lower body cuddled hers. With each circle he pressed into her skin, her resistance faltered. Words along the lines of "I'm fine" sputtered in her mouth and never came out. Her senses screamed with the need to look back over every piece of information and see what tiny speck of evidence might have been missed or lost. She also needed to kiss Josh. She couldn't figure out how to do both.

His news served as a deathblow to her hopes. It sapped part of her strength. But Josh's arms felt so right. As everything fell apart she clung to him and somehow managed to stay on her feet.

Bracing her hands on his shoulders, she applied just enough pressure to get him to lower his mouth to hers. "Please . . ."

"Deana." That was the only word he got out before their lips touched.

Energy raced through her at the kiss. Her mind wiped clean of doubts and arguments. For that moment she didn't think about her family or all the loss suffered by the Armstrongs. She fell straight into feeling, opening up her body and mind to something other than a blinding grief so powerful it swallowed up all else.

She licked and tasted, letting her body grow more accustomed to the sensation of having him this close with his warm breath in her hair. The bulge against her stomach and low groan vibrating in his throat told her he felt the same. Whatever they had—whatever this attraction was—its pull grabbed them both.

And she did not want to let go.

Chapter Sixteen

The kiss started out gentle. Josh wanted to comfort Deana and wipe the crushing sadness from her eyes. As his mouth passed over hers again and again, he realized he needed something from her, too. This was no longer about beating back the desire he had for her or soothing her fears and pain away. It was about giving in to his attraction and taking her.

Right woman.

Wrong time.

Still, the kiss went on. He stole small breaths, but his mouth never left hers for long. His tongue dipped inside her lips, seeking out a richer taste of her. The idea of being separated or breaking off the contact raised his fight-or-flight instinct.

Here, now, her, couch. The combination seemed so simple.

With his arms locked around her waist, he steered her back to the overstuffed sofa. A groan rattled around inside his chest as their mouths moved over each other. He lowered her to the cushions and her back. One thought burned into his brain: no more clothes blocking their way.

His mouth slid down the long line of her neck to her collarbone, tugging aside her shirt as he went. After a few tries to reach skin, he gave up. It was easier to tunnel his hands up from the bottom. Only took a second and then his fingers found warm, smooth flesh.

His lips traveled back to the exposed vein on her neck. He sucked hard, feeling her blood pound harder through her body the more excited she became. When his palms finally found her lacy bra, tight nipples pushed against the flimsy material to meet him. Rather than fight with the back clasp, he dragged the cups down, letting her breasts fall into his waiting hands.

He had to taste her. Abandoning her neck, he flipped her shirt up and lowered his head to her breasts. She flinched when his tongue traced the rough raised skin of her scar.

"Does that hurt?" He panted out the question between sharp breaths.

"No." As if to back up her answer, fingers speared through his hair and held him tight against her.

He didn't need a spoken invitation. With infinite care, he moved his mouth back to her breasts. Licking and kissing, he treated her soft skin to the reverence it deserved. He took turns sucking the tips into tight peaks and soothing his fingertips over the puckered edge of the scars, as his fingers plumped and caressed her pale skin.

Damn, she was so hot and responsive that he almost came right there. Forget the foreplay. He wanted to be inside her now.

"Josh?"

"Yeah, baby."

"We need to stop."

Hell no. "Not now."

"Please." She pushed against his chest. "I need to sit up."

She struggled to do just that. Against his weight and with his mouth covering her, she scrambled to a sitting position.

"What are you doing?" he asked, because he had no idea what game they were playing now.

"I just need a minute."

He needed to go faster and she needed to slow down. Talk about being on different wavelengths. "Right now? This is when you decide you need a break?"

She grabbed a handful of her shirt and pulled it down. She didn't try to replace the bra or hide her face. "I can't—"

"You definitely can. I sure as hell know I can." He stayed straddled across her thighs more because he couldn't move than to hold her there. "So, what's the real problem here?"

"A woman has a right to say no."

He tried to calm his breathing and sound reasonable even though he felt anything but. "Agreed."

His quick response seemed to throw her. Her mouth fell open and then shut again.

"Is it the scars?" he asked.

"You are obsessed with those." She continued to press her hand over her breasts even though the shirt covered every inch of skin worth seeing.

"Only since you won't talk to me about them."

"It's just that I . . ."

He slipped his hand under her chin and forced her to look at him again. "What is it, baby?"

"We don't even like each other."

Only a woman would care about something like that. "For a smart woman you can get your information pretty damn wrong."

"Meaning?"

He gestured toward the area where their bodies met. "I think we were doing okay."

She rolled her eyes. "You're treating this as a joke."

"Do I look like I'm laughing here?" Hell, he could barely sit with the erection pressing against his thigh.

"I'm not one of your one-night stands. I can't just go to turbo power. I need some time."

So that was it. This evidently was a woman thing. Some weird insecurity or shyness. The realization took part of the sting out of his frustration. Well, fine. If she needed to get to know him, to touch him and explore for a while, he would indulge her.

First, they needed to clear up a little misinformation. She had it in her head he didn't respect or care about women. She couldn't be more wrong.

"It's obvious your opinion of me in relation to women isn't very high," he said without moving, forcing her to deal with him instead of getting up and running as she clearly wanted to do.

"That's not true."

"Then lay back down."

She frowned up at him. "Does that guilt trip work for other women?"

She was determined to tick him off. He refused to let her win this verbal battle. "Do us both a favor and stop spouting off whatever it is you think you know about my love life."

"I have the report, Josh."

Now there was an argument guaranteed to piss him off. "This is not about other women or your detectives or anything else. This is about us."

"Did it ever dawn on you that I might not want you?"

He snorted. "No."

"How do you fit in the car with that ego?"

He raised an eyebrow. "Oh, please. Give me some credit for knowing a woman's body."

"Your talent in that department is obvious."

At least they finally agreed on something. "Then trust me."

"To do what?"

Not what he wanted. Far short of what he wanted. "Explore. Get to know each other."

Her grip on her shirt eased. "That's it?"

"You don't have to sound so damn relieved."

"I asked to slow down, not stop."

"And I'm complying." He held up his hands to let her know she could leave if she wanted to. He would hate it, but he would deal.

"You're sure?" she asked.

Hell, no. "I told you before that I can control myself."

With her arms still locked in her shirt she eased back into the cushions. Her wide eyes grew even wider as she stared up at him. "This seems like a bad idea."

"Just relax." His fingers slipped under her shirt to the bare skin on her belly. "You're a beautiful woman."

"Hmmm."

He wondered if he would have to pry her hands off her shirt. If he hadn't sensed she needed this, needed to feel special and comforted tonight, he would have given up, gone to the guesthouse, and took in three or four hours of cold showers.

His fingers moved higher until he hit the blockade of her arms. "I've already seen the scars and your breasts."

"I know."

"Not afraid of them, either."

Still clenched. "Uh-huh."

"Everything about you is a turn-on." And that wasn't a lie. Hell, even her snotty disapproving frowns sent his lower half bucking.

"You're such a guy."

"Because I like breasts?"

Her arms relaxed but didn't fall to her sides. "Because you'll do anything to see a pair."

"Just yours. Don't want to see any others at the moment."

This time he got his palms under her bra. When his thumb flicked over her nipple, she jumped but not in surprise. He could feel a flush of heat burn through her. After two more passes her arms slid down her body to fall against the couch cushions.

"That wasn't so bad, was it?" he asked.

He inched the edge of her shirt up, taking care to let her protest. Instead, her gaze locked on his face. When he worked the hem up and tucked it under her chin, her arms tensed as if she wanted to cover herself again.

He refused to let her hide. His fingertips traced the lines from the tops of her breasts up to the center of her chest. "Tell me."

"About the scars?"

"How did you get these?"

"Car accident," she said as her breaths grew shorter and more labored.

"When?"

She hesitated a few beats. "Ten years ago."

Not at all the answer he expected. "You were twenty."

"Nineteen."

Her fingers moved to cover his. She didn't shrug him off or pull away. Instead, she balanced her palms on the back of his hands as if guiding him.

Josh caressed her breasts, loving the smooth feel of her,

and then moved back to the scars. "This could have been serious."

Her body snapped tight, killing her relaxation and the mood. Deana gripped his hands. "Okay, that's enough."

"You can tell me."

She tried knocking his hands away. "I just did."

"Not all of it."

He didn't fight her this time when she tried to move. Sliding over, he made room for her to sit up beside him. He noticed she hadn't adjusted her shirt. She just balanced her head against the back of the couch.

"I can see why you're so successful with women. That concern comes off as really genuine," she said.

Ah, the ice queen had returned. Well, he wasn't buying it. "If that's your big attempt to push me away, you need to try harder."

She rolled her head to the side to face him. "I'm not like you."

"Patient?"

"Carefree."

Showed how little she knew about him. "You seem to think I jump on every woman I see."

"You don't?" She actually sounded confused by the idea.

The reputation followed him everywhere. Committed relationships weren't his thing, sure, but he never treated a woman wrong. He believed in mutual satisfaction. How he ended up as the shallow "out to touch any breast regardless of the owner" loser in her mind, he didn't know.

Anger edged up on him out of nowhere. This scenario wasn't about sitting there instead of enjoying each other in bed, though that part didn't make him happy. This was about her hiding behind stupid gossip rather than saying what she really meant.

"I'm living in your guesthouse, watching out for your nephew, and giving a shit about your life for one reason."

"Which is?" she asked.

"You. There's one common denominator, Deana. It's you."

Her eyes grew wide. "When did you stop hating me?"

He didn't know when, he only knew it happened. "I have no damn idea."

His sharp words fell into silence. They two sat there, leaning against the couch and staring at the ceiling. Nothing in particular felt uncomfortable about the quiet, but it didn't feel right, either. Despite that neither rushed to fill the talking void.

After a few minutes, Deana adjusted her bra and pulled down the shirt to cover her flat stomach. "You still thirsty?"

He needed something. He just wondered if anything or anyone but Deana could satisfy it.

Chapter Seventeen

The next morning Deana sat at her breakfast table and looked across at Brad Nohea's shiny bald head. He wore a short-sleeve dress shirt and thin tie clipped tight enough to choke him. Maybe that explained his flushed red face.

Deana was more concerned about the vicious excitement that bounced off him and soured the mood in the room. After fifteen minutes of listening to the guy spout off a list of Josh's supposed faults and past crimes she regretted her decade-old decision to stop drinking. Also vowed never to answer her doorbell again. Clearly nothing good came of unwanted guests, especially if those guests wore badges. She had no idea how Josh worked at the DEA for this idiot for all those years.

Josh. Now there was trouble. Not the kind Brad kept whining about but the type that promised to take her life, turn it upside down, and then shake hard until something important fell out. Like her common sense.

He had stayed with her for hours the evening before. Touching turned to a sort of peaceful calm. They sat together and watched television, ate, and talked about every careful subject that popped into her head. When he finally retired to his own house across the lawn he didn't even try to steal a good-night kiss. Nothing sexual, but very safe.

She now hated safe.

She had played her life within the rules and without any room for mistakes for years, thinking that would remove the stain from her past and redeem her actions in her family's eyes. While she was busy polishing her martyrdom crown she lost almost everyone she cared about. Now she wondered what else she had missed.

When a man like Josh walked into your life and showed an interest, did you run? Her answer up until two weeks ago would have been yes. Hell, yes. Not only did you run, you packed a bag and found the first fast-moving vehicle out of town. A man with his reputation, a man so strong and self-assured, could bring only turmoil.

But what she felt last night in those quiet moments between the rush of sexual excitement and the pathetic need to chatter to make him stay with her longer struck her as something worth exploring. And that scared the hell out of her.

"Ms. Armstrong?" Brad's angry voice boomed through the glassed-in breakfast nook.

Deana looked up and studied the man's pinched frown. She wondered how much of the conversation she'd missed. She doubted any of it really mattered. "Sorry?"

"I'm trying to make you understand the gravity of the situation."

She guessed "situation" was another way of saying Josh. "Go on."

The lines around Brad's mouth eased a little. Deana

guessed he was trying to stay calm despite whatever raged inside him.

"I happen to like Josh," Brad said, his tone sounding the exact opposite of his words.

Yeah, sure he did. That's why Brad showed up today to belittle Josh. A severe case of like. Right.

"I can see where women find him charming." Brad's laserlike stare bored right into her as if willing her to agree with him.

"I'm not sure what to say to that." She also was not quite ready to admit how much *this* lady liked him.

"Josh has been my subordinate for years. He has a problem with following rules and acting within the law. That has been a problem on Kauai. If it weren't for the intervention of his friend, the police chief there, Josh would have been out of DEA a long time ago."

"You're talking about Kane Travers?" Funny, but that one struck her as a complete by-the-book guy. No way he lied just to protect Josh.

Brad stared at the full mug of cooling coffee in front of him. The same one he asked for but hadn't touched since sitting down. "There has been some suggestion that in order to cover his mistakes, especially his most recent actions in a civilian-involved shooting, Josh might try to implicate others. That he might feel the need for revenge in having lost his job."

There it was. She understood the point of the visit now. Brad feared word about his incompetency was getting out. "I thought Josh quit."

"His termination was only a matter of time. He left to save face."

"Why are you telling me all of this?"

Brad balanced his weight on his elbows and leaned in

closer. "I know you hired Josh to look into your nephew's . . . situation."

People always did that. Tried to sugarcoat the facts with pretty words. "You mean conviction."

Brad nodded and then rushed on as if he had a prepared speech and had to get the words out before he forgot them. "My fear is that Josh gained his position with you through inappropriate means."

This guy could say a whole mouthful of words without actually saying anything. "Are you a lawyer or something?"

Brad's mouth slammed shut. "Uh, yes. How did you—"

"Just wondering." She waved her hand. "You were saying something about me being used by Josh."

"I believe he played off your vulnerability in your family situation and is using exaggerated versions of his work, and possibly false allegations of why he was let go at DEA, to win your trust. Frankly, I'm concerned you're being used."

"By Josh?"

"Yes."

"Interesting. May I ask you something?" She traced the inside handle of her coffee mug.

"Of course."

She thought Brad's look of concern was a nice touch. Totally fake but certainly did fit with the rest of the crap he was spewing. "Do I look like someone who would allow herself to be taken for granted?"

Brad's face fell. "Well, no."

"I have a great many resources at my disposal."

He sat back in his chair. "Of course."

"I know a lot of people. Important people." She stopped there, letting her words sink in. Letting the worm squirm.

"Sure. I just—"

"Members of congress and the governor. The same peo-

ple who might not appreciate knowing a government employee is using company time to fly between islands to plead
his case and cover his tracks."

Brad shifted in his chair. "That's not what—"

"Of course it is." This time she tapped the mug against
the table. "You want me to believe the worst of Josh."

"I'm trying to help you. Warn you."

"I read the papers. I have an opinion on how Josh was
pushed out of the DEA and why. Want to hear it?"

Brad started huffing and puffing. "That's not why I'm
here."

"It's exactly why you showed up today. Despite what
you've been saying and all of your attempts to the contrary,
public opinion is not on your side. And Cassie Montgomery, the woman Josh shot, the sister of the dead helicopter pilot, publicly sided with Josh. She insists Josh saved
her and that you—yes, you—caused her brother's death by
placing him in danger."

"Ms. Montgomery is distraught."

"She's on a mission to restore Josh's name." Deana took
a nice long drink just to make Brad a bit more uncomfortable. If the way he grabbed on to the edge of the table with
enough force to claw through the wood were any indication, her plan worked. "And I agree with her."

"Look, I don't know what Josh told you—"

"He didn't tell me anything about you. Didn't have to.
Unlike you, he doesn't have anything to hide. He's not trying to sway people's views."

"I can't disclose what happened in Josh's hearing, but if
you had heard the testimony you would feel differently
about this," Brad explained. "I assure you."

"I doubt it."

"Any coffee left?" Josh slipped into the room and leaned against the door frame.

At the sound of his voice, Deana jumped a bit in her chair. That was nothing compared to Brad's reaction. He turned from a stuttering man with a target on his chest to one bubbling with fury.

But because she wanted Brad out of there and figured Josh's presence would make that happen, she ignored Josh's failure to knock. "Help yourself."

"Windsor?" Brad looked from Josh to Deana and back again. "What are you doing here?"

"I came over for breakfast."

Brad nodded, slow at first then much faster. "Oh, I see what's happening here."

Josh walked over to the sink and saluted with the coffee pot before he started pouring. "Me getting some coffee."

A feral smile crossed Brad's lips. "You two are—"

The pot landed against the counter with a thud. "I'd stop right there if I were you," Josh said.

"Josh is working out of my guesthouse," she said, hoping that tidbit of information would stop the testosterone battle she sensed looming on the male horizon.

Brad stood up and backed into the doorway where Josh had stood. "I gotta give it to you, Windsor. You always did have a way with women."

She was out of her chair before Josh could take the second threatening step in Brad's direction. "I have this."

The flat line of Josh's mouth inched up. "Sure?"

"Definitely." She winked at Josh before turning back to Brad. "One word, one innuendo, one nasty rumor about Josh and I will destroy you. I have the connections and the money."

"Do not threaten me, Ms. Armstrong," Brad said.

"And do not underestimate me, Mr. Nohea. If you want a fight I will give you one."

Brad glanced past her to Josh. "You let women fight your battles these days?"

Josh didn't move; he stood there sipping his coffee. "She seems to be doing fine."

"Unbelievable." Brad scoffed. "Never thought I'd see the day when Josh Windsor got led around by his dick."

"That's enough," she said.

Josh had other ideas. He slowly set his mug down. "We can go outside and I'll show you what I can do with my fists."

Brad laughed, clearly enjoying whatever story he was concocting in his head. "Don't you need your benefactor's permission for that?"

"I don't know about any benefactor, but I certainly think you could use a punch or two," she said.

"I'll pass." Brad shot Josh a superior look. "And I'll find my way out."

Josh fought the urge to follow Brad out to the yard and pound the shit out of him. Drowning him in the pool seemed like another possible solution. Josh figured anything to work off the energy surging through him would work.

He had stood in the hall outside Deana's kitchen and listened to her defend him. Without any explanation from him, she believed he got screwed at DEA. She had him investigated in the past and knew his record for walking awfully close to the legal line, yet she refused to fall for Brad's lies. Being the smart woman she was, Deana knew Brad was fishing for information and refused to give him what he sought. For that, a fierce pride moved through Josh. Having someone trust him to that degree felt good. Damn good.

It was the part where she used her position to push people around and get her way that pissed him off. He was not some dumb kid who needed a mommy to run in and rescue him. And the fact she thought everything could be solved with the power of money reminded him about the woman who once tried to ruin him.

"Why did you let him in?" Josh asked.

"He had a badge."

Josh leaned against the counter and watched her dump the coffee from Brad's mug in the sink. Watched her look everywhere but at him. "And you wanted to know what my former boss would say about me, right?"

She stared through the window and out over the ocean. "I admit to being curious."

"Learn anything interesting?"

She finally looked at him. "That Brad Nohea is a jackass who likes to blame others for his inability to do his job."

Josh didn't know he was holding his breath until it left him in a rush. "None of that is news."

She sat back at the table and fiddled with the neckline of her high-cut sweater. "Why don't you tell me why you're so ticked off."

It took a minute for the words to register in his brain. "How do you know I am?"

"I can see it in your stillness, in the stiff way you're holding your body." She pointed at his face. "That stern look where all of the happiness leaves your face."

"Impressive."

She smiled. "You're not that complex."

"You know me so well?" What scared him is that it sounded as if she did.

"I've been around you enough to tell when you're winding up for a fight. I guess I want to know why all of that is aimed at me and not Brad."

Her smarts never ceased to amaze Josh. It was one of the sexiest things about her. That and those mile-long legs.

"Is it just an automatic reaction?" he asked.

"What are you talking about?"

"That part where you start highlighting your connections and ability to destroy people." And there was the one thing he hated about her.

"Ah, so this is about money again." She nodded. "Figures."

"I didn't say—"

"You want to talk about this? Fine. We will." She tapped her fingers against the table. "I was lucky enough to be born into a family with money. I never had to worry about food or shelter or education. I don't apologize for that."

It was as if she saw straight into his past and was picking at the wounds. "I didn't ask you to."

"But you want me to feel guilty about it. Forget that my brother and sister-in-law were beaten to death. Forget that my father heard the news and dropped over dead from a heart attack. Forget that my mother had a breakdown or that my nephew is in jail. You think my biggest shame should be the amount of money in my bank account."

In his mind there was a connection between all that had happened to her and the money she had piled in accounts, but to say that suggested her suffering was somehow deserved. No matter what she had, she didn't ask for the parade of deaths that had followed her. Still, he hated her background and willingness to use it to get what she wanted.

Rather than fight, he said what he should have said from the beginning of the conversation. "Thank you for not buying into Brad's bullshit."

"The way I see it you can be a jerk," she said.

Looked like she wasn't buying his gratitude. "Yeah, thanks for that, too."

"But you're not the guy Brad thinks you are."

Josh wondered what he was. He used to be a DEA agent and a damn good one. Now he was stuck in this in-between status, not knowing where he fit or what he wanted separate from wanting Deana. "Not everyone agrees with that assessment. In fact, there's an entire administrative board that thinks I should have turned in my badge and gun long ago."

"They're wrong."

Something in her tone sent a cold shudder through him. "Don't."

"What?"

He could tell from the way her mouth dropped open but her eyes still sparkled that she knew exactly what he was saying. "Do not help me get my job back by going to the Board."

She just stared at him.

"I'm serious, Deana."

"I can see that."

"Are you hearing me? I don't want you to throw your name around and fix this for me."

She hesitated for an extra second. "Whatever you say."

Crisis averted. At least he hoped that was true. "Remember that line when I stop by for a visit tonight."

That suddenly, the temperature in the room shifted. All the hatred that followed Brad into the house and all the frustration that remained after he left evaporated in a flash.

Heat flared behind her eyes. "What about practicing it on me now?"

He cursed her timing. "I'm meeting someone."

"Oh."

"Not a woman." Telling her more would only lead to trouble, but he didn't want her to think he was chasing other women while he was with her. "And not important."

"Oh, I think it is or you would just let me know what it's about."

He weighed his options. It was either tell her or run the risk of having her follow him all over town and mess up his plan. "Promise me you'll stay calm."

"You probably shouldn't preface whatever you're going to say with that sort of comment. Kind of makes it an even bigger deal."

"Frankie Butler."

She stood up. "I'm coming with you."

So much for letting her in on his plans. He vowed not to make that mistake again. "No way."

"Wrong answer."

Josh put his hands on her shoulders to keep her from picking up her purse and climbing into his car. "If Frankie sees you, I won't get anything out of him."

She bit her lower lip.

"You know I'm right," Josh said.

"I could hide."

"I would know you're there, and I need to be able to concentrate."

"You're laying it on a little thick, don't you think?"

"I need to do this alone."

She rested her hands on his belt buckle. "But you'll come back and tell me what happened with Frankie?"

"Yes." He leaned in and kissed her.

"Promise?"

"I have plans for that and more this evening."

Chapter Eighteen

"Why should I tell you anything?" Frankie sat in the booth at the diner and scarfed down a hamburger.

Josh saw the baseball cap pulled down low with dirty blond hair peeking from underneath, the faded sweatshirt, and the fingernails bitten to the quick, and he wondered when Frankie last had a decent meal. When he last got through a day without taking some drug to pass the hours.

Did anyone even give a shit about this kid? He had a house but was never there, a fact that didn't seem to bother his mother. Reaching the kid required a patchwork of calls and contacts and a lot of help from Eric. Convincing Frankie to meet proved impossible until Josh offered a meal.

"I figure it's about time you told someone the truth about what happened that night," Josh said.

Frankie wiped his mouth on his sleeve. "Already did that."

"Tell me what you told Eric Kimura."

The kid stopped chewing. "Ask him."

"I'm asking you."

"All I said was that Ryan liked to talk big and throw his money around."

"You mean his parents' money."

"Ryan hated his dad and all the rules. After the bust a few years back the guy clamped down hard." Frankie popped a few fries into his mouth. "Ryan couldn't piss without permission."

"What exactly did Ryan say to you about his parents?"

"That he knew how to get the money." Frankie shoveled the food into his mouth one hand after the other.

"Meaning?"

"Come on, man. You know," he mumbled over a mouthful of food.

Josh did. "Did Ryan brag about killing them?"

"Nah, I'm saying Ryan liked to talk. That's all. He got high and said things."

"And what did you do?"

Frankie swallowed hard. "Nuthin'. I didn't have anything to do with what happened at that house."

"Chace Armstrong ran you off. Told you to stay away from his son." Josh decided to touch on the part only Eric knew and shared in confidence. "Word is Ryan's dad smacked you around to make his point."

"No."

"He banged your head off a wall and gave you a concussion."

"So?"

The way Frankie said the word, with so little emotion, told Josh what he needed to know. The scene between him and Chace had been bad. Possibly even the type that crushed egos and spiraled out of control.

"It had to piss you off to have him throw you around like

that. Word is he did it in front of one of your friends. Seems Chace was trying to send you a message," Josh said.

Frankie shoved his plate away. "You're not laying this on me, man."

"Then give me another way to look at this."

"What?"

"You ever hear about Ryan having an accomplice? Someone who acted as a lookout?" Josh stared at Frankie, hoping for eye contact, but the kid looked all around the diner. Spent almost thirty seconds watching the traffic outside the window before he finally answered.

"No."

"Hard to imagine a loudmouth like Ryan keeping his plans to himself. I'm thinking he told a friend."

"He didn't have any." Frankie's jaw clenched. "His dad saw to that."

"Except you."

"Nah, man. I wasn't allowed in his house."

Josh understood Chace's actions. The man saw his son going downhill and panicked. Pulled the strings tight and held on. The idea that loving his kid might have gotten Chace killed was not a new one but was always devastating. Josh had seen it all before. It was an unbelievable chain of events that happened over and over across the country. Kids couldn't appreciate having a safe home. Parents couldn't control all the influences bombarding their kids.

"His dad blamed me for getting Ryan into drugs," Frankie said.

"But that's not how it was."

Frankie's anger festered beneath the surface, showing itself in the darkness behind his eyes and the grinding of his teeth. "Fuck, no. The drug-running was Ryan's idea. He was bored and wanted more money than the crappy amount his dad gave him access to. Thought it was funny to go to all of these prestigious events with his family and then get high after."

"But killing is something else. It's bigger and takes more planning."

Frankie shrugged. "I guess."

"Everyone agrees you're the smarter of the two. Ryan couldn't manage that sort of scene on his own. He liked to pretend he knew what was going on, but he didn't."

Frankie's teeth snapped together. His words sounded as if they were pulled from him. "Don't know what you're talking about."

"If I were that smart friend I would have contacted the prosecutor and made a deal."

"I didn't get no deal."

"But you told your story first. You beat the polygraph. Smart kid like you, in and out of the system your whole life would know how to do that."

"Didn't take a poly."

Of course not, because the police had already focused on Ryan. "Did anyone ask you?"

"Look, man. I know you're hanging with Ryan's aunt and all, but you're looking in the wrong place. Ryan was on his own on this one. I didn't want any part of his plan. Drugs was one thing. This? No, man."

And that was the piece of information Josh both wanted to hear and dreaded knowing. It suggested Frankie knew about the murder before it happened. Also meant Ryan planned the whole damn thing, probably even asked Frankie for help to get the deed done.

Sure, Frankie could be working a new scam, trying to get Josh to believe one thing about Ryan when another was true. But Josh sensed the truth. Frankie's demeanor hadn't changed. The kid didn't even know he handed Josh a piece of the puzzle. Josh's job now was to follow the evidence. That meant following Frankie.

"So you think he did it?" Josh asked.

Frankie ripped a stack of napkins from the holder on the table. "Doesn't matter much since he's rotting up in Halawa."

Josh began to think that was exactly where Ryan was going to stay. Forever. "His aunt thinks he should be freed. I'm wondering if maybe she's right."

"You mean out?" Frankie twisted a paper napkin around his finger. The knot was tight enough to turn his skin white at the edges.

"I figure after spending some time in lockup Ryan might be more willing to talk about his co-conspirators. If he's protecting someone, now would be the time for him to say something. After all, you said he likes to talk."

Frankie's face turned as white as his strangled hand. "Ryan says he didn't do it."

"I'm betting he did and that he had some help."

For the first time in more than ten minutes Frankie made eye contact and didn't look away. "Why?"

"Just a feeling."

Frankie waited a few more seconds and then threw his crumpled napkin on the table. "I gotta go."

Not a surprise. Josh hadn't expected to hold Frankie's attention for as long as he had. Josh also planted the seed in case his feeling that Frankie was involved in the murders turned out to be true. No better way to flush out the truth than to set the conspirators against each other. Eric had tried, but the evidence pileup against Ryan made it unnecessary to go looking for more killers.

"Thanks for talking to me," Josh said.

"Whatever." Frankie took off without looking back.

Josh watched the kid rush out of the diner and break into a jog once he hit the street. *Perfect*. That was exactly the plan. Now to follow him.

Josh dropped money on the table and waved to the waitress as he headed for the door. The rental car sat only a few feet away. He could climb in and follow Frankie and . . . Deana. There she was—in the front seat of his car.

Chapter Nineteen

Deana knew Josh was going to be pissed. She anticipated hearing a great deal of swearing and yelling. He better understand that she wasn't afraid to throw it right back at him. As far as she was concerned he could get mad and then get over it.

Even though their relationship had expanded into something that at its core she refused to name, they had a business transaction to finish. That's why she followed him and slipped into his car. Whatever happened tonight, well, that didn't have anything to do with today. She intended to keep the two parts of her life separate. This was for Ryan. Later would be for her.

Josh slid into the driver's seat and slammed the car door behind him. "Get out."

Gruff with his voice low and furious. Yeah, Josh's reaction didn't disappoint; it was exactly as she expected.

"Hello to you," she said.

"Door's unlocked. Go." His voice stayed deadly soft. It conveyed his anger just fine. So did his white-knuckle grip on the steering wheel.

He could rip the thing right out of the dash for all she cared; she wasn't moving. "No."

"That wasn't a question, Deana."

"Look, I promised not to interfere with your meeting and I didn't."

He slammed his hand against the wheel. "Do you think I'm kidding here?"

"I think you should use those keys and drive."

"Where?"

"To the place you planned to go until you saw me sitting here." She could read him now. That satisfied look on his face as he watched Frankie run off faded the second his eyes met hers. Whatever he was searching for from the meeting he got.

That realization both thrilled her and scared her. He had made it clear he wouldn't simply find the answer she wanted. He would find the real answer.

As much as she believed in her heart Ryan could not have caused the bloodbath at his house, a part of her had begun to doubt. She remembered the calm way Eric declared him guilty. Heard the concern in Josh's voice as he listed the evidence against Ryan. Her instincts screamed for her to hang on, but she worried that those same instincts had failed her.

"I can't do my job with you in the car." Josh stared at Frankie's retreating figure, breaking only to glance at her.

"The car will run just fine with two people in it." She folded her arms across her chest just to let him know she didn't plan to budge.

"Not if I don't turn the key."

She watched Frankie disappear around the corner. "You're wasting time. You're going to lose him."

"Who?"

"Don't play dumb; it doesn't suit you."

Josh leaned back in the seat and kept his hands on the wheel. His arms stretched until they were perfectly straight. Any stiffer and he might break a bone.

Deana decided to stick with the basics. "You have a plan. You always have a plan."

Josh swore then stuck his keys in the ignition. He pointed one finger at the center of her forehead. "Not one word."

"Whatever you say."

Josh eased the car into traffic. "As if you would follow a direction."

"I'm not good at being ordered around."

"No fucking kidding."

She caught a glimpse of Frankie's sweatshirt ahead as he climbed into a dirty old pickup truck. "I thought he was on probation."

"That's what his record says."

"Then how can he drive?"

"He can't."

"Did anyone bother to tell him that?" Frankie squealed the tires as he pulled out. "Do you know where he's going?"

Josh shot her his best frown. "I have an idea, yeah."

"Care to share?"

"You're not going to like it."

"I haven't liked much about Frankie from the moment I met him."

"This won't be much different, since I think he's going to visit Ryan."

Her stomach fell past her knees. That was a nightmare scenario. Ryan had enough trouble without keeping in contact with his drug buddies on the outside. "Why?"

"Frankie knows something."

"About Chace and Kalanie?"

"Yeah."

They drove in silence for a few more minutes, far enough to keep from cluing Frankie in to their presence. While Josh drove, Deana tried to sort out all the conflicting facts running around in her head. When Frankie's truck made the last turn and headed for the drive leading to the prison, Deana knew Josh had information he wasn't sharing. Information, theories—something. Knowing her world could fly apart at any second made her nerves click to life.

Josh pulled into a visitor's space at the front of the building but in a lot opposite the side where Frankie left his truck. Josh let the car idle as he stared at the building.

"Will Frankie be allowed to see Ryan?" she asked.

"No."

Finally, some good news. "You're sure?"

Josh thumped his fingers against the wheel in time with the beat of the music from the radio turned so low that she could barely hear it. "I checked the approved visitor list before I left to meet Frankie. Also made sure that Frankie's name could never be added."

"That's a relief, but . . . why?"

"I don't want them to talk to each other."

Her blood turned icy. Everything inside of her froze. "For any reason in particular?"

Josh turned to stare at her. Wariness had crept into his bright blue eyes. "Cutting off contact will make Frankie desperate. When that happens he'll come looking for me and I can get some of my questions answered."

She knew what those questions were. They were the same ones that played in her mind those brief moments before she kicked them out again. The same ones she refused to nurture and ask.

"You think Ryan did it." She didn't raise her voice or accuse. She just wanted to know if all of the work in reading transcripts and reviewing evidence and talking with Eric and meeting Ryan did anything to sway him.

"I think Frankie knows more about what happened and Ryan's role in it than Frankie is willing to admit."

It wasn't the exoneration she hoped to hear, but it was enough to ease the heaviness closing in on her heart. "That's not an answer."

"That's the only one I can give right now." Josh put the car in reverse and started to pull out of the space.

"I thought we were waiting for Frankie."

"He'll be out in a second. We need to be somewhere else or my plan to scare the shit out of him will never work."

She knew something about those feelings. Had lived with them for what felt like forever.

"I don't want it to be true," she said, her voice so soft and small that she barely recognized it.

"Of course not."

Her mouth fought with her brain. She had carried the secret for so long, kept it locked away from everyone except those who were there that night and agreed to forget.

"He's your nephew." Tension left Josh's shoulders and voice. He no longer talked in booming tones. "Whatever else Ryan is, he means something to you. You remember the innocent kid. It's a matter of love and loyalty. No one expects you to condemn him."

Exhaustion swept through her. Playing the role of the perfect daughter had grown so tiring. Hiding and pretending weighed so heavy. "That's not it. Well, not all of it."

Josh's grip on the wheel loosened. "What does that mean?"

She traced the back of her hand down the window. "I could have stopped his drug use."

"Don't do that. Don't give Ryan a way out of his mistakes by taking on all of this guilt. He made the choices, not you."

Josh flashed her an angry scowl, but she knew the fierce emotion wasn't directed at her. He was in full protector mode, throwing his body in front of anyone or anything that might harm her. The man might want to push away his rescuer tendencies, but they rose to the surface automatically.

She wondered if he would be so kind and supportive once he knew the truth. "I could have spent more time with him."

"Deana—"

"I should have explained how life is about moments and choices and that all of the money in the world can't buy your way out of the worst of those."

"He was too young to understand that lesson. Hell, most grown-ups don't get that one."

"Like my family?"

He pulled the car onto the shoulder of the road and cut the engine. With one hand resting over the wheel he turned to her. "Anyone who thinks you don't know the difference is an ass. For the record, consider me a recovering ass."

Of all the things he had ever said to her, that small concession meant the most. "I don't claim to be perfect."

"You're not."

She smiled despite the sadness churning inside of her. "Always the sweet-talker."

"You aren't Ryan. And you're not responsible for the stupid choices he's made."

"But I have to admit to my own. I should have done that for Ryan, told him I understood what it was like to want to break free from the Armstrong name. That escaping would not make him forget all those lectures about owing something back to the community."

Josh rested a palm on the back of her seat, close enough to touch her if he wanted to. "Escape how?"

"Drugs, alcohol. Anything that would disgust the good people who attended those charity functions and big parties at the house."

"Why do I think you're not really talking about Ryan now?"

The lessons fit, but she was most definitely talking about her own life choices. "I left Hawaii to go to college. Thought I could forget about being one of *the* Armstrongs. Thought I could go somewhere and not have my parents' friends see me and report back. I wanted freedom."

"That's what college is for."

"No lectures on being a poor little rich girl?"

He wrapped her hair around his finger. "Doesn't sound like this was about shopping or having the most expensive car. You wanted to find your identity."

Feeling his gaze on her, she leaned her head back against the seat and closed her eyes. Somehow it felt right to finally talk. Sharing something so personal with Josh a few days ago would have been unthinkable. Now it seemed natural.

"I was nineteen and drinking all of the time." She remembered the rush of doing something forbidden and how good it felt to fall into a state of nothingness. "I experimented with drugs. Thought I was so cool because I was living this adult life that I could never have on an island where everyone knew who I was."

He traced the outline of her ear with his thumb. "I've never seen you drink."

"I don't. Not now. Not after climbing behind the wheel drunk off my ass at nineteen and hitting another car."

"Deana."

She could hear the law enforcement hardness move into his voice. She did not dare open her eyes for fear of seeing the distaste she suspected he now had for her. "I wasn't in control that night. I drove too fast and put a pregnant woman in the hospital."

"Was she okay?"

"She delivered early, but the baby was fine."

"That could have been—"

She pushed forward. "But I killed my best friend."

His hand stilled in her hair. "What?"

"She was in the front seat with me. Went through the windshield." Despite all the years that had passed, Deana could still remember those moments right before the crash. The two girls were laughing and singing as loud as they could to some song on the radio.

If she closed her eyes Deana could remember Laurie that way. Deana blocked the other image. The one her father forced on her when he shoved the accident photograph in her face and demanded she stop drinking.

"Damn, Deana. I'm sorry."

She turned her head and looked straight into Josh's soft blue eyes. Saw all the compassion and sadness there. No pity. No anger. Just worry for her.

During the past year with Eric she had hidden the truth. He knew about the car accident and that a friend died. She didn't tell him about her role out of fear of his reaction. Eric had a political career ahead of him. Being saddled with her secret would have been too much.

But the accident marked her. Changed her. She didn't even try to make Eric understand that part. Now that she had shared with Josh, the weight inside her lightened. She didn't experience a great rush of mutual understanding like that portrayed in movies, but she did feel a shift. Slight but it was there.

"She was thrown. I was trapped in the car," Deana said.

"The scars."

"I didn't wear a seat belt. My body crashed into the steering wheel and the windshield shattered on top of me."

"You're lucky to be alive."

Deana rolled her head from side to side against the headrest as she forced the words up her throat and out of her mouth. "The night is a blur. Sirens. Crying. The school's dean rushing to my side and telling me not to answer any questions until the lawyer arrived. Later at the hospital, everyone was there, but the unbelievable pain in my chest took my breath and my head refused to clear."

She remembered it all. Her teeth had chattered as waves of freezing cold moved through her. Flopping between being numb and being terrified, she waited for her father to arrive and then watched him handle everything. It was not until the plane took off to take her back to Hawaii that the rush of tears started. They hadn't stopped for hours.

"What happened after the hospital?" Josh asked.

"Nothing."

He pressed his fingers under her chin and turned her head to face him again. "That's not possible."

There was no reason to hide the rest. The answer would shore up his feelings about her and her family's wealth, but the context was important if Josh were to understand how everything unfolded with Ryan. "After several surgeries I spent some time in a rehab hospital due to a hip injury. Spent an additional thirty days in a an alcohol treatment center. I eventually reenrolled in college in Hawaii."

His thumb smoothed over her lips. "Anything else?"

In his own way Josh was asking about criminal charges. Trying to ask without offending her.

"You were right when you said money can buy a great deal. Throw enough of it around and you can make anything go away." Deana wanted to believe she differed from her parents in this major aspect. They fell back on money. She had spent her adult life trying to use money for good rather than to get her way. But the more she analyzed the facts and listened to Josh's perception, the more she saw just how deep blood ran.

When it came to helping Ryan on the drug charges, she had been willing to sacrifice Josh and use all her resources to do it. When Brad Nohea went after Josh, her immediate response was to use her position to control the government hack. Even though she lived with the reality that ignoring responsibility led to backbreaking guilt, she followed the same path and used the same threats to get her way.

Rather than hide behind her hypocritical statements, she had to face the truth. Even if that meant losing Josh's respect. "In case you're wondering, the price for a dead daughter is about a million dollars. That's all it takes to make criminal and civil charges disappear."

Josh dropped his hand.

She refused to let the loss of contact stop her. "I'm not sure what other promises were exchanged or how many checks were written. At the time I didn't want to know. I was nineteen and thought that having my parents rush in and fix everything was a good thing. The fact I never had to go to jail and my records would be expunged seemed like such great thiings."

"And now?"

"It wasn't until years later, when the guilt got worse instead of better and the silence and buried records were all I could think about that, I understood what a disservice we had done to Laurie. That I realized I should have paid a higher price for my mistakes."

"Your friend?"

Deana nodded. "Despite that, I watched my brother do the same thing for Ryan. Hell, my mom and I did our own form of throwing our money around against you to make the drug charges disappear."

"I remember."

But did he forgive her? Deana exhaled, trying to clear her head and push her mind to finish this. "I thought we were helping Ryan. I had hoped he would change."

"You wanted him to become focused and driven, like you."

"I wanted him to stop using."

Josh exhaled loud enough to fill the car. "Ryan isn't you."

"He could have been."

"No. The memory of what happened stayed with you because you knew it was an awful thing and something for which you should have paid a high price. Because you're decent." Josh stroked the back of his hand against her cheek. "You've lived your life since then half hidden behind your scars paying penance and punishing yourself."

"I wouldn't—"

"Do you honestly think Ryan would ever carry that kind of guilt?"

"I . . ." She didn't. Ryan always possessed a grander and skewed sense of what he deserved more than other kids. He wasn't content to be lucky in life and make the most of that. It was almost as if he wished to punish his family for all he had because it still wasn't enough.

"If the point is that you think you somehow could have

stopped the murders by letting Ryan face more hardship on the drugs, drop it," Josh said.

"It's not that easy."

"Ryan was a first-time drug offender. Say a few apologies and he would have gotten probation, which he would have sailed through because the kid can pour on the charm when he needs to. But none of that would have kept him from hanging out with kids like Frankie or from carrying around that sense of entitlement." A very real pain showed in Josh's usually clear eyes. "Or from picking up that bat and trying to take his inheritance early through violence and without ever earning anything through his own hard work. It's not who he is."

A tear seeped out of the corner of her eye. "You're convinced he's guilty."

Josh wiped away the wetness. "I haven't seen anything to suggest he isn't."

"I got a second chance."

"And you've paid the price for that in other ways for years." Josh leaned over and gave her a long, lingering kiss. "Let's go get your car and go home."

"You're not repulsed?" She hated to ask, but needed to know the answer.

"I'm sad for the kid you were. And . . ."

"Yeah."

"Impressed with the woman you've become."

She couldn't ask for more than that.

Chapter Twenty

Josh barely let Deana unlock the front door before trapping her against the wall and kissing her senseless. He wrapped his fingers around her wrists and held them next to her head. Not that she fought him. If anything her mouth was hotter, more insistent, than his.

His legs tangled against hers; the rough material of his pants rubbed her bare legs under her knee-length skirt. What he wanted was to drop his pants and feel his skin against hers. He settled for separating her legs with his thigh and sliding his knee high against her, gently caressing the crotch of her underwear until she groaned against his lips.

"Josh, we need—"

He broke off the kiss and balanced his forehead against hers. "Jesus, woman. Do not tell me you need more time."

She kissed his cheek. "You've been so patient."

"You're killing me."

She threw him a sexy little pout. "Poor baby."

Damn, he wanted her. "I'll wait however long you need me to wait, but I'm hoping like hell the answer is something along the lines of four minutes instead of four days."

She licked the outer edge of his ear, then whispered, "I stopped the kiss to suggest we find a bed."

Thank God.

"That okay with you?" she asked.

He was fine taking her right there against the wall. Fast the first time worked for him. They could go slow the second time . . . and the third. "I'll go anywhere with you if you do that tongue thing again."

She did. With her mouth on his ear and her body pressed hard against him she had him hard and panting. So did that hand of hers as it slid out from under his and went exploring. Those fingers walked down his chest and landed on his fly. No games. No waiting. Just her palm cupping his erection.

"Where's that bed?" he asked in a rough voice.

She pushed away from the wall and slipped out of his arms before he could stop her. Swaying hips. An evil seductress smile. After two steps, she held a hand out to him. "Are you coming?"

"In about two seconds, if you keep looking at me like that."

"I bet you can hold out for longer than that."

His fingers entwined with hers. With a gentle tug, he pulled her back into his arms. "I've been waiting, taking cold showers, counting backwards from two thousand for days."

She wrapped her arms around his neck. "Guess that means you don't hate me anymore."

The words brought with them a quick flash of guilt. For a guy who fought his entire life not to be judged by his background, he sure jumped fast to do that to Deana.

"I like everything about you."

Her eyebrows inched up. "Everything?"

"I plan to like certain parts of you very much all night long." He backed her down the hall toward the bedroom. "I'll start with those breasts. Round and perfect for my hands. I've been fantasizing about those since the pool."

"Hmmm."

"And those legs. Hot-damn-legs." He cupped her backside and pressed her close against the bulge in his pants. "I stayed up last night imagining how they'll feel wrapped around my waist."

Josh inched her skirt higher on her thighs. By the time they reached the bedroom he had the material balled in his fists and dragged up to her waist. He glanced around enough to make sure he didn't trip over a piece of furniture. He saw flashes of a white comforter and big pillows, but the decorating style was the last thing on his mind. Tasting her owned the top spot.

"How about we try that thing with my legs now? Sounds fun." Deana asked the question right before she lifted one leg high on his hip.

The move gave his hands the access he craved. One hand stayed on the small of her back while the other slid down her butt to the lacy edge of her panties. He did not stop until his fingers dipped into her wetness.

Her head fell back as his forefinger traced the creases between her legs. Immediately her scent filled his head. Salty and womanly. Perfect, like the rest of her.

He sat down hard on the bed and gathered her on his lap. Her knees hit the mattress on either side of his legs and her mouth never left his.

As his hands roamed over her ass and his fingers plunged deep inside her she did a touching tour of her own. She grabbed his shirt and pulled it off his shoulders and threw it on the floor. Nails raked across his bare back. Her hot mouth traced a line over his collarbone.

Hell, she was on fire. Forget the conservative clothing and snotty attitude. Deana was pure woman in the bedroom. Sexy and giving, she knew what she wanted and did not hide it. He loved that in a woman.

He fell back against the bed with her sprawled on top of him. While she trailed a line of kisses down his chest, he ripped her shirt off. Not pulled, not tugged, actually grabbed it and heard it tear. Buttons bounced as he stripped it off her, leaving only a purple lacy bra behind. The thing pushed her breasts over the top, treating him to an eyeful of creamy flesh.

She lifted her head and smiled down at him. "You owe me a shirt."

"I'll buy you a damn closet full." Anything to get her out of those high-necked clothes. Hell, he'd shred every outfit if he thought that would force her to buy something more sexy.

Forget the shirts.

She should wear only that bra. Ever.

Josh could see her dark nipples through the thin material. Unable to hold back, he reached out to feel the weight of her smoothness in his hand. Her nipples immediately tightened.

"You're very good at that," she whispered against his neck.

"I have many skills."

"So do I." She sat up, straddling him.

Fast hands went to work unbuckling his pants and grabbing for his zipper. Clicking sounds filled the room as she lowered the zipper and then slid her hand deep inside his underwear. His lower body bucked when her hand covered his erection.

"This is going to be fast," he said, his voice rough with need.

"I'll take whatever I can get." She lifted up on her knees.

He put his hands on her waist to stop her. "Where are you going?"

"To get the condoms." She stretched over him and opened the drawer in the cabinet beside the bed.

The position put her breasts in his face. He didn't squander the opportunity. He sucked on her nipples through the bra. Deana didn't sit back down. She just waited there, her head forward and her hair brushing over his chest as he learned the feel of her.

"That feels amazing." She turned the last word into three long syllables.

"I agree."

While he licked he watched her strain against his mouth. From this position he could see every inch of her long, lean body. And those matching purple panties. He wanted those damn things off and planned to remedy that the second she crawled on top of him again.

She sat back down on his thighs and leaned in to kiss him hard. There was no guessing about her intentions. Her need matched his. This woman appreciated desire and seduction as well as he did.

She threw the condom packets on his chest. There had to be twenty of them.

"Uh, baby. You know I'm not sixteen, right?"

"Thirty-five isn't old, and I'm betting you'll do just fine." He skimmed his hands up her legs. "Aw, shucks."

"I bought them the day you agreed to work with me."

He stopped on his way to the part of her he wanted to touch again. "Really?"

"I knew then."

He waited for the panic to set in. For the idea to send him running. It had the opposite effect. Josh realized he felt the same way about Deana. He fought it, didn't want the feelings, but he knew deep down they'd fall into bed sooner or later. But, hell, she hid her side well enough.

"Are you going to keep staring at me, or are you going to take off my panties?"

"That's an easy one." He flipped her over onto her back.

After one last kiss on her mouth he traveled down her bare body, kissing and licking as he went. Now that he finally had a full view of her chest, he stopped and paid extra attention to the area. His lips traced the scar and followed it down to where it ended between her breasts.

Deana didn't push him away or try to stop him. No, she tunneled her fingers through his hair and pulled him even closer. By the time he moved to her stomach, he had her back arching off the bed and her ankles digging into his butt. She held him tight enough to crack his spine. And he loved every minute of it.

Adjusting her legs, Josh slipped down even farther and inhaled her sweet fragrance. She was wet. Had been since they hit the front door.

"Are you ready for me?" He asked the question as he peeled those tiny panties down her legs. Inch by inch he dragged them off her, revealing tanned firm skin.

And that wasn't all she hid. He could see the small line of hair left from waxing. He brushed his hand over her smooth skin.

"Beautiful," he whispered as he lowered his head. Seconds later his mouth was on her, his tongue in her.

She thrashed and moaned as he learned every inch of her with his lips and fingers. With two fingers, he dipped inside her, stretching her until her internal muscles convulsed. When he lowered his head and sucked on her clit a tremor moved through her. Every inch of her body pulled taut, including her fingers, which were stretched out and grabbing the white sheets.

"Josh . . ."

He still had his pants on. In two seconds he eased away from her and stripped off the remainder of his clothes. Naked and ready, he looked up and saw her holding a condom out to him.

"Now, Josh."

She didn't have to ask twice.

With his hands on her knees, he eased her legs back against her chest. He wanted to feel all of her. In one swift movement he entered her, plunging deep inside. Her body tightened around him. She was wet and clinging and her body pulsed around him until he thought he'd pass out from the pleasure.

Her head pushed into the pillows, treating him to her uncovered neck. He could see her swallow and fight for air as he pushed into her, retreated, and pushed again. When her body clamped down on him again he lost the ability to see anything.

The sound of their harsh breaths filled the room. Smells of their lovemaking mixed with the groan rumbling up from his chest. And she wasn't quiet, either. As he went faster, she chanted his name.

Her body stiffened, but she didn't find her release. It was as if she were holding back, trying to savor each feeling. He couldn't wait another second, but he wanted her with him.

His finger barely touched her clit before she exploded. The chant turned into a scream that shook the bed.

The orgasm rocketed through her, making her pulse even harder against him. The pressure sent his body bucking. When he pushed into her one last time the tension pulling inside him snapped. His entire body broke apart as the orgasm tore through him.

His last thought was he didn't want to return to the guesthouse tonight.

Chapter Twenty-one

Deana opened her eyes and stared up at the slatted wood ceiling. Arms out to the side and legs like jelly, she hadn't made one move on the bed since Josh collapsed on top of her a few minutes earlier. She tried to talk now but gave up when she couldn't muster the air to speak.

The emotional unburdening in the car. The wild lovemaking now. One led to the other and they both felt so right.

"Wow." That was the only word she could think of to say.

"Exactly." Josh rolled off and fell into bed beside her. "I'm not sure I could move if I had to."

"I vote we stay here until we need food. Then we call someone to get it for us."

"This is one of those times when it would be helpful to have Mrs. Chow around."

"Where is she?"

"With my mom."

"She's working for her?"

"I told you, she's not a maid."

He lifted his body up on one elbow. "Ready to explain who she is?"

Deana decided to stop torturing him. "She worked for Chace."

"Ah, she's the live-in housekeeper who was visiting relatives the night of the murders. I saw a note, but the name was different."

"It's the difference between her legal Chinese name and the one she goes by, Mrs. Chow. She didn't have anywhere else to go."

"So you took her in." He reached out and laced his fingers through hers.

When he kissed the back of the joined hands, she melted. Ladykiller Josh Windsor sure knew how to make a woman feel special. And his reputation for knowing his way around a bedroom was well deserved. She wondered if she should pay a little more attention to gossip from now on. Well, not if it was about Josh's future conquests. No way did she want to hear about them. The thought sucked all the joy out of her, so she pushed the image away.

"Why are you tensing up?" he asked.

"I'm not."

He propped his upper body up and hovered over her. "Try again."

She decided to ask the question that nagged her since their car ride to the prison. "I'm just surprised at how well you took the news of my accident."

"I'm a balanced guy."

She pressed her hand against his cheek. "I'm serious. After all of those snide comments about money, I figured you'd at least give me the old 'I told you so' lecture."

He pretended to be offended. "That doesn't sound like me."

"Uh-huh." She dragged her hand over the stubble on his

chin. It was as if he had a permanent shadow. Facial hair never turned her on before. Then she met Josh.

"You said something about expunging your records. Were any charges ever brought?"

"I pled to reckless driving. Since that wasn't a serious offense, at least nothing compared to murder, the lawyers were able to seal and eventually expunge the records. Finding any record of it would be near impossible."

"But not totally."

"There were people who knew the truth. That always leaves open the potential from someone to talk. More criminal charges, no, but there is a lingering possibility someone would find out the story and spread it around. Having that type of information on one of the Armstrong family could be good for a reporter's career. Scandal, money and misuse of power always sell."

"How did Eric take the truth?"

That came out of nowhere. It took her a few seconds to process being in bed with Josh and hearing her ex's name. "Eric?"

"You know, the man you used to date."

She pinched him in retribution for the sarcasm. "He doesn't know."

"How is that possible?"

"Oh, he knows the scars came from an accident. The rest I kept to myself." She tucked the sheet under her arms. "Didn't think his prosecutorial sensibilities would handle the truth all that well. Also had his political career to consider."

"I'm not convinced that's true."

Eric was just about the last topic she wanted to talk about. "I'm trying to figure out why *you* don't care."

Josh reached for her hand and kissed it again. "Let me

ask you this. If the accident happened today, if you got drunk and lost control and someone died as a result, would you look to your money and power to get you out of trouble? Would you run around hiding the records and paying off reporters to stay quiet?"

Her defenses rose before she could shut them down. "I don't drink anymore. I wasn't lying about that."

He put his fingers over her lips. "Stop. I get that. What I'm asking is would you stand up and take responsibility?"

Deana had asked that question every day since Josh walked into her life. The easy answer was an unequivocal yes. She believed the person she was today would handle the fallout better than her nineteen-year-old self, no matter how horrible the results. At the same time, she had learned from the past few weeks that her first inclination was to whip out her checkbook and begin issuing orders. Now she had to wonder whether she had learned very much at all in the years since the accident.

She thought about lying but went with the truth. After what they just shared, Josh deserved that much. "I hope so."

"That's not the strongest denial I've ever heard."

"My initial reaction is to say of course I'd do the right thing. But life is not that black-and-white." When his stare remained unreadable a frisson of panic raced through her. She rushed to explain. "I know you live your life by these rules and that's easy for you, but the rest of us grapple with doing what's hard when it's hardest to do so."

He smiled. "You do know you're arguing with yourself, right? I haven't actually said anything to disagree with you."

"I'm just saying I hope I'm the type of person who would

stand up and face the consequences. I want to believe knowing what I know now I'd make different choices."

"Deana—"

"But the other way, pulling strings and calling in favors sure isn't hard. It doesn't require any kind of sacrifice." She turned to face him head-on. "So, what if I took that road instead? What if I'm not the person I think I am and didn't deserve the break I got?"

Josh's smile grew even wider.

His reaction took her by surprise "What?" she asked.

He rubbed his thumb over her collarbone. "You."

"My what?"

"Most people would insist there's no moral dilemma. They would ignore human nature and act noble. But it would be fake because most of us would take the easiest road out of trouble."

She had no idea what he was trying to say. "Kind of makes you worry about the world, doesn't it?"

"You're not telling me what I want to hear or what you think you're supposed to say."

"I can't figure out if you're complimenting me or not."

He laughed. "I'm just saying it's easy to say you're a hundred percent sure of what you would do in every circumstance, but life doesn't work that way." He cleared his throat. "In other words, I'm agreeing with you here."

"Really? Because it's kind of hard to tell."

"You're being honest, Deana." He kissed her nose. "That's a good thing. It's the hard thing."

Enough with the small little pecks. She wanted a real kiss. Leaning up she did just that, because right then she couldn't do anything else.

"After all of those comments about money I expected

you to be . . . I don't know, disgusted," she said when they finally broke apart.

"I don't want to be judged on what I did when I was nineteen. Can't imagine you do, either. And if you hadn't changed since then, if the death didn't haunt you, that would be one thing. That would make you one kind of person. The kind I could write off. But the real answer is that the Deana Armstrong I've come to know would step up. Sure, you might be tempted to hide behind the checkbook, but you're not really that person. Not deep down where it counts."

"Which?"

"The type who could forget about killing someone and move on. You've already proven it." He traced his thumb over the long line of her scar. "This shows that."

"A scar isn't much compared to the price Laurie paid."

"True, but it's been a long time. Why not get plastic surgery?"

Deana heard that question from her mother a million times. The scars influenced what type of clothes she wore and for her mother a neckline to the chin was a pretty big sin. "It's a reminder."

"You carry that here." He tapped a finger against her head. Then against her heart. "And here. You don't need a physical sign of what happened."

"You working for the plastic surgeon now?"

The grim line of his mouth showed he planned to ignore her joke. "It's as if you want to be disfigured."

"The scars don't bother me." She had endured them for so long they were now a part of her. Staring at them in the mirror each day helped her remember.

"Maybe not, but you only keep them to punish yourself." He delivered his assessment in an even tone. His fingertips continued to caress her skin. His eyes were filled with understanding.

But the entire scene made her twitchy. The comment hit too close. Deana didn't want to talk about her or Laurie or punishments. She had told Josh the truth to knock down the walls between them. He accepted her without judg-ment—something she never believed could happen since it was so much more than she deserved—but he wasn't letting it go. He wanted to dissect and analyze.

If he could, so could she.

"You should talk about self-punishment," she said.

He pulled back slightly. "Is that girl code for some-thing?"

"Woman code. And why haven't you challenged Brad Nohea?"

Josh's mouth fell open. "Why the hell are we talking about that jackass all of a sudden?"

"You mentioned Eric."

Josh actually sputtered. "That's different. I like Eric."

Deana refused to be pulled off topic. "Brad is engaged in some strange campaign to ruin you. Hell, he gave me all sorts of information about what's wrong with you."

Josh's hands were off her now. "When did we start talk-ing about me?"

"Come on, you and I both know Brad should get fired over his actions, or at least demoted." She sat up and rested against the headboard. "He should not be a supervisor."

"No arguments here."

She wrapped an arm around her bent knees. "So, push back. Don't let him get away with the lies."

Josh exhaled. "We're really going to talk about this now?"

"Seems like a good time."

Josh lifted the sheet and stared down at his lap. "I can think of other ways to burn through a few minutes of empty time."

The offer was tempting but so was the conversation. "We were talking about Brad."

"You sure know how to kill a mood." Josh scooted up and joined her at the top of the bed. They touched at their upper arms, but that was it. "The hearing is over."

"It was suspended. The charges would have been dropped if you had fought back. Enough other people showed up to vouch for you." When he frowned, she rested her palm on his thigh. "Told you I read the paper."

"Sure that last bit didn't come from the P.I. you hired to follow me?"

"Maybe."

He glanced down to where her hand lay on the white sheet. "Sure I can't convince you to try another one of those condoms?"

Just as tempting the second time around and even harder to ignore. "Brad needs to be removed from his position. He's a danger."

"No, he's just a desk jockey. His job is to balance budgets and grant leave. When it comes to the field, he's clueless."

"He cost a man his life. Under your theory, a real adult takes responsibility for that no matter how easy it is to hide behind regulations."

Josh covered her hand with his. "Clever woman, throwing my words back at me like that."

"It's a gift."

"You have others. Can we get back to those?"

If she let him, Josh would have her on her back and this

conversation would be a memory. If she didn't sense how important this was, she might have let that happen. "Right now Brad's hiding behind you."

Josh threw his hands up in the air. "Man, you are not going to let this go."

"He put a non-agent in danger and then he tried to shuffle the paperwork or do whatever it is desk men—"

"Jockeys."

"—do. Why not stand up to that, Josh?"

He let out an exaggerated groan. "It's complicated."

"As you've pointed out, I'm smart. Explain it to me."

Josh balanced his head against the headboard. "You win."

About time. "Took you long enough to come around and see things my way."

"It's just that . . ." He stopped, as if he were searching for the right words. "You ever get so tired of fighting and having to prove yourself that you decide it's enough? I busted my ass for that department. I did every assignment that crossed my desk, volunteered for the work no one wanted, and tried to fix Brad's mess by getting him to come clean with the NTSB and DEA about enlisting an innocent man's help and then leaving him without any protection."

"Those are good things," she said, repeating Josh's phrase back to him.

"Yeah you'd think, but the way I was treated proved otherwise." Josh shook his head. "I should have earned some goodwill by now. To be dragged in front of that damned board . . ."

"So, this is about your sensitive ego?"

The blank expression returned. "That's not how I see it, but I guess you could look at it that way."

She was missing something. Josh's self-esteem seemed as healthy as the next alpha male's, but being ticked off about something so stupid and to let that end his career? She didn't comprehend that reasoning at all.

"I think you feel guilty," she said.

"You been talking to my shrink?"

The news stunned her. "You see a therapist?"

"I did while I was at DEA. Had to since I shot someone. It's a requirement to get the gun back. When I quit the agency, I dumped the therapist."

Josh was damned good at leaving. He was a man who walked away. As far as she could tell, only Kane, Annie, and Derek ranked as worthy of keeping around. That realization sent a ball of frustration bouncing around in her hollow stomach.

"You left the DEA, Brad, the job, the therapist, the pension. Dump anything else recently?"

"A carton of milk?"

Deana pulled the sheets up higher on her throat. "I'm trying to make a point."

"So am I."

"Which is?"

"That I'm ready to try another condom." He fished one out of the rumpled sheets and held it up in front of her.

"We're having a rational adult discussion."

"We can do that lying down with me inside you." He leaned over and pushed her back until she slid down into the mattress. All those moves and he never even touched her.

"You're impossible."

"And you're very tempting."

He touched her then. Kissed her throat as he tugged the sheet away.

She figured she'd made her point or as much as she could right now. Besides, his mouth felt so good against her skin. "Maybe a little less talking wouldn't be so bad."

"Always said you were a smart woman."

Chapter Twenty-two

"All roads lead to Ryan." Kane made the statement as he looked over the whiteboard Josh had set up in the small living room of the guest cottage. There were photos and writing and lines connecting everything together.

Josh understood it all. It was morning and all the coffee in the world couldn't make the evidence come out another way.

He sat on the chair and watched the rain pound on the grass outside the window as he tried to figure out what he'd missed. The need to find a missing piece took on more importance after his wild night with Deana. They agreed to separate out the personal from the investigation. That proved to be damned impossible.

Even now he sat here going over the evidence and all he could think about was how Deana looked when he surprised her in the shower this morning and the pleasures they unleashed on each other as the water ran cold.

"You make an even more convincing case than the prosecution did." Kane pointed to the list of red flags Josh had written on the board.

"Between calls and visits I've talked with Ryan three times now. Each time I believe less of his story," Josh said.

"Eric always maintained that the kid's demeanor kept the spotlight on him."

"Ryan doesn't show an ounce of remorse. Except for some well-placed acting it's like he doesn't give a shit his parents are gone, let alone the disgusting way they died." Josh thought back to his last meeting with Ryan and felt his stomach clench in fury. "The kid's emotions seesaw back and forth, but there's never a time when the sadness seems genuine. He doesn't talk about them. Doesn't cry. Doesn't do anything but tell everyone how he got screwed by his aunt's ex-boyfriend."

"A true narcissist."

Josh balanced his ankle on his opposite knee. He tapped his pen against the rubber sole. "That's how most people describe him. Hell, I talked with police officers who were there that night, teachers and administrators from school, parents of Ryan's classmates. No one ever said they thought Ryan was innocent. Not one."

"We both know the usual perpetrator in cases like this is a family member. You can't make the evidence say anything different if it's not true."

The thumping in Josh's head grew louder. "What the hell makes a kid choose this option? He had a family who loved him and all of the potential and opportunities in the world."

Kane frowned. "You don't know what was happening in the household."

The pen slipped, making a long blue pen mark on the white bottom of Josh's sneaker. "You're blaming Chace and Kalanie for this?"

"No."

"Sure as hell sounds like it."

"Ease up." Kane sat down on the coffee table in front of Josh with his elbows resting on his knees. "Think maybe you're too close to this one?"

"This isn't about Deana."

"I'm thinking it has something to do with the fact you're sleeping with her."

Josh threw the pen on the small table next to his chair. "What, was it on the news or something?"

"I've known you a long time."

"That just reminds me how old you are."

"Young enough to beat the shit out of you if needed." As if to prove his point, Kane sat up and flexed. "I'm ready when you are."

"Let me grab some breakfast first."

Kane blew out a long breath. "Look, I can see you're frustrated and on edge."

"I think I've been a pretty good host this morning."

"There's enough adrenaline pumping through you that you could lift this house."

Josh knew where Kane was going and refused to make it easy to get there. "And you equate that with me having sex?"

"It's how you act when people you care about are in trouble. I saw it when I first met Annie and you were unsure of her. I've seen the two times someone has pointed a gun at my head and you were standing right there."

"Don't go thinking I give a shit about you."

Kane smiled. "The feeling's mutual."

Josh didn't say anything because he didn't have to. He understood Kane and vice versa. If one of them ran into trouble the other would come running. That was the unspoken deal and it now extended to Annie and Derek.

"What does the evidence say?" Kane stood up and went back to the board.

"That Ryan did it. That he must have gotten his friend Frankie to help, but the kid balked at the last minute."

"The idea of a multiple murder scene will do that to some people."

Frankie was there that night. Josh would bet his entire bank account that Frankie removed Ryan's bloody clothes and the murder weapon. "I'm going to get Frankie to confess to his involvement."

"Jesus, how stupid is that kid?"

"What do you mean?"

"The case is over and no one is looking at him. If he keeps his mouth shut, he gets to walk. If he talks, Eric will bring him up on charges."

Yeah, that was the big problem. Josh thought he had an answer, but making it work would take a team with some unwilling members. "I have a plan."

"Is it legal?"

"Mostly."

Kane took his badge out of his pocket and dropped it on the table. "Tell me."

"I have to convince Eric to help me."

"Eric, as in Deana's ex?"

"Despite what she thinks, Eric is one of the good guys."

Kane nodded. "I don't disagree, but he's also got political aspirations. Letting a kid get away with murder is not on Eric's 'things to do to get into office' list."

But Josh had one factor in his favor. "Eric still loves Deana."

Kane's frown deepened. "And you're going to use that against him."

"Wouldn't you?"

"Depends on whether or not you want to give Deana a reason to hate Eric instead of you."

The blow landed right in Josh's gut. "Low blow."

"But an honest one. You're setting Eric up to be the bad guy in this scenario."

Josh refused to weigh the morality of his plan. "Eric already plays that role in Deana's eyes."

The skin pulled taut across Kane's cheeks. Josh knew the look. It was a mix of disappointment and fury. Josh had seen Kane direct it at other people. Being on the receiving end sucked.

"You're talking about making Eric take your fall for giving the bad news so you don't have to," Kane said, his voice shaking with anger.

Leave it to Kane to drill down to the base of the plan. Josh wanted closure for Deana. He also wanted to come out of the situation without having her hate him. It was selfish and sick and he couldn't stop building on the idea. "Yes."

"Damn it, Josh. You're better than this."

"I can't walk away from the investigation and I have no idea what to do about Deana."

Kane shook his head. "At least be honest about what's happening here. You don't want to let Deana go and you're afraid your findings will push her away."

Josh had to get the conversation back to the case. Talking about Deana didn't get them any closer to an answer. Didn't wipe that shocked look off Kane's face, either.

"The prosecutor's office put the evidence against Ryan together in a tight ball. I took it apart, separated it all out, and tried to make it work another way. It doesn't." Josh had stayed up thinking it through while Deana slept. Still nothing came to him. "Ryan had the motive, means, opportunity, and will."

Kane hesitated for a second before dropping into the chair across from Josh. "Ryan's a little shit."

Relief poured through Josh at the change of topic. Fighting with Kane was never a good idea. "A murdering little shit. The alarm code, the claims of sleeping through the attacks, spending the money after, and wanting it so much in the first place. And that doesn't even count the fact that the only DNA and fibers found at the scene belonged to Ryan."

"That could be explained by the fact he lived there. Found the bodies."

"Yeah, I had hoped to find that the police focused only on that and excluded some other piece of evidence. Combined with the fact Ryan didn't have any blood on him and there weren't any bloody clothes found anywhere in or around the house, there seemed to be some daylight on the idea of the killer being someone else."

"Because the killer had to be drenched."

Josh's mind flashed to the crime-scene photos. He'd seen some awful things during his career, but the brutality reflected in those pictures screamed with hatred. He couldn't imagine Deana seeing it and being able to function again. But she did. She had somehow identified the bodies and buried her family, including her father, and then went on with her life. That kind of strength humbled Josh. If that sort of violence had happened to someone he loved, forget about eating or doing anything else. He would have turned the world upside down seeking vengeance.

"The blood is where Frankie comes in. He knows what happened or he helped Ryan," Josh said.

Kane looked up from the file in his hands. "Any chance Deana is right and Chace's partner did it?"

"He had motive, sure. But from looking at his dealings it's clear the guy was spending all of his time covering his tracks on the fraud issue. He had a solid alibi for the night of the murder and there's no money trail leading to him paying someone else to do it."

Kane read from the paperwork. "The officers who questioned Olive the night of the murder say he appeared stunned by the news. Could be an act. After all, why run?"

"Probably because he knew the finger would point at him."

Kane closed the folder and dropped it on the coffee table. "Hmmm."

"What?"

"Nothing." The way Kane crossed his arms over his chest telegraphed something.

"Just say it."

"Forgetting about Eric for a second—and I haven't, so don't think that conversation is over—how is Deana going to handle your conclusions?" Kane asked.

That was the question that haunted him. Even after all the sex, when his body had relaxed and she drifted off to sleep beside him, his mind raced in search of a solution to a seemingly unsolvable problem. "She knew this finding was a possibility from the start."

"That was before she started sleeping with you."

Josh closed his eyes and groaned. "How the hell did this get so complicated?"

"Women do that."

Josh didn't see Kane, but the laughter was hard to miss in his voice. "Never used to."

"I have faith you'll figure it out."

Chapter Twenty-three

Deana knew she shouldn't be in the guesthouse without Josh. She had promised him privacy, but something pulled her here today. After visiting Ryan she wanted to be in a place that filled her with something other than sadness. Right now anywhere that reminded her of Josh erased the pain.

The rooms carried Josh's masculine smell. The citrus scents of shampoo and aftershave brought to mind his hands and how well they moved over her. They had spent the past two nights in her bed, keeping the work as distinct as possible from the case. And what amazing nights those had been. The bed, the shower, the pool. They had been all over each other.

For hours at a time she had forgotten about her life and the murders and every horrible thing that had happened over the past two years. She had never enjoyed that sort of mental freedom before with Eric or anyone else. But with Josh all of the badness fell away. Without words he forgave her for how she treated him in the past and convinced her the guilt over the accident no longer needed to occupy her every thought. She needed to remember. She didn't need to wallow.

Special gifts from a special man.

She walked over to the huge whiteboard in the middle of the living room. The thing was hard to miss. She had no idea where a person could even get something like this. Knowing Josh, he charmed it out of an unsuspecting school principal nearby.

She smiled at the thought. Then her gaze wandered to the images tacked across the top. Violence assaulted her from every angle. Crime-scene photos that distorted her brother so much she couldn't tell if the mass lying there was a human or an animal. A picture of Ryan. Pages from transcripts. She looked away before the stark loss overcame her.

And then she saw Josh. Standing at the door, keys in his hand.

"Hi," she said in a shaky voice. When Josh didn't move or speak, she tried to fill the void. "How long have you been there?"

"Long enough to see you snooping around." The judgment was there on his face, in the starkness of his eyes. He put the worst spin on her actions. She wanted to know why. What had happened to the unselfish lover from last night? "That's not what I was doing."

He threw the keys on the table next to the door. "Care to tell me what you're looking for?"

"You."

His frown didn't move. "On the whiteboard?"

"Oh, well, that." She glanced at it and then looked back at Josh's grim face. "I saw it and—"

"We had a deal."

"What?"

"You agreed not to come in here." His words were short and choppy. It didn't take a genius to see he was pissed off.

"Why are you so angry?"

"I don't know, Deana. Maybe it's because you're sneaking around in here."

"Sneaking?"

"Or maybe it's because I just got back from visiting Ryan and found out you saw him right before me."

His reaction was so disproportionate to her offense. None of his comments made sense. "So?"

"Why were you there?"

Josh clearly wanted a fight. Fine, she'd give him one. She hadn't done anything to deserve his wrath. Even if she had, no one talked to her that way. Not while they stood on her property and accepted her paychecks.

"I don't like your tone." That was a complete understatement, but she was trying to hold her anger in check.

"Is that an answer?"

She breathed in nice and deep and grabbed for a few more minutes of calm. But why she was bothering to do that she wasn't sure. "Look, I don't know what's wrong with you."

"You don't?"

"Did I do something to tick you off other than walk into my guesthouse and visit my nephew? Those seem like pretty petty offenses to me."

"And here I thought after sleeping together we'd be more in sync." Josh's shrug matched his flippant attitude. "Guess not."

His words cut through her. All the excitement at seeing him drained from her body, leaving behind only a rumbling emptiness and a load of rage that had nowhere to go but in his direction.

"Until you get your ass back under control, I'll be at my

house." Deana stepped in front of him and reached for the doorknob.

"That's where you should have been instead of being in here."

He thought he could run her off with a few nasty words. Maybe that worked for scared teens in prison, but not with grown-up women. No way.

She turned back to him. "You want to know the truth?"

"Are you capable of telling it to me?"

Every syllable struck at her and threatened to knock her off her game. He did this. He made her vulnerable to his shots. And she let him.

"I visit Ryan every damn week. Have since he's been in that hellhole. You see, someone in the family has to go, and my mother won't. Couldn't figure out why for the longest time, but I think I finally have. She's terrified Ryan might say something that will convince her he killed his parents. She never admits that, of course, but I know."

The anger drained out of Josh's face. "Deana—"

Too late. She pulled away from him when he tried to touch her arm.

"You wanted to know why, well here it is. I go because there is no one else to go. Everyone else is dead." Fury raced through her veins, giving her the energy she needed to get through this fight. "I came here because after all that dragging despair I wanted to feel alive. Happy. I stupidly thought seeing you would do that. Trust me, I won't make that mistake again."

Deana brushed past Josh and opened the door.

"Wait," he said.

"No thanks."

He pressed his hand against the door next to her head and held it shut. "Please, Deana."

"I'm leaving."

He buried his nose in her hair. "I was being an ass."

"True. Now let go."

"The day sucked and then I saw you here and jumped to conclusions. I was out of line."

"Step back so I can open the door." The words were tough, but the heat behind them had faded.

She wanted to run before he saw just how vulnerable she was to him. But standing there wrapped in his arms with his cheek next to hers wore her down.

"I'm sorry." He whispered the words against her ear.

"For being an ass?"

"For acting like one."

He turned her around. She tried to look everywhere but in his eyes, but he wasn't having it. He lifted her face, cupping both cheeks with his hands.

"I wasn't snooping," she said.

"I get that."

Then he was kissing her, deep and long. The kind of kiss that turned a woman's knees to liquid and her common sense to mush. It went on, his mouth slanting over hers.

Deana tried to catch her breath and get her bearings. She wanted to hold him away from her emotionally. She didn't need another unloading like the one he just treated her to.

When he lifted his head again, she only held a thin line on her resistance to him. "Are you done acting like an ass?"

"For now."

"Well, at least you're honest."

"I just don't want you in here. I wasn't kidding about that part."

Well, that said it all. She needed to leave. "Fine."

Josh stopped her before she could pull away again. "Hold up. What I mean is that this room is filled with death. There are photos in here you should never have to see. Hell, I didn't know your brother and sister-in-law and I don't want to see them."

Even though a part of her thought there was more to his anger than protecting her, his words made sense. But his rescue instincts weren't necessary this time. "I lived it, Josh. I was at the house that night."

"And you shouldn't have to go over it all again in vivid color. Your mind deserves to heal."

She dropped her head on his shoulder. "It never goes away."

"But it can fade." He brushed a hand through her hair. "Give it a chance to slip into the back of your mind."

"There's an awful lot I need to store there in the dark. The accident, the murders . . ."

"Let me give you something to fill the rest of your mind. A good memory this time."

"Like?"

"You, me, naked . . . any of this sound familiar?"

"Oh, that. I'm not sure good is the right word."

"How about a round of mind-blowing sex?" Before the words left his mouth he treated her to a long, hot kiss.

The man excelled at kissing. Curl-your-toes, hide-your-daughters kissing. The kind where the short breaths lingered long after his lips left hers.

"You're not proposing sex after that display of masculine ridiculousness, are you?" she asked.

He had the grace to blush. "Yeah, I kind of was."

"I thought you didn't want me in here."

"There's nothing in the bedroom but some clothes and furniture. That seems like a safe place to forget about everything but each other."

Sounded like an excellent plan to her. Much like the one

she had when she unlocked the door and let herself in. "But the condoms are back at my house."

His eyebrow lifted. "You think you're the only one who invested in a box right after you tracked me down?"

"Why, Mr. Windsor, I had no idea you felt that way."

"Bullshit."

"Very charming."

"I'll show you charming." He swung her up into his arms.

The move came so suddenly and without warning that she almost lost her balance and sent them both crashing into the wall. Somehow he maintained his footing.

Then he stood there.

"Now what?" she asked.

"I'm not totally sure. Never done this before."

"That's disappointing." It actually was more like the exact opposite of disappointing.

A grin broke across his lips. "I'll consider that a challenge."

Chapter Twenty-four

Half an hour later they had stripped down, thrown the pillows all over the floor, and opened that condom packet. Deana vowed to fight with him more often if that's what it took to get him whipped into a sexual frenzy.

She gripped the headboard behind Josh's bare shoulders and straddled his lap. "You ready for me?"

Josh waved the condom in front of her face. "If you don't ride me soon, I'll . . ."

"Yes?" She kissed the stubble on his chin.

"Explode."

"Well, we can't have that." With her lips kissing along his jawline, she reached down between her thighs and rubbed her thumb over the tip of his erection.

Josh's fingers dug into her hips in response. "Damn."

"It's tempting to torture you for a few more minutes." She eased her hand up and down his length.

"Hmmm."

Faster this time. "How am I doing?"

"Killing me."

"That's my evil plan." She squeezed her palm tighter.

"I'm a dead man." When his head fell forward and a mumbling moan rattled in his throat, Deana figured she almost had him where she wanted him.

It had been this way from the beginning. The man gave as much as he took. His hands and that tongue could inflict a huge amount of pleasure. But now it was her turn.

"I'm not going to last much longer," he said, his voice rough around the edges.

"Good."

She brought him to this moment. When they entered the bedroom earlier she had slid onto the bed and gone to work on his zipper. After a few minutes of wrestling with his pants, the two hit the floor and his hands slipped into her hair.

It had not taken very long to bring him to the edge. Taking his erection deep into her mouth almost did it. The sucking and licking only made him burn hotter. He was full and panting and begging her to change places with him in no time.

Deana had ignored all of it and continued to pump him with her hands and mouth, taking control of the lovemaking. But now was the time for fulfillment. With the condom on and his fingers pressing inside her and her breasts rubbing against his broad chest, the woman was ready.

The fighting and arguments dissolved into a whirlpool of need. This. Them. It was more than a matter of heat and bodies. This was about a need she didn't even know she had until he walked into her life and turned it upside down. With him she could enjoy and know she would be safe in his hands.

Every cell in her body begged her to go faster. Desire clawed at her stomach as she slowly slid her body down on top of him. With him lodged inside her, she began to move. She shifted her legs to adjust to his fullness before lifting up and plunging down again. The bed creaked in time with the rhythm of their bodies as she rode him. She was slick and primed for an orgasm.

From the way Josh's hands held her hips, helping her move up and down, he was ready, too. The faster she went, the harder his breaths puffed against her naked chest. When a dark growl escaped his mouth she knew he couldn't hold back much longer. She lifted her body one last time, tightening everything inside her and clamping down on him until he yelled her name.

As his body jumped, he wrapped his arms around her waist and pulled her tight against him. With his back arched, he pushed even farther into her. As his lower body started to buck, every muscle in her body stiffened. A spring wound through her to the point of snapping. Then it popped.

Her body let go as the orgasm ripped through her. She barely heard her own scream over Josh's shout of satisfaction. After the last ripple moved through her, she collapsed into him. His chest was hot and slick. The thumping under her ear moved faster than her heart.

"Did I thank you for stopping by today?" His joke came out between staccato breaths.

She wanted to punch him in the stomach for revenge but lacked the strength to lift her fist. She settled for nibbling on his nipple.

He jumped in response. "Much more of that and I may pass out."

The feeling was mutual. "I don't want that."

He kissed her forehead before staring into her eyes. "What do you want?"

"You."

*   *   *

That had been a close call. Only now after two bouts of sex did the anxiety at having gone too far stop spiraling through Josh.

He had walked into the guesthouse and seen Deana studying the whiteboard . . . and lost his fucking mind. With the mocking call from Brad still playing in his head he saw only that Deana was exactly where she promised not to be.

Random thoughts about her using him to gain access to information, and old trust issues about her and her money, came rushing to the surface. The call, the look on her face, seeing her name on the visitation log, and having to deal with Ryan's extra-surly attitude. Josh felt it all back up on him until he exploded all over her.

Then he saw that hurt in Deana's eyes. Her spine went stiff and her chin snapped up, but all the toughness in the world couldn't hide how much his harsh words wounded her.

Old habits died hard. That young kid who watched his mother turn tricks and grew up determined not to be used or taken for granted again reared up and demanded attention. The privileged part of Deana's life reminded him of all those promises he made years ago. The main one: never depend on a woman again. Hard to keep that straight while he lived in Deana's house, accepted her money, and slept in her bed.

How in the hell could something so right feel so wrong?

Josh knew he owed Deana some sort of explanation for his behavior. A partial was the best he could do. "I talked with Brad today."

Deana turned and snuggled against his side. "Good lord, why?"

"I filed a request to reopen my hearing."

She shot up, sitting next to him and not even noticing that the sheet had dropped to her waist.

Well, he noticed and took advantage of the moment by rubbing his thumb over her puckered nipple. "Brad got word and called to let me know he planned to destroy me."

She rolled her eyes. "There is just nothing likable about that guy."

"Nothing that I could ever find."

She sat up and crossed her legs in front of her. The new position gave Josh a great view of every part of her from the waist up. Also had the negative of putting her about a foot away from him.

"How did he get to be in charge of you?" she asked.

Josh wondered why he started this conversation rather than just enjoy having Deana in his bed. But he could fix that mistake. He slipped the sheet down until it rested low on her hips. A few more inches and he would be able to see all but her knees.

"Let's talk about something more interesting," he said.

She pinched his upper arm. "Tell me."

"Ouch!" Josh rubbed the injury. "Damn, woman."

"The easiest solution is to answer my questions about Brad and his stupid threats."

"Or never start the conversation in the first place," Josh mumbled.

"Too late." Deana folded her arms under her breasts until her softness plumped above.

"Brad got injured and pulled a desk job."

"How?"

"A drug raid gone bad. Happened years ago. Word is Brad was a good street agent back then. Being a dick helps

in dealing with drug dealers. The bad guys don't exactly like
the suit types."

"If you say he was good at something at one time I'll believe you, but it's hard to imagine."

Josh fell back into the only remaining pillow on the bed
and folded his arms behind his head. "After that he worked
his way through the government chain. DEA owed him
and he paid his dues, so when the Hawaii gig came up he
got it."

"Nothing like rewarding idiocy."

"Welcome to government service."

She unfolded her legs and lay down on top of him. With
her hands on his stomach and her chin on top of her palms,
she smiled. It was the kind of look a woman gave a man
that meant he had the green light.

"So?" She asked the cryptic question and then stopped
talking.

"Yes?"

"What made you decide to challenge Brad?"

She wanted credit. He loved that about her. No guessing
what was in her mind. He could see the emotions play
across her face as clear as could be.

"Well, I got this lecture from a bossy—"

"You!" She pinched his arm again. This time he saw it
coming and moved in time to keep her from getting a good
chunk of skin.

Josh slipped his hand behind her neck. "You're right.
Brad lied and misused government resources. I'm not saying
I wouldn't have done the same thing, but I *would* take re-
sponsibility for having it all go bad."

"And Brad's flailing around trying to save his butt."

Brad was making empty threats and claiming he had

enough information to bring down Josh and Kane. The last part gave Josh more than a minute of hesitation. He was willing to take the risk, but asking Kane to do so was too much. But there was nothing to spill. Brad was the one with dangerous secrets, not him and certainly not Kane.

"He'll fight you to the end, won't he?" she asked.

Josh massaged her neck. "Brad isn't the type to give up his power easily."

"And you're not the type to back down from a fight." She kissed Josh's chest. "Sounds like the perfect combination."

Chapter Twenty-five

"How is the investigation going?" Eric asked the question a few days later as he slumped back into his big leather chair.

"Depends on what you want the outcome to be." Josh dropped his notepad and pen in his lap.

"How about we try the goal of truth and justice."

Josh marveled at how Eric could say shit like that without sounding like a lying dumbass. Most prosecutors guarded their win-loss records with a fervor that bordered on insanity. Eric actually believed keeping innocent people out of jail was more important than a score. It was one of the many reasons Josh respected the man. It was also the main reason Josh wondered if Eric could really handle the political positions he craved.

Being the governor or whatever else Eric had on his career to-do list required a great deal of game playing. Lots of hand shaking. Rounds of parties. Deals with people he wouldn't piss on under normal circumstances. Josh knew Eric couldn't stand that environment. Good men with morals found it hard. It would be interesting to see if clean and re-spected Eric survived the political baptism.

"Your office did a solid job on this case," Josh conceded.

"Good to know."

"The evidence fit and all angles were covered."

"Except Olive."

"I got lucky on that one." Josh chalked that one up to having resources others didn't.

"Maybe. Still, I appreciate you closing that loop and tracking him down."

"Your people turned over everything. No corners were cut. It's as clean a prosecution as I've seen."

Eric nodded. "That was my order on this case. Err on the side of providing too much information but no favors to Deana and her family."

That was the part that killed Eric's relationship with Deana. Josh wondered if he would have made the same call in Eric's position. The case was huge and the crime unimaginable. Eric stepped out of it and watched from afar. That was the smart thing to do. Fair and reasonable. But if it meant losing Deana forever, Josh wasn't sure he could have done the job.

"The trial attorneys also kept me out of it, so I never had to testify to what I knew as the boyfriend." Eric stretched back in his seat. "Not that the compromise did me any good with Deana or my staff."

"She have any idea what you sacrificed for her?"

"No." Eric's gaze was thoughtful and a bit guarded. "So, is there a 'but' somewhere in your summary of my office's conduct? Am I about to go to court on a motion by you to reopen the case?"

"No."

Eric's chest fell and the hardness in his jaw eased. Josh guessed this was what relief looked like.

"That's good news." Eric glanced over at the flashing lights on his phone. "Right?"

"I think you missed something."

"So, not right. I figured as much." Eric's chair fell forward again with a thud. "Is it a piece of evidence?"

"An accomplice."

"What?"

To keep his hands busy, Josh tapped his pen against his notepad. "Frankie."

"You think he did it?" Eric had already begun shaking his head. "I'm telling you we talked to that kid several times. I knew him from previous cases. There's no way that kid put something like this together."

"Agreed."

Eric's mouth opened and then closed again. It was another few minutes before he said anything. "I confess you lost me."

"I think Frankie is the person who hid the murder weapon and Ryan's clothes."

"You *think*?"

"I have some circumstantial evidence. Nothing concrete and nothing that would hold up in court."

"Just what every prosecutor likes to hear."

"Here are copies of my notes." Josh slipped a file out of his stack and slid it across the table to Eric.

Eric didn't bother to open it. Josh took that as a sign of trust.

Eric stared at his fingers for a few seconds. "I knew that Ryan was guilty. I turned that case over so many times looking for holes and couldn't find any that convinced me he was innocent. But I admit there was a part of me that hoped you'd find a different answer."

"You're not alone."

"Maybe we just didn't want to believe a kid could slaughter his parents."

That was part of it. Josh knew family dysfunction. He also knew having a strict father didn't justify murder. "We wanted a different answer for Deana's sake."

"Yes, of course." Eric wiped a hand over his face. "How did she take the news?"

"She doesn't know yet."

Eric let out a low whistle. "I don't blame you for waiting. The fallout won't be pretty. She's very invested in Ryan's innocence. I think it preserves Chase's memory for her somehow."

Josh knew it would be a bloodbath with him slammed against the floor. "I need a favor."

"Sure. Name it."

Josh didn't waste time looking for an easy way to start the conversation. He jumped right in. "Immunity."

Eric's eyes popped. "What the hell are you talking about?"

Josh underlined his plan in his notebook. "I want you to give Frankie immunity so he'll talk. There's no reason for him to say anything without it."

Eric's shook his head. "Why in the hell would I do that? What lawyer would?"

"You don't have any evidence to charge the kid, so you won't be any worse off than you are right now with the immunity."

"You mean when I'm out of a job?" Eric shoved the file to his right. "I can get the evidence. That's how this works. We have a theory and we'll test it to see if we can make it work."

"You haven't been able to hang anything on Frankie so far. That's not going to change."

"Haven't really been trying. I can remedy that right now." Eric reached for the phone.

"We both know you would have pinned it on this kid if you could have. You got nothing."

Eric's hand slipped off the receiver. "Then why are you so certain about this?"

"I just am." Josh could feel the truth down to his feet. He wanted to come up with a different response. Would have given anything to make that happen.

"That's not an answer, Josh."

Josh moved to the edge of his chair. "Then let me give you a reason to go along with this."

"I'm listening."

"Deana."

Eric started shaking his head. "Josh, I can't—"

"She needs this. She deserves to know the truth no matter how terrible that is or how we have to get it for her. She can't move on without it."

"Let me get this straight." Eric put his elbows on the table and folded his hands together. "You want me to let a vicious killer loose so you can get laid?"

"This isn't about my relationship with Deana."

"Josh, come on. I have eyes."

"What does that mean?"

"All anyone has to do is look at you to see this is ripping you apart. You fell for her. Now you're worried she's going to hear the news, get pissed, and dump you."

"That's not it."

"It is. I understand. *Believe me,* I get it."

Josh refused to compare the relationship he shared with Deana to the one she had with Eric. "This is different."

"You're looking to lay the news on someone else's doorstep. Sorry. I played the role of bad guy once where Deana was concerned. I'm not doing it again."

The truth hit Josh with the force of a car. "You're still in love with her."

"I'm trying to make you see reason."

Josh hated being right about this. He wanted to believe both Deana and Eric had moved on. That whatever they had long ago had faded into nothingness. Seeing the stricken look on Eric's face explained it all. The man would take Deana back if she only gave him a chance.

"I notice you didn't deny it," Josh said.

"Whatever I had with Deana is over. Has been since before you entered the picture." Eric's hand tightened. "This isn't about jealousy."

Josh sensed that was exactly the emotion at play. "It's not about my relationship with her, either. We both know I can tell her whatever I want and she'll continue to believe Olive did this or had someone do it."

"And?"

"She deserves better." Josh believed that down to his soul.

"My job is to put the guilty behind bars, not appease the conscience of one resident. If Frankie is a killer, he needs to pay." Eric scoffed. "You saw the crime-scene photos. You really think anyone should get away with that?"

But that wasn't the point and they both knew it. "You. Love. Her."

"That's not good enough."

Josh noticed Eric didn't even bother to deny it that time. "You can't get Frankie. Dig all you want. I tried."

"Maybe you missed something. You are fallible."

"You know I didn't. Hell, I turned over everything and looked at it in new ways because I wanted Frankie to be the killer. And I'm not alone. You do this deal and Frankie talks, you can settle any conspiracy theory that's out there and quiet the few people who claim Ryan is a poor little rich kid who got a raw deal."

Eric tapped his finger against Frankie's file. "None of these are reasons to grant immunity."

Josh fell back on his best argument. On the only one that mattered. "Do it for her."

"What about my pledge to the people of Hawaii?"

Josh heard it in Eric's voice. The higher pitch. Yeah, the other man was wearing down, getting close to giving in. Josh vowed not to let up until Eric did.

"You're not violating anything. The actual killer is behind bars and you can assure everyone of that fact. We're talking about a kid who made some of the evidence disappear." Josh said the words like they didn't mean anything, but deep down he knew the circumstances made both Frankie and Ryan guilty. It didn't matter who swung the bat. They both killed Chace and Kalanie.

"Besides, I have every confidence you can spin this to your favor," Josh said.

Eric's cheeks reddened. "I'm not using Ryan's case to score political points. Never have and never will."

"Jesus, Eric. I know that. But you know what this case does to her every single day. In one night Deana lost her entire family, you, and her faith in the system. Hell, she couldn't move on or put it behind her. You of all people know that."

"She's not as weak as you think she is," Eric said.

"She's not weak at all."

A silence filled the room. Neither of them rushed to say anything. Josh sensed pushing harder at this point would only destroy the progress he had made. Eric had to come to the decision on his own.

"If I do this, I control it." Eric started out slow, his voice low as if he were weighing each word. "Frankie comes in and gives a statement. I record it and I get to use it in Ryan's appeal or in any other way I see fit."

"Agreed."

Eric pinned Josh in a dark-eyed stare. "You know you're providing the final piece that will ensure Ryan never gets out of prison."

The reality of that fact rumbled around in Josh's stomach. "I know."

"Whether I administer the blow or you do, Deana will never forgive you."

The words kicked him in the gut. "I know that, too."

Eric nodded. "Is it true on top of the Ryan situation that you're taking on Brad?"

Josh let out a long exhale. He felt as if he dodged a disaster. Somehow he managed to convince Eric. Now he had to work on Frankie to get him to agree.

"Not one of my brightest ideas, but yes. Brad needs to step up on this."

"I think it's a good idea," Eric said. "You don't follow the rules, but you aren't the man Brad claims you are."

The praise made Josh uncomfortable, but he appreciated Eric's words. "Thanks."

"And if all goes well, you'll get your old job back and can return to Kauai."

The idea hit Josh like a kick to the stomach. For some reason getting back to his regular life no longer sounded like a good thing.

"In the meantime"—Eric grabbed for the phone and started dialing—"I'll do what I need to do to have Frankie brought in."

"I do the questioning," Josh said.

"This is your show. I'll stand behind the glass and watch."

Chapter Twenty-six

Two days later Josh sat across from Ryan in the tiny room at the prison and listened to the kid ramble on about his innocence. Since Josh had Frankie's statement to the contrary in his hand, and it spelled out exactly how much planning went into the murders, it was hard not to reach across the table and shake the shit out of Ryan.

Ryan killed his parents. Even did a test run the week before to check the timing and make sure Frankie could get in and out without being seen. They had the information because Eric had kept his promise. He brought Frankie in, had a lawyer there to assist the kid, and had the court reporter administer the oath. Two hours later Josh knew the truth.

The entire thing turned the coffee in Josh's stomach to acid. Sitting there and letting Ryan go on was harder than Josh expected. The plan was to catch the kid off guard, let him think he had Josh convinced. Then pounce.

"I talked with Frankie yesterday," Josh said, not waiting for a break in Ryan's nonstop chatter.

Ryan's face went blank. "What?"

"It wasn't the first time. I met with him before." As soon

as Josh said the words the air in the room turned heavy. The mood grew darker. Josh could almost see the invisible barrier slam down in front of Ryan's eyes.

The kid was not stupid. He had to know too many conversations with Frankie spelled disaster.

"Why?" Ryan asked, his voice as tense as his shoulders.

"He had a run-in with your dad right before the murders. That made Frankie a prime suspect. Besides, he had a history with you."

Ryan exhaled hard enough to make a sound. "Right."

"And then there's the fact Frankie was there that night," Josh said.

"What?" The kid kept picking at a slice in the table. The nerves were coming out in the fidgeting and flat line of his mouth.

"At the house. Your house. He admitted to all of it under oath, Ryan."

Ryan's hand clenched into a fist. "He's lying."

Josh noticed Ryan didn't even pretend not to understand. "You seem to be getting pretty upset."

"Because Frankie is lying and you're falling for it."

"I didn't even tell you what he told me yet."

"I . . ." Ryan's gaze darted to the side. "Well, I thought you meant he turned on me to save his own ass."

"If someone told me Frankie admitted to being at the house the night of the murders, my first inclination would have been to think Frankie confessed. You jumped to another conclusion."

"Wait, you're saying Frankie confessed?"

"You've been pushing him as the killer."

Ryan knocked his fist against the table. "That's not true. I told you Olive did it."

"You made a big mistake by turning me on to Frankie.

You put him right in my path." A typical misstep of a juvenile offender. Josh knew Ryan picked the most obvious other parties to blame, never thinking that one of those options could backfire. "You had to know Frankie wasn't smart enough to hide the truth forever."

The chair screeched across the floor as Ryan stood up. "Whatever he told you was a lie."

"Sit down."

"Make me."

"You don't want me to get up. You sure as hell don't want me to put a hand on you right now." Josh kept his palms on the table to keep from strangling the little bastard. At this point the need to unload and punish ran deep.

"You think you scare me? I'm in fucking prison." Ryan pointed toward the hallway. "You can't do anything to me that's worse than being in here."

"You're wrong about that. Sit down." Josh figured Ryan must have seen the danger looming in front of him, because he dropped back into his chair.

Ryan threw his hands out to his sides. "Happy?"

"You still haven't asked what Frankie said."

"So tell me." Ryan folded his arms in front of him. "Go ahead."

The angry-kid persona had stepped to the forefront. Ryan replaced his "poor me" whining with the tough-guy act.

Every part of this kid pissed Josh off. He no longer bought anything Ryan said. The benefit of the doubt was gone. Lost it when he took a bat and beat his parents to death. He didn't get to act innocent after that.

"We found the clothes," Josh said.

"What clothes?"

Ryan acted dumb, but he knew. Josh could see it in the way his eyes grew wide.

Not so tough now.

"The bloody clothes. Frankie led us right to them. He had them bagged and hidden. I'm betting you weren't counting on that."

"They're not mine."

Ryan unraveled before Josh's eyes. The kid wasn't asking the right questions. Everything he said, every way he said, told Josh that Ryan knew what was coming before Josh said a word. Ryan knew things only the killer would know.

"You probably told Frankie to burn the clothes. Turns out the drug dealer was a bit smarter than we all thought, because he kept them. Said it was for protection. From you."

"I'm in here."

"Good thing he kept everything, because now we can do some testing."

Ryan was constant motion now. Between the toe-tapping and hand-wringing he could not sit still. "I don't know what you're talking about."

"Sure you do. You were in the courtroom and heard your attorney talk all about DNA and how the prosecution didn't have it." Josh hesitated for emphasis. "That was then. Now, they'll have it."

"Frankie is a liar."

"Clothes and DNA don't lie."

"They aren't mine!" Ryan's shout echoed off the walls.

Josh waved off the guard before he could storm into the room. "We have more. Your drawing. Seems you made a diagram of your house so Frankie would know where to hide and how to get in to retrieve your clothes after the murders."

This time Ryan pounded both fists on the metal table. The thing bounced from the force of his shot. "They belong to Frankie, not me."

Ryan could deny all he wanted, but it was over. Josh expected to feel some sense of relief. Sadness washed over him instead. So much loss because a spoiled brat decided he deserved more than his responsible parents would give him. People dead and a family broken for no good reason. The waste made Josh ache for Deana.

"After we look through the thousands of photos your parents took of you—yeah, the people you hated enough to destroy loved you so much they documented every inch of your life—"

"Stop saying that."

"—and we talk to your grandmother and aunt, we'll be able to show that the clothes are yours. Your DNA will be inside, too. Also helps that you and Frankie aren't even close in body type. You probably have three or four inches on him, so they're not his, either."

"Listen to me." Ryan reached across the table. Even called up that weepy face he used when he pretended he cared about something. "Frankie is setting me up."

A liar to the end. Caught and trapped, Ryan kept throwing out whatever he could think of so he didn't have to own up to everything he'd done.

Josh actually hated the kid. Didn't feel one ounce of pity for him. "Did I mention we have the murder weapon? Bet there's all sorts of DNA evidence on that."

The last of the kid's defenses fell. He scrambled to his feet, gesturing and swearing. "You son of a bitch. You work for me."

Josh remained in his seat. "I work for your aunt."

"You think she's going to let you treat me like this?" Ryan asked, his voice filled with righteous indignation.

"She'll only back a loser for so long."

Ryan's mouth twisted in a feral glare. "The dumb bitch couldn't even hire the right stooge to get me out of here. Unbelievable."

That was the one step too far. Ryan could get as pissed as he wanted at seeing his cover break. He couldn't go after Deana. Josh would not tolerate it. "I told you once before not to speak ill of your aunt."

Ryan threw his hands in the air and he paced the four-foot space next to his chair. "I don't give a shit if you're screwing her."

This time Josh did stand up. "I warned you."

"You gonna hit me or something, old man?"

"Wouldn't waste my time." Josh tucked his pen behind his ear. "I'm going to leave. You see, someone has to tell your grandmother and aunt before the press conference."

"Frankie is talking to the press?"

"The prosecutor is presenting the evidence as the final proof that you should be in here." Josh picked up his file. "Forever."

"You—"

The kid launched his body at Josh. Josh blocked the shot and shoved Ryan into the wall. To keep him there, Josh put his hand around the kid's neck and held him against the wall. Despite the fury flowing through Josh, his brain clicked on and sent a message to his hand not to squeeze too tight. Just enough to hold Ryan steady. Not enough to inflict the kind of damage Josh wanted.

"If you want to take me on, you better start lifting weights while you're in here." Josh pushed back, knocking Ryan's head against the cement, just hard enough to keep him from squirming. "After all, you're going to be in here a long time."

"When I get out of here—"

"That's the point, Ryan. You're never getting out." Josh let go.

Without Josh's steadying hand Ryan slipped down to his knees. He grabbed his neck and wheezed for a few dramatic seconds. "Deana will hate you for this."

"Probably."

"She'll bury this report."

"It's too late for that. The prosecutor is running the DNA tests and the news will be all over the papers." Josh balanced on his haunches so he was eye level with Ryan. "No one is going to believe you now except the whacko women who love men in prison. It's over, kid."

"You're not going to win." Ryan snarled his comeback.

The kid finally got something right. "No one is."

Josh sat in his car outside the prison for a good twenty minutes before he wrestled his rage under control. He'd never wanted to kill a kid before, but when he looked at Ryan he saw only the eyes of a destroyer wrapped in a lanky kid package. Ryan took everything and explained nothing.

And he made Josh question everything he believed to be true. Josh had seen serious dysfunction in wealthy families before. Worked on cases where spouses killed each other because it was cheaper than divorce. Worked on others where well-off kids turned to drugs and crime as a way to escape. Watched people with money do unfathomable things to make sure their bank accounts stayed fat.

In all of those cases he could point to greed or abuse or a terrible home life to fill in the blank as to why the people did what they did. Here nothing made sense. Chace was strict. Kalanie was quiet. From every report, Chace didn't throw his money around. There were no abuse or addiction issues.

Ryan started out a happy kid in a healthy home with parents, grandparents, and an aunt who loved him. They sheltered him from the harsh parts of life and showered him with love. They gave him what he needed but never so much that they would create the kind of evil kid Ryan turned into.

Josh tapped his fingers against the steering wheel and watched other cars pull into the parking lot. Ignored the stares from the passersby. The sunshine seemed misplaced on such a dark day.

He never expected to be this pissed off at finding out he was right. Ryan had everything and blew it. Josh hated the kid for not seeing that.

Josh had experienced the other side of growing up. Never once did he look to a baseball bat to fix his life. Just proved life was so fucking unfair. Some kids had everything and appreciated nothing. Other kids lacked everything and turned out fine.

Then there was Deana. Beautiful, strong-willed Deana. She fought an internal battle against her money. He verbally beat her up at every turn about her checkbook and she took it. But somewhere in the past week his view of her changed. He didn't feel like an employee or a friend. Those descriptions were far too tame for the images that flashed through his mind every time he thought about her. There was no longer a moment when he *didn't* think of her.

And now he would deliver the news that would break her.

He turned the facts over in his head, trying to think of a way not to have the blame fall on him. But that wasn't his style. He wasn't Brad Nohea. Josh stood up and took the consequences. In this case that meant losing Deana. She had dumped Eric when he delivered Ryan news she didn't like.

She deserved a man like Eric. She deserved a family that wasn't crippled by loss. Josh could only give her closure. It wasn't enough to keep her, but it might be enough to save her.

Chapter Twenty-seven

Deana heard the front door open and fought off the urge to rush into the entry and welcome Josh home. She hadn't seen him for almost twenty-four hours. He called twice to say he was following a lead in the case. After that nothing.

Her biggest concern should be with whatever Josh found that kept him so busy and how it might help Ryan. Her motives turned out to be much more selfish. She missed him. After only a short time he had come to play such a big role in her day that not sharing a meal or having a few minutes to talk left her feeling a bit lonely.

The man knew his way around a bedroom and a woman's body. All those stories about him treating his dates well and leaving them satisfied weren't wrong. Deana now understood why she had not been able to get a single woman to tell tales about him. His relationships might have been short, but they were not meaningless.

At least that's how it was for her. The easy response would be to write her relationship with Josh off as a fling. But this went beyond sex. She could lock away her time with him and put it in the back of her mind, then get back to her regular life. That would be the wise thing to do, but she couldn't get excited for that choice.

"Hello." Georgianna called out her greeting as she walked through the house.

Deana peeked around the corner and out into the open foyer. "Mom?"

"Where is he?"

Her mother straightened her silk blouse as she talked.

"Who?"

"Your investigator." The older woman plastered her best Georgianna Armstrong society smile on her face. It was the one she used when she stepped onto a stage to raise money for a cause.

Deana knew the difference between the real one and one for show. "Mom, I honestly don't know what you're talking about."

"Mr. Windsor—"

"Call him Josh."

"Very well, Josh called and told me to meet him here." Her mother sat down on the couch and tucked her legs to the side. "Frankly, I was not pleased at being ordered around."

"He does that sometimes," Deana mumbled.

She talked with her mother, but her mind wandered to somewhere else. Josh called a meeting and forgot to include her. She hated being left out. Worse than that, being taken for granted that no matter what she would be there waiting for him. Deana had grown accustomed to having him around. That didn't mean waiting for him by the door with his slippers.

"If he is going to be a private investigator he needs to

work on his client skills. When one is paying for services one expects a certain level of respect."

Her mother was in rare form. Deana guessed the snide comments and over-the-top attitude had more to do with worries about the subject matter of Josh's meeting than the way Josh called it.

"First, he's not a PI. He's a DEA agent." Deana hoped that last part was still true.

"I thought he got fired."

"Not quite, but it really isn't important. I'm more concerned with why he called you. What exactly did he say?"

"That he had news on Ryan's case." Georgianna's eyebrow raised in the condescending way she had perfected. "I thought you were watching over him? Hasn't he explained all of this to you?"

Watching? Yeah, that was one way to describe what they had been doing. If Deana told her mother, the poor woman would have a heart attack. Despite her outward polished appearance and paid driver, her mother didn't care what people did for a living. No, that wasn't the issue. Georgianna Armstrong would be horrified that her only daughter dared to live in sin with someone. That sort of thing did not sit well with Mom's old-fashioned sensibilities on love and marriage.

Love. Deana hated to use the word, but it fit. The feeling budding inside her could only be identified as one thing. Love. Deana knew it. She'd known it for days. The racing sensation inside her chest. The thrill at seeing Josh walk through the door. The smile that shot straight to her heart every time.

"Deana? Is something wrong?" her mother asked.

Other than the fact she wanted to vomit? Everything and

nothing. Loving a man who flipped through women was damned dangerous. Thrilling but stupid.

"Josh didn't call me." That fact hurt more than Deana wanted to admit.

"That's not a loss. His phone manners are terrible."

"You could be a bit less judgmental about him."

"I doubt that." Her mother looked in the distance to the foyer. "By the way, your investigator-slash-agent is at the door now. I can see him in the side window."

That familiar feeling of happiness zipped through Deana. She had become a blithering idiot where Josh was concerned. She actually sat there waiting for him to come in. How her life got to this she did not know.

The doorbell chimed. Josh hadn't stopped before coming in since that first night he moved into the guesthouse.

When she opened the door he stood there, his muscular frame taking up the entire entry and blocking the sun behind him. A dark tension hovered around him. That smile that made her world spin a little faster was gone. In its place he wore a severe frown like the one he treated her to when she first propositioned him in the courthouse.

"What's wrong?" she asked.

"I need to talk with you and your mother."

Deana gestured toward the family room. "She's here—"

"Good." Josh walked right past and kept moving until he stood by the couch.

No welcoming kiss. Not even a hello.

Dread moved through her. So did a good deal of pissiness. He barged into her house without saying a word. And damn if he didn't have her running after him. She hated that.

Loving this man was not going to be easy.

"Josh, what's going on?" she asked from a few feet behind him.

"I finished the investigation." He stood by the huge glass doors to the outside with a folder in one hand. Gone were the jeans. He wore a suit. Looked professional.

Deana knew what was coming. She had seen a fixed jaw and drawn cheeks on every person who ever delivered devastating news. A feeling of dread washed through her. Whatever Josh held would knock her to her knees. She knew that as sure as she knew her own name.

"Olive was a dead end. Nothing traced him back to the murders."

The older woman snorted. "I don't see how that's possible."

"Mom, let Josh finish."

"Ryan's friend Frankie was a different story." Josh opened the file and took out a handful of papers that he handed to her mother. "He confessed to helping Ryan that night."

"With what?" Deana asked.

Josh's skin pulled even tighter around his eyes. "Disposing of the clothes and baseball bat Ryan used on his parents."

Her mother threw the papers on the coffee table without looking at them. "Frankie is lying."

"Ryan said the same thing, but the tests are clear. Initial test reports place Ryan at the scene holding the bat. The lab is working on the DNA, but there isn't any doubt. Chace's and Kalanie's blood are on the clothes and Ryan's skin cells are inside. The pants and shirt are his."

The entire room tilted as pounding dizziness crashed over Deana. Her mind scrambled as thoughts piled one on top of the other. She didn't realize she had sat down until she felt the couch cushions beneath her.

"What did this Frankie say?" she asked.

Josh swallowed a few times as his gaze searched her face. "That Ryan had been planning the murders for weeks."

Georgianna touched her hand to her forehead. Her fingers shook. The strong, vibrant woman Deana knew collapsed in on her self. Deana knew her mother would have rolled into a ball and cried if Josh weren't standing there delivering the horrific news. They both would have. That's what happened in the hospital as she waited for miracle news on Chace.

"You can hear the details watching Eric's press conference, though I would recommend against it," Josh said.

The news about Ryan had barely registered and now this. Deana didn't understand what one had to do with the other. "Eric?"

Josh shifted his weight from one foot to the other. "He helped me get Frankie's story."

"He never did believe in Ryan's innocence." Her mother gulped in the air as she spoke.

"And he wasn't wrong." Josh stared at the floor. "I'm sorry the news isn't better."

He delivered his report in a flat voice. Stood there in his tie and read off a list of atrocities as if they never shared more than a cup of coffee.

It was all too much. The rumbling in her chest exploded into a fireball of fury. "That's all you have to say?"

"I'm only the messenger."

"That doesn't mean you have to enjoy your job so much." Deana knew the accusation was unfair, but she didn't care. The emotions bubbling inside her needed an escape.

Josh clenched his teeth together. "I am only—"

"Does it bother you at all?" She stepped in front of him and poked her finger in his chest. "Do you feel anything when you look at me and deliver this news?"

"I told you my work could end this way."

He did. He warned her and tried not to get involved. He stepped back and performed the work as promised. But he wasn't the target of her rage. She was.

Deana had started down this road, all but forced Josh to help her. She was so sure the jury got it wrong. Believed with everything inside her that she could fix the mess Ryan made of his life. All she wanted was to give him another chance. She got one, why shouldn't he?

She dropped her hand. "I can't do this."

"I want to see." Her mother grabbed the remote and turned on the television.

Eric's image filled the screen. He didn't look any better than Josh. Both were ragged and tired. Eric's voice even dragged as he spoke.

Shutting out Eric's words, she turned back to Josh. "Does Ryan know?"

"I told him this morning."

Another piece of the puzzle fell into place. "I tried to see him today."

"I blocked your access."

"Why?"

"You needed to hear this from me."

Josh was protecting her. Through it all his first thought was to protect her. She held on to that bit of hope as the world spun out of control around her. "You wanted—"

His face hardened even more. "Ryan would have sold you a sob story and mixed up the facts. It was important you had the report and the real story before he got to you."

Hope fizzled in her chest. This wasn't a rescue. It was a hard life lesson.

"And now that I did my duty, I'll leave." Josh didn't wait. He walked back through the family room and out the door before Deana knew what was happening. He didn't walk. He stalked, almost jogged, to get away from her.

Not this time. She did not intend to spend her life running after him. If he had a problem, he needed to stand and fight. Mr. DEA Agent was so big on the truth then it was about time he learned this one.

Chapter Twenty-eight

"Josh, stop." Deana called after him as his feet hit the driveway.

He heard her. The desperation in her voice almost stopped him, but he kept walking.

"Josh!" Her voice slipped to frantic.

Damn her. As usual her timing was one beat off. He wanted a quick exit, not a long discussion filled with hate-filled lectures about how he ruined Ryan's life.

She was angry and had every right to be, but he couldn't be her target on this. He had vowed to stand there and take it. But seeing her knees buckle, watching the blood drain from her face, battered him like being in a ring with a champion boxer.

They needed time to grieve, or plan, or do whatever it is they would do without him there to watch. He owed them the right to hate him. Someone had to take the blame. He knew he fit that role in this scenario. But Josh would give anything to go back in time and ignore all references to Frankie. Finding him was the key to the investigation.

And to the end of what he shared with Deana.

"I said stop," she said as she grabbed his arm. "Do not ignore me."

Her angry rich-girl voice had popped back into place. The sound tore at him.

"I did what you paid me to do." Not that he intended to keep one dime of the money. This was never about a salary.

"After everything that's happened that's all you have to say to me now?"

"I don't know what you want from me."

"You seemed to know when we were in bed." Deana got up in his face. "Is that the problem here? You can only connect with a woman in a prone position?"

She wanted to hurt him. The words spilled out of her from a place of anguish. He understood, but that didn't mean he could listen to it. He opened his car door.

"I'll get my bags out of the guesthouse tonight," he said.

"You're actually leaving?" She sounded shocked at the idea.

Even though every vein and bone and muscle in his body begged him to stay. "It's time for me to go back to Kauai."

"So, that's it? You drop your bombshell and run?" She shoved her hands against his shoulder.

The loss of control was so unexpected that he didn't move. He stood there and took it. "Don't do this?"

"What, make you give a shit about someone?"

The comment struck too close. "I investigated. I'm done."

"Do I even get a second to process what you said?"

"You made your feelings clear, Deana. Your immediate response was exactly what I expected. You blamed the messenger." The anger came out of nowhere. He viewed leaving now as something he was doing for her, giving her space. But disappointment filled him, too.

He saw the look of distaste on her lips as he recited the facts. She turned all of her anguish and pain on him. Made him the bad guy.

"You walked into my house without warning and told me there's no doubt my nephew killed my brother. You think maybe I could have more than three seconds to come up with a satisfactory reaction for you?"

Josh struggled to get the conversation back to Ryan. He could handle a conversation about blood and murder much easier than one about them. "Deana, this is simple. Your nephew is where he should be."

"You think that's a simple answer?"

Josh took the one step he needed to separate them and get her life back on track. "And you should talk to Eric."

She pulled her head back as her eyebrows snapped together. "About what?"

"He was doing his job. He tried to make all of this run smoothly for you."

"What are you talking about?"

"He's a good man. You should give him another chance."

Her jaw dropped. "You want me to be with Eric?"

Hell no. Josh didn't want her with anyone but him, but that was the wrong answer.

"Eric bent the rules to make sure you could have a final answer about Ryan. He provided Frankie immunity so he would talk." It actually hurt to get the words out. Josh rubbed his chest to ease the ache.

"If he's so amazing, maybe *you* should go out with him," she said.

"He's the right guy and he loves you."

"What about you?" She drilled right to the bottom of the problem. Gave him a way to stay in her life.

He shut the avenue down as fast as she opened it. "I did my job."

"That's all it was?"

The sadness on her face tested him. "Yes."

All emotion left her face. "Then leave the guesthouse key on the table by the door when you go."

Chapter Twenty-nine

The next day, Deana unlocked the guesthouse and walked inside. The scent of Josh's aftershave hit her before she could close her senses to it. She glanced around and recognized the jeans he wore the day before in the pile of dirty clothes in the corner. His paperwork and that horrible whiteboard were still there.

He delivered his news and bolted as if he had wheels on his shoes. Despite the rush, he hadn't moved out yet. The weasel was off somewhere but still in town. Not seeing his car, she knew it was safe to come over.

Safe. That was a laugh. Exhaustion weighed down every part of her. The day ranked up there as one of the worst. She had watched her usually calm mother fold in on herself at hearing Josh's news. Only a few minutes ago Deana had to drag her mother away from the television to spare her from the replay of Eric's business-like recitation of what happened that horrible night. The endless speculation started all over again on the news.

But seeing Josh walk out as if it were so easy to leave her was the last straw. Deana had cried until her eyes burned.

She knew from experience the scratchy throat would go away. The sinking feeling in her chest would take longer.

When she finally came out of her daze she realized the phone had been ringing all day. Annie and Kane called, Eric, family friends, her attorney. Talking was the last thing she wanted right now. She needed facts, which is how she ended up in the guesthouse.

Josh laid it all out in his conclusions, but she thought looking at the whiteboard and seeing how he came to them might help her to understand. Last time she was here she saw the whiteboard and tried to ignore it. Her goals were different then. This time she did more than scan it. She read through the documents, flipped up the papers to see what was written below. She even forced her eyes to the photos.

The blood and horror. Ryan had done this. She hadn't seen the test results, but she knew Josh and Eric would only take such a strong and public stand if they had the evidence to back up their statements. The final DNA testing would be in soon. She wanted to hope for vindication, for a mistake or that Frankie was lying, but she didn't have the strength for that. But the sense that Ryan was paying for someone else's crime had disappeared. She believed the prosecution now.

Ryan killed them, handed the bloody clothes to a friend, and crawled back into bed to wait for morning. The kid she loved, the same one she took to football games and taught to swim, committed an act of unimaginable violence. The realization erased every good memory that came before. The taint stained everything now.

She closed her eyes and let the tears fall. Wetness rolled down her cheeks. She cried for everything lost and for knowing too much. At least with unanswered questions dwelled hope. She had listened to Ryan cry and believed him. Just showed she didn't know anything about the male gender. Ryan and Josh had taught her that difficult lesson.

"This is where he worked, I suppose," her mother said. She walked into the small two-room structure with a tissue clenched in her fist and glanced around.

"Mom, you shouldn't be in here. There are photos—

"You don't need to protect me." She picked up Josh's sweatshirt off the small sectional. "I guess I was wrong."

"About?"

"I thought he was sleeping at your house."

Just when Deana thought her mother wasn't paying attention, she proved she knew exactly what was going on around her. "Mrs. Chow came to live with you so I would have room at the guesthouse for Josh."

"That was the excuse you gave me, yes. But I'm not blind. All of that energy bouncing between you had to go somewhere."

Deana wasn't comfortable talking with her mother about sex. Didn't want to talk about Josh at all. "Let's talk about something else."

"Why? I'm not that old, my dear." Georgianna joined her daughter in front of the whiteboard. "It's even more awful when someone puts it together like this."

"You don't need to look at it."

"I've seen the photos. Made myself look at them at the trial. Seemed to be the least I could do to honor your brother."

Sometimes Deana forgot she wasn't the only one suffering. Her mother mourned in relative silence. She kept up her society appearances and ran her charities, but the sadness in her big brown eyes was tough to miss.

Grief flooded through Deana and knocked her back until it was hard to stand. "I'm sorry, Mom."

Georgianna put her arm around Deana's shoulders. "For what?"

"Everything. For hiring Josh. I don't know." Deana buried her face in her hands as she struggled to maintain her composure. "The idea that Ryan could do that."

"I always knew."

The three little words shifted Deana's world. She lifted her head and stared at the woman who raised her and forgave her for the worst. "What?"

"From the time he was arrested."

"Mom, what are you saying?"

"Oh, I didn't want to believe, of course, but I could sense it. There was something in the way Ryan acted and how he carried himself. At first I made excuses, saying he had an extra burden because he found the bodies. That wasn't it. I know that now."

Deana's mind rebelled against what she was hearing. She had spent so much time wanting and hoping, worrying about her mother falling apart and waiting for her to get out of bed again after her father died. All that time her mother was more in tune with the truth than anyone else.

"You never said that before," Deana said.

"How could I? To admit Ryan killed Chace was to admit Ryan was some sort of animal. That somehow this family bred a child so filled with hate that no love could reach him."

Deana reached up to her shoulder and squeezed her mother's hand. "This isn't your fault."

"It's not yours, either."

Her mother was only half right. Deana knew she had opened the door and invited the deathblow. "Josh's part in it is. I found him. I convinced him. I paid him. I ended up providing the final evidence against Ryan."

"It would have happened sooner or later."

"But the news would have come from somewhere else."

"Ah, I see." Her mother showed a sad smile.

"Care to share?" Deana asked.

"Do you know why I fell in love with your father?" Georgianna rubbed her daughter's back as she spoke.

Deana tried to keep up with the careening topics but couldn't. "What?"

"Do you?"

Remembering her father made Deana both happy and sad. They lost him too early. "He used to say it was because you were afraid of bald men and he had a full head of hair."

"I married him because he made me laugh."

The longing in her mother's voice made Deana even more sad. "Mom."

"He didn't have money, certainly couldn't dance. Oh, I dated a lovely man before your father. He was so beautiful and refined. His family owned a chain of exclusive boutique hotels. You know the type. He owned his own tux and drove a fancy car. His shoes were always shiny and he never dressed out of fashion."

Deana thought of her father's disheveled look and smiled. "Sounds the complete opposite of Dad."

"Your father didn't know a shrimp fork from a plastic one. But he loved me, good parts and bad, and when he smiled at me the world made sense. I decided I could go a lifetime without dancing if I could have that smile every day."

The love was right there on the surface. Deana could hear it in her mother's voice. She thought back to her parents' life together. She hadn't appreciated them or their tight bond when she was younger, but the adult version recognized the relationship for how special it was. They held hands and kept a weekly date night. They didn't get everything right, but they taught their kids about marriage through example.

Chace saw what their parents had and tried to replicate it. He married the woman he loved. Kalanie worked in a bank when she met Chace. She didn't have anything, but they had each other.

Deana rested her head on her mother's shoulder and let the tears fall. "I miss them all so much."

"Me, too. Desperately."

The women stood there in silence, comforting each other, lost in their memories, until Georgianna spoke. "I bet Eric can dance."

The comment was so out of context, Deana had to shake her head to make sure she heard it right. "What?"

"Eric strikes me as a man who would always know what fork to use at a fancy dinner."

Deana had no idea what that meant. "I guess."

"Now that Josh Windsor. Hmpf." Her mother almost snarled when she said his name. "I doubt he could take a few steps around the dance floor before he fell over his big feet."

Deana didn't want to think about Josh. "I have no idea."

"But he does have a nice smile."

Now Deana saw where this was going. Her mother circled back around but Deana slammed on the brakes. "Since when do you like Josh?"

"I like a man who knows how to smile."

"He's not the one." For a few minutes Deana had toyed with the idea. She had been dumb enough to fall for him. Spent a few more minutes hoping he returned her feelings. He convinced her that wasn't the case when he walked out of her house and got in his car.

"Are you looking for a dancer?" her mother asked.

"No."

"The world is full of dancers."

"I don't think that's true."

"Sure it is. The men who can waltz in and sweep you off of your feet. They move in and out of your life with ease. A man who makes you laugh, who possesses a smile that warms you from the inside out, now that's rare."

Deana didn't doubt that piece of advice. It was her mother's end goal that confused the hell out of her. "I can't believe you're trying your hand at matchmaking. Not now, not after everything that happened today."

"I'm your mother and want to see you happy." She brushed the hair off Deana's shoulder. "Some days I wish I would just see you smile."

"It's been hard."

"But it's time for you to concentrate on you."

"With Josh?"

"I didn't say that. I'm just talking about men who can dance."

Deana laughed. "No, you're not."

Her mother smiled. "No, I guess I'm not."

Chapter Thirty

Deana glanced around Brad's small office and wondered why the hell she had come to see a guy she viewed as a buffoon. Other than the fact he called and asked for a meeting, there was no good reason to be there.

He mentioned something about having a mutual interest. Since the press kept stomping all over her driveway and the phone kept ringing, she decided a side trip to Kauai might not be a bad idea. Hiding for a few days was better than moping around the house.

"Here you go." Brad put a cup of coffee in front of her.

She fingered the DEA stamp across the mug. "Thank you."

"I'm sorry about your nephew." He slipped into the chair across from her. "Many of us hoped the prosecution got it wrong."

A door slammed shut in her mind. "I'm not here to talk about Ryan."

Brad nodded. "Of course."

"I'm actually not sure why I'm here. You were pretty cryptic on the phone."

"We have something in common."

She found that hard to believe. "What would that be?"

"Josh Windsor."

The last person she wanted to think about. The same man that lived in her head and refused to get out. It was all that talk about dancing and smiling. Her mother planted this seed. She saw something in Josh. She mentioned him three times at breakfast that morning.

But her mother didn't know what it was like to love the man. Deana did. He pushed her away. Even tried to get her to go back to Eric. The memory of that one sent a crack of pain through her temples.

Josh was good and decent but behaved like a complete ass half the time. The rescuing tendencies added to his appeal. They also promised he would do what he thought was right even when it was most definitely wrong. Included in that was the way he followed through on his threat to leave Oahu.

He was back in Kauai. That's where she was at the moment. She tried to tell herself there was no correlation between those two facts. She didn't come here for Josh. But she glanced across the table and knew she certainly hadn't traveled here to see Brad.

"I hear Josh is contesting his suspension," she said.

Brad's lips pursed together in a frown. "He was fired."

Brad seemed determined to stick to that story even if the facts said something else. She had some experience with that mentality and knew it wasn't healthy. "That's not what the newspaper said."

"They got it wrong."

Yeah, sure they did. "I see. So, tell me what you have in mind for me."

"I know you must feel betrayed by Josh."

She did but not for the reason Brad thought. "And?"

"I am giving you a chance to, let's say, feel better about your situation."

"You mean to get revenge."

Just as she suspected. The little rat actually thought she would turn on Josh. Deana couldn't figure out if the man was desperate or mentally ill. Maybe that's what happened when a man wore a tie pulled that tight. Any minute his head might pop off and slam into the ceiling.

"He used you," Brad explained in slow words as if she were a fragile child. "I tried to warn you, but you were reluctant to listen, which was understandable."

"Gee, thanks."

Brad folded his hands on top of the files stacked in front of him. "I'm saying I know what it's like to deal with Windsor. He has a way of making you feel as if he's listening and that he'll do the right thing by you."

As far as she could tell, that was the only honest thing Brad had said. "Technically, Josh did what I paid him to do."

"We both know you had a specific goal in mind when you took on Josh. He made promises he could not possibly keep but failed to warn you of that fact. He knew that when he took your money."

She regretted agreeing to this idiotic meeting. "What is it you think I can do?"

"Josh has a vendetta against me. I forced him out of DEA. Now, I gave him every opportunity to adjust his behavior first, but he wasn't interested. He is not a man who can follow rules."

"I'm trying to imagine someone adjusting any part of Josh."

Brad sipped on his coffee, making an annoying sucking sound that ripped through her skull. She was going to need a bottle of aspirin before the return flight home.

"Now that Josh is looking at a long road of unemployment, he's decided he wants back in at DEA. The only way for him to do that is to target me," Brad said.

"And you're looking for?"

"A witness. Some help with legal strategy."

Good lord, the idiot wanted money. "The administrative hearing is an internal process and unrelated to me."

"It doesn't have to be."

She wanted to roll her eyes but refrained. "Interesting."

"What's interesting is that Brad here thinks this meeting is an appropriate use of government funds." The door opened and Kane stood right there with Josh directly behind him.

The dark and light of their looks intrigued her. The laser-like stare from Josh's blue eyes filled her with a different sensation. She kept telling herself she was immune to him, that she could see him and tamp down on her feelings so that all he saw was indifference. But she hadn't counted on him looking so bad.

The scruff on his chin was darker and fuller than usual. Lines now marked his forehead. She had no idea what that meant, but she knew the loving joker who played in the bedroom and made her fruit smoothies for breakfast was not the same shell of a man standing in front of her.

She knew from the news he had been working nonstop. Eric had made him testify under oath. During all of the turmoil he had moved back into his condo and started going after Brad in earnest.

"I am meeting with Ms. Armstrong." Brad's smile stretched from cheek to cheek.

"Why?" Josh asked Brad the question but stared at Deana.

"He wants me to testify against you."

"Stupid little fucker." Kane's assessment rang through the room.

Brad gestured to the door behind the other men. "If you two will wait in the hall—"

Deana had experienced enough nonsense for one day. Whatever game Brad was playing, he could do it alone.

She stood up and took her bag with her. "There's no need. We're done here."

Brad's smile faltered. "You and I have more to discuss."

Josh stepped into the room. "About what?"

"You, actually," she said.

Josh's mouth thinned. "If you hate me, fine. But don't do this, Deana."

Is that what he thought? Could he really not see her feelings right there in front of him? "Brad called the meeting. Not me."

"This is not the time," Brad said.

"You, shut up." Kane stopped pointing at Brad long enough to stare at Deana. "Why are you here?"

"I wanted to see what he had to say."

Josh went off again. "Give me a break, Deana. The guy hates me. You're furious with me. You knew what he was offering before you got on that plane."

"Ms. Armstrong has a serious complaint about you," Brad said.

She was not about to let Brad Nohea, jackass extraordinaire, talk for her. "You have a complaint. I have a plane to catch."

Kane glanced around the room. "Maybe we should take this outside. Let Brad, here, get back to work."

"Ms. Armstrong and I are not finished."

"Yes, we are." She aimed her best glare at Brad. "You are on your own. I have no intention of getting involved in your case against Josh."

"Sounds like you're done here," Kane said.

Brad cleared his throat. "We'll talk about this another time."

"I wouldn't count on that if I were you." She walked to the door.

Kane shifted out of her way but not before giving an almost imperceptible wink. Josh proved more immovable. With his palms resting against both sides of the doorway, he blocked her way.

She looked up at him, refusing to back down again. "Excuse me."

"You're not working with him." It was a statement not a question.

"Correct."

"How long are you on Kauai?"

She glanced at her watch more for something to do than to check the time. "Only a few hours. It's time for me to get back home and back to my life."

Josh held his guard position for a few more seconds, then moved to the side. "Have a safe flight."

Here she hoped he'd want to stop her. Maybe want to see her. They never had a chance to say good-bye or end it smoothly. They jumped from full speed to full stop.

She walked down the hall to the elevator, forcing her legs to take each step. Walking away from him was even harder this time.

Her eyesight blurred as she punched the button. When she felt a presence behind her she sucked back the tears and turned around. Kane stood there wearing a smile that seemed way out of line for the situation.

"I thought you had a meeting," she said.

"It was a setup. That's why I came along. The idea that Brad suddenly wanted to have a rational discussion with Josh and called him in didn't ring true."

"You're a bodyguard."

"I knew Brad had some surprise in mind and I had to make sure Josh didn't kill the guy. The paperwork would have been terrible."

"So, this was all about timing," she said.

"I'm guessing Brad wanted Josh to see you here. Thought it would torture the poor lonely bastard."

With Annie at home or wherever she was it looked as if Kane had taken up the matchmaking role. It was cute but not going to be effective.

"You can rest easy. I have no intention of testifying against Josh," Deana said.

When the elevator door opened, Kane put his arm out in front of her to block her way. "Why?"

She thought about telling Kane to move but could tell from strained look on his face that it would be futile to try. "His DEA job is not my battle."

"That's not really an answer."

It was taking all of her energy to stand there when everything inside of her screamed "go back in and shake some sense into Josh." "It's the only one you're going to get."

"Have you forgiven him?" Kane asked. "Does he matter to you at all?"

If she wanted to get on the elevator she would have to go through Kane. She glanced at his broad shoulders and stiff stance and decided that wasn't going to work. Kane wanted to talk. He was the wrong man, but she'd take anything at this point.

"Why would he need my forgiveness?" she asked.

"For telling you the truth."

The door rolled shut again with her on the outside. After the thud, silence filled the hall.

She tried to find the right words. When those didn't come, she went with the feelings kicking around inside of her. "I blame him for not sticking around to talk about it."

"He's not a great communicator. Not one of his strengths, but he has others."

"He's a stubborn ass with an anti-money issue."

"That, too."

"Where is he now?" The question slipped out before she could stop it.

Kane shrugged. "With Brad, I guess."

"Is that smart?"

"Probably not for Brad, but Josh can handle himself for a minute or two." Kane's smile grew. "And you're changing the subject."

"No offense, Kane, but this isn't your business."

Kane leaned one arm against the wall. "Josh is my concern."

"He made his decision."

"He's an idiot."

Deana found her first real smile in days. "I'm not disagreeing."

"Are you really leaving Kauai today?"

"Yes." The temptation to hang around and see if Josh would come to her pulled at her. The only thing that stopped her was the idea of sitting alone in an empty hotel room staring at the phone. She refused to be that pathetic and needy.

It was time to go home. Her mother needed her. She owed Eric a return phone call. The poor guy sounded almost frantic in this afternoon's message. And she had to visit Ryan. The last one would be the hardest. Even though everyone insisted she now had closure, she was more confused than ever. Ryan had called collect twice. Both times she lifted the receiver thinking she'd tell him off. Instead, she refused the charges both times. Couldn't talk to him. Didn't want to. Understanding him would take a long time. Forgiving him was even harder to see.

But she was too tired to tackle that problem today. Seeing Josh again sucked the life out of her. That carefully built wall around her heart crumbled when he walked into that room. She missed him so much.

"Any chance I can convince you to stay?" Kane asked.

"None."

He nodded. "Fair enough."

She hit the elevator button again.

"Will you do me a favor?" he asked.

"Not if it has anything to do with me giving Eric a chance as a boyfriend."

Kane looked appalled at the idea. "What?"

"That was Josh's brilliant plan for my love life. He all but made the call to set our next date."

Kane muttered something about idiots with badges. "Man, he sucks at this."

The elevator bell dinged. This time Kane didn't try to stop her, so she stepped inside.

Kane stepped into the opening. "He'll come to his senses."

That was a promise she knew Kane couldn't keep. Josh did what he wanted when he wanted, and he didn't want her. She had the broken heart to prove it.

"Good-bye, Kane."

The elevator alarm started blaring.

Kane stepped back. "I'll see you soon, Deana."

Chapter Thirty-one

"May I make a suggestion?" They were the first words Kane spoke since leaving Brad's office. He had waited until they hit the parking lot to open his mouth.

Josh couldn't blame him. The meeting hadn't gone well. Then again, that wasn't a surprise. Josh knew Brad had some dumb trick in mind when he called the meeting. Josh expected to get drilled on old cases. He never thought he'd walk into the office and see Deana.

How the hell was he supposed to recover from that? Her pale skin and red eyes hinted at how tough the past two days since the press conference had been. Hell, she had even forgotten to pull her shirt up high and left the top two buttons undone.

Josh shrugged. "Go ahead."

"Get your head out of your ass." Kane stopped at the hood of his truck.

"Excuse me?"

"Head in ass. Remove it." Kane pointed to the body parts as he said them.

If the goal was to piss him off, Kane was doing a good

job. Josh almost welcomed the rush of anger. He hadn't felt anything but empty for two days, the exact number since he had seen Deana.

"Anything else?" he asked in a tone that suggested there better not be.

"I have more."

"May as well say it."

"Fine. Get on a plane, go to Oahu, and beg her to forgive you."

If only life were that simple. "Are you done?"

"I'm sure I can think of a few others things you can do. Places you can go."

"I was thinking the same thing." Josh tried to open the passenger door but Kane used the remote to lock it.

"I'm not ready to leave."

Josh turned around and faced Kane. Let his friend see he was not in the mood for this right now. Or ever. "What the hell is wrong with you?"

"I thought this one would be obvious, but never tell the woman you love to go date another guy." Kane threw up his hands. "Jesus, Josh. What the hell is wrong with you? You told her to go back to Eric? Why?"

Hearing Deana's name linked to Eric's made Josh's stomach roll. He was the one who put it out there because, deep down, he knew she belonged with Eric. That didn't mean he ever wanted to see it or hear about it.

"How do you know about that?" Josh asked.

Kane smiled. "I notice you didn't deny the love part."

Didn't because he couldn't without lying his ass off. "I'm not getting into this with you."

"Yes, you are."

Josh tried the door again, but it was still locked. "Unlock the fucking door or I'll walk home."

"You're nowhere near your house, so give it up."

"Fine." Josh jumped on the truck's hood. "Say whatever you have to say."

"First, get off my truck." Kane pointed to the ground. And he wasn't kidding. To him the truck was sacred.

"You're a pain in the ass about this truck." Josh mumbled.

"I'll remember that the next time I want to kick your Mustang."

"Touch it and die." Josh slid off the truck.

"Exactly. Now, on the issue of Deana."

Josh held up a hand as if that would somehow stop the conversation. He understood what Kane was trying to do, but this was killing him. Josh didn't need a lecture. He needed space.

When a guy went hours without sleep and saw a woman's face every time he closed his eyes, he was in trouble. Josh passed that point a day ago. He could hear her voice, smell her, remember some of the things she said and start to smile. Despite all of his vows to remain neutral to her, he wasn't. He had fallen stupid in love with her.

"I don't want to talk about her." He muttered the comment under his breath because he was too exhausted to do anything else.

"Like I give a shit about your feelings on this."

"Kane—"

"What are you doing?"

Josh exhaled nice and loud. "Trying to get home."

"You know what I'm talking about. Why are you here and not there with her?"

In his weaker moments, Josh wondered the same thing. "I did my job. It's over."

The word sliced through him. This doing-what's-right thing was cutting him from the inside out.

"Sell that to someone who doesn't know you."

"I don't want to talk about her."

Kane's mouth flattened. The fire behind his eyes banked. "Because it hurts?"

"No."

"Josh, come on. I've been there."

Josh thought back to the beginning of Kane's relationship with Annie. The poor bastard had been hooked from the start. This was different. He and Deana started out in very different places. He now knew she was not the ice queen she pretended to be. That didn't make them right for each other.

"I'm not you. This won't work," Josh said.

"Because she has money?" Kane looked as if he were ready to yell. "Let that shit from your past go."

"This isn't about that."

"Of course it is."

"Deana took in an old Chinese woman who needed a place to stay. She fought for Ryan when no one else would. She tolerates the idiot crowd on Hawaii just so she can raise money for good causes. She stood up to Brad."

"Since when do you know so much about her?"

A slight blush stained Kane's cheeks. "The usual way."

The invasion into Deana's privacy ticked Josh off. If anyone other than him could track down the information on her accident, it would be Kane. For some reason, Josh didn't want that getting out. "You investigated her?"

"I checked her out. There's a difference."

"Not really."

"I wanted to know what you were dealing with."

After all those hours of being numb, a new emotion churned through Josh. Frustration. "Not okay."

"Yeah, that's what Annie said." Kane shook his head. "But I don't care what either of you think on this. That kiss I witnessed on the porch that night was not one-night-stand action. I had to check on Deana after that."

"And?"

"There are holes, but we all have holes." Kane shrugged as if it didn't matter.

Josh sensed his friend knew more than he was telling. He was an observant guy. He had to have noticed the beginnings of Deana's scars peeking out from under her blouse. But whatever Kane knew, he wasn't sharing it.

Kane was protecting him. The realization blew the frustration away, taking the anger along with it.

Josh decided Kane deserved the truth in return. "The last man who delivered bad news to Deana about Ryan got the boot. She dated Eric for a year and now can't stand to look at him."

"Why?" Kane asked.

"What do you mean, why? I just told you."

"You added one and two and got sixteen."

Josh reached for his pen in his shirt pocket and realized he didn't even have a pocket. "I'm not in the mood for math."

"But you are in the mood for a cigarette. Happens every time you get in a tough situation."

"I quit years ago."

"And now you're addicted to pens."

Exhaustion swept through Josh a second time. "Can we go now?"

"Did you ever bother to ask Deana what happened with Eric?"

"I'm guessing that means you're still not going to open the door." Josh tried it just to make sure. Still locked.

"Good observation."

"Then, no," Josh said. "I didn't ask her because it's obvious."

Kane made a sound somewhere between a growl and groan. "You're an idiot."

"Eric filled in the blanks."

"The same Eric she dumped?" Kane took a step closer and put his hand on Josh's shoulder. "Look, I get that you're running. I get that she's not who you thought you'd end up with."

"So, we're done here."

"I also know that you love her."

Something deep inside him, buried under his heart and soul, rushed to the surface. "You wanna know the truth, Kane? She deserves better."

"That's not true. There's no one better."

That one comment stopped whatever had begun whipping around inside him. It humbled Josh. "Kane, I—"

"Go to her. Ask her whatever you need to ask and then ask yourself if you can live every day here knowing she might be with someone else. It will eat you alive, Josh."

Bile rushed up the back of his throat, but Josh swallowed it back. "It's not that simple."

"You're making it hard." Kane squeezed Josh's shoulder and then let go. "You're sure she's going to say no or tell you to go to hell. Rather than guessing, find out the truth about how she feels and what she wants."

"The truth is going to suck."

Kane nodded in Josh's direction. "Look at you, is what you're feeling now any better?"

Josh looked down at his untied sneakers and frayed jeans. Maybe it was that simple.

Chapter Thirty-two

"I didn't expect to see you again," Georgianna said as she opened Deana's door to Josh's knocking.

"The feeling is mutual." Josh glanced past the older woman in search of the younger version. "Is she here?"

"Deana?"

"It is her house."

"Is sarcasm the way you want to play this, Mr. Windsor?"

He wasn't sure he wanted to wade into this area at all. If not for Kane's meddling and the hole the size of Canada in his chest, Josh knew he would be back at his condo or over at Derek's house right now.

But staying away proved impossible. Kane planted the seed of doubt in Josh's head. Here he thought he was doing the right thing by pushing Deana to Eric. Maybe . . . well, he didn't know what the answer to the maybe was, but he was here. Desperate and uncertain but in love. Stomp-on-your-heart, steal-your-sleep-and-your-sanity love.

"Why did you come by today?" Georgianna asked. "Do you need the whiteboard back?"

Score one for the older woman with the sharp tongue. "No."

"I see." But she didn't move.

For a small woman, Deana's mother could certainly throw her weight around. She somehow made her petite frame take up the full doorway. Unless he planned to knock her over, Josh was stuck standing there, which he guessed was exactly her point.

"I need to talk with your daughter."

"I believe you've been quite clear in your comments so far."

He had no idea what the hell that meant. "Can I see her?"

"Maybe it would be better to continue any additional conversation through the mail. Maybe you could write a note on your bill."

He felt the wallop as sure as if she had kicked him. "This is personal."

"I will not allow you in if you plan to berate her."

As if it was even her house. "Why would I do that?"

"You didn't exactly show yourself to be chivalrous the last time you were here."

The comment came from out of nowhere. Josh struggled to remember what he had said other than the truth. "You both needed to know what really happened that night. It was my hope having the information might help the healing process."

She waved her hand in front of her face. "I'm not referring to that. I'm talking about the delivery."

"What?"

"Not what you said. How you said it."

Josh knew what the word meant, but he never considered that to be an issue. He had wanted to get the words out and then leave before Deana started throwing her weight around and blaming him for the press conference. "I still don't see your point."

"Most men would be more compassionate when delivering terrible news to the women with whom they were living."

Shit.

"Do you understand now, Mr. Windsor?"

"I stayed in the guesthouse," he mumbled, trying to figure out how he had messed up this badly.

"Not at night."

The shocks just kept coming. "Deana told you that?"

"I have been around long enough to know when my daughter is involved with someone."

"Involved?" Such a tame word for what they had.

"You can't be this simple, Mr. Windsor."

"Apparently I can."

Her eyebrow arched. "Do you dance?"

She had lost him totally that time. "Excuse me?"

"Can you dance? Ballroom, anything?"

"No."

A look of satisfaction crossed Georgianna's lips. "Deana is out by the pool."

"Alone?"

"Who else would be here?" Georgianna traded positions with him, leaving him standing inside and not knowing how he got there. "And Josh?"

Hearing her use his first name made him suspicious. "Yeah?"

"You should smile more."

He had walked into an asylum. He glanced around and discovered it was an empty asylum. Looking through the family room, he could see Deana sitting by the pool. She wore a one-piece suit and what looked like a scarf around her waist. Her hair whipped around in the breeze as she watched the water.

She was so damn beautiful it hurt to look at her.

Seeing her here he knew he could never let her go. Money or not, power or not, he loved her. He wasn't good enough for her, didn't deserve her, but that didn't matter. The idea of any other man touching her burned a hole through his stomach.

The job didn't matter without her. Nothing did. How had he been so damn dumb not to see that? Kane said it would be simple. Josh never expected it would be as clear as looking at her again and knowing.

Now he had to convince her.

Deana knew he was in the house. She felt his presence the moment her mother opened the door. Deana picked up bits and pieces of the conversation, but had no idea what was happening in there, which scared the hell out of her.

Mother was in a feisty mood, clearly unhappy it had taken Josh this long to come to the house. Deana never thought he would come at all. Despite her mother's predictions to the contrary, he was there, walking across her family room and opening the door.

She had to blink a few times as she watched him come out on the deck to make sure the moment was real. "What are you doing here?"

The butterflies buzzing in her stomach refused to die down. Either the sun or seeing his face made her dizzy. He wasn't smiling. Tension pulled at his mouth. Dark circles colored the area under his crystal-blue eyes. Those strong shoulders slumped and the polo shirt hung from him as if he had lost weight in only a few short days.

And he had never looked more handsome.

"I was talking with your mom about dancing," he said.

Deana groaned on the inside. "It's just a stupid theory."

"What theory?"

"What?"

His eyes narrowed. "She asked if I could dance."

Relief soared through Deana. Her mother had not embarrassed her. She had only harassed Josh.

"And you said?" Deana asked.

"No." Josh took the seat next to her and laid his palm on the table beside hers. "Is the question code for something?"

"Sort of."

"Hmmm."

Looked as if she was going to have to lead the conversation. She hoped it ended up where she wanted to go. "You didn't tell me why you came today."

Even as she dared to hope, she fought back the pending happiness. He could have stopped by to pick up his notes or deliver his bill. There were any number of awful business-like purposes that could have brought him to her doorstep.

And if he mentioned one of them he was going into the pool headfirst.

"I grew up without money." That was it. He said the words and then let them sit there.

Deana didn't know what to say.

"No money." Josh stared at his hands. "Like 'my mom turned tricks to pay for food' kind of no money."

Sadness washed over Deana. She closed her eyes and mourned the scared little boy he once was and said a prayer of thanks for the fine man he had become. "Josh."

"The military was a way out and the only chance for an education, so I took it."

She moved her hand until it touched his.

He stopped flexing his fingers the second she got closer. "That led to the DEA and who I am today."

"I like who you are today."

"You're right. I rescue people for a living. It's ingrained in me." He took her hand then. Folded his fingers over hers.

The touch sparked her body to life. "And you balk when someone tries to do the same for you."

"I'm not used to depending on people." He finally looked up again. "That little kid inside never goes away. That reflex to fight against people with power and to assume folks with money don't appreciate it or deserve it is hard to kick."

Everything opened in front of her. It was all so clear now. Every time she pushed or mentioned payment, she verbally poked him, touching on the one thing sure to make him push her away. She reminded him again and again that she stood for everything he hated. "Ryan's actions certainly don't help how you feel."

"He's not you. I don't put that on you." Josh's intense gaze drilled into her as if he were willing her to believe him.

She did, but she also knew he had jumped to so many conclusions that his knees should hurt. They weren't perfect, as anyone who read a newspaper could see, but they weren't soulless monsters, either. She didn't live the life he thought she did. The house had nothing to do with money and everything to with having a place that reflected the peace she chased for so long.

If they stood any chance of being together, she needed him to understand and accept her for who she was. "You think my family spends its time at the country club picking out suitable mates to breed the next generation."

"I never said that."

It was an exaggeration, but the analogy made her point.

"My dad didn't come from money. Kalanie came from even less. My parents loved each other. I never doubted that. Never had a chance to since it was right there and plain to see when I was growing up. It was the same way with Chace and Kalanie. It's part of the reason losing them so early hurts as much as it does."

"I don't doubt their love for each other."

"But you are selling it short. You are seeing the checkbooks and ignoring everything else."

Josh opened his mouth twice and closed it again before speaking. "Possibly."

Hope bloomed inside Deana. If they could both separate out the money from the rest, they had a chance. "They had relationships based on feelings and respect, love, and commitment. Money was a bonus but not the basis."

Josh turned her hand over between his palms. "Eric . . ."

"Is the wrong man for me." She knew that down to her toes. She had not spent one second thinking of Eric since she met Josh.

"You pushed him away because of Ryan," Josh said.

Deana sighed at all of the wrong assumptions between them. "You're only half right. Eric and I never would have worked. My accident was always going to be a secret between us. I never felt comfortable telling him."

"He would have understood."

"He is looking at a lifetime of campaigns and political maneuvering. I was a liability." She drew Josh's hand to her face and ran the back down her cheek. "And it was a life I didn't want."

"What do you want?"

"My answer hasn't changed."

Josh dragged his thumb across her bottom lip. "Which is?"

"You."

He closed his eyes. "You could do so much better."

"I don't agree."

When he opened his eyes again, they were clear. No sadness. No doubt.

He loved her. She could see it written on every inch of his face. That softness around his eyes and slight lift to his mouth spelled love. She knew because she saw those same emotions in the mirror every morning. Even through all the sadness and pain, she loved him.

And he loved her back. Joy flowed through her. A weightlessness she hadn't felt since before Chace died spilled through her.

"There's so much baggage between us," he said.

She refused to let him throw another wall in their path. "Kiss me."

"I—"

She didn't wait for him to make the move. She leaned in and took his mouth in what she thought would be a gentle touch. But cool and detached never worked for her. Within seconds the kiss turned hot.

It was as if a dam broke inside him and all the emotions came pouring out. He held her face in his hands and his mouth passed over hers. In between he mumbled words and promises.

She lifted her head and tried to calm the thumping in her heart. "What did you say?"

"I love you." He trailed his fingers across her jaw. "Simple words, but they do the job."

"You love me." She repeated the words, relishing in the sound and taste of them.

"I think I started falling when you walked up to me all

buttoned up and snotty in the courthouse." He kissed her again.

"Remind me to save that outfit."

"I was stupid and insensitive and scared to death."

"Mr. DEA Agent was afraid of something?"

He grew serious. "Of losing you. Of getting so close that I wouldn't be able to walk away from you again."

"But you did."

"Not in my head. Not in my heart."

She melted right then. "Josh."

"The feeling never went away, Deana. No matter how much I tried to push it out and forget you, I couldn't. I'll never be able to live without you."

"I love you."

He swore. "About time. I thought you were going to make me work for it."

"I thought about it." She wrapped her arms around his neck. "Decided to put you out of your misery."

"Then never leave me."

All of the pain washed away. "Never."

He hugged her close with his chin on the top of her head. "What are we going to do about Ryan?"

Her mind went blank. "I don't know."

"Your mother?"

That one was easy. "She likes you."

Josh snorted. "You've got to be kidding."

"I'll explain about the dancing later."

"My point is that we have a lot to navigate. Ryan and then there's my job—"

She lifted her head and kissed his chin. "Don't forget your issues with money."

"Yeah, all of that."

"Then we'll figure it out together."

He winked at her. "I'm going to hold you to that."

"I'm counting on that, babe."

And she was counting on him. Forever.

If you liked this book, try Jami Alden's
UNLEASHED,
out this month from Brava . . .

He did a double, then a triple take.

No fucking way.

His breath caught and his nostrils flared as he took her in. He knew the thick black waves spilling to her waist, the mouthwatering curves elegantly draped in black wool. Her dress went from neck to wrist to knee and should have been modest, but only served to highlight the lush swell of her breasts, the deep curve of her waist, the sexy flare of her hips. The heels of her black pumps tap tapped their way down the concrete steps and headed in his direction.

He dragged his gaze up to her face. Her luscious mouth was painted red and set in determined lines. Even though the sun was hidden behind a thick layer of clouds, like him she wore sunglasses, her oversize frames hiding half her face. As though, like him, she didn't want to chance anyone getting a peek into her soul.

Caroline fucking Palomares.

No, he reminded himself. Caroline fucking Medford.

Raw emotion spun up inside him, threatening to take him

down. Lust. Anger. And a bunch of other crap he wouldn't touch with a ten-foot pole.

As she strode toward him, shoulders back, hips swinging like she had every right to be walking back into his life, today of all days, he struggled to put the lid back on the swirl of emotion struggling to break free. He reminded himself savagely of who she was. Caroline *Medford*.

Wife of James Medford, rich attorney twenty years her senior. The same James Medford who could give her the affluent lifestyle he hadn't realized she coveted until it was too late.

The same James Medford she may very well have killed to keep herself in fast cars and high fashion.

She was not the seventeen-year-old who'd promised she'd never leave him when she gave him her virginity. She was not the twenty-year-old who'd sobbed when he'd announced his plans to join the Special Forces after he graduated from West Point. She wasn't even the twenty-two-year-old who'd told him to fuck off one final time before walking out on him without another word.

As she drew closer he focused on those differences. She was thinner, for one, he noticed as she got closer. And older, her mouth bracketed by fine lines that came from stress and age. Not to mention the wardrobe. He bet her outfit topped out at over a grand, even more if you counted the purse. A far cry from the wardrobe of a girl from a working-class neighborhood who shopped at discount stores and went to private school on scholarship.

She was nothing like the girl he'd known, and he was nothing like the dumb kid who'd entertained romantic illusions like true love and happily ever after.

He took of his glasses, feeling a smile curl his lips for the first time in several days as she stumbled a little.

She was off center. Just the way he liked it. And he was in perfect control. Because Caroline Medford meant nothing to him.

And don't miss Brava's Christmas anthology,
KISSING SANTA CLAUS,
featuring Donna Kauffman, Jill Shalvis, and
HelenKay Dimon, out this month.

Turn the page for a preview from Donna's story,
"Lock, Stock, and Jingle Bells."

"It's been a long day, and there's a lot to do." Holly lifted the bag. "Thank you for this, it was very thoughtful."

"If there's anything else I can do to help—"

"You've already gone above and beyond the call of duty here."

"Like I said, it's what I do, and I saw the light on." Sean tried a smile. "I also make a good listener. Family my size, you learn early. It can't be easy, leaving England, coming back to your hometown, taking over the business."

She held the bag a little closer to her chest, like a shield, but didn't say anything.

"If it helps, I know a little something about that."

She dipped her chin, and he found himself reaching out to tip it back up again. "Hey, I didn't say that to make you feel bad. But I do know about having plans derailed and a life you never thought you'd end up with being dumped in your lap."

She stared into his eyes and for the first time he felt he was really looking at Holly Bennett.

"You probably think I'm being a bit of a spoiled brat,"

she said. "I mean, you came home because of an unspeakable tragedy, while my parents just retired. Which, at their age—"

"Yes, but most parents don't retire and head off to a new life and dump their old life on their only child."

She tilted her head slightly. "I thought you and my parents were friends."

"We are. I love your folks. But that doesn't mean I automatically vouch for all their decisions."

"Did you regret coming back to run your family restaurant? You seem—"

"Happy? I am. Very. And I didn't necessarily expect to be. Turned out that all my training has benefited me just as much, if not more, in taking over Gallagher's as it would have if I'd gone off on my own in D.C. like I planned. But I was lucky. I was already heading in a direction very similar to my folks, and their folks before them. It was more a detour down the same path, than a whole new journey."

"If you had come back and hadn't been happy . . . would you have stayed anyway?"

"I don't know. I have the benefit of coming from a very large family. So, it's possible I'd have trained one of them, or a handful of them, to take over, and I'd have gone back to my original plan of opening a more upscale establishment. They'd have only been a few hours apart, so it's possible I could have run one, and overseen the management of the other."

"Why didn't you go ahead and do that anyway? Have your cake, and all that?"

He smiled easily. "Because I am happy here. I learned why it was that generations of Gallaghers have cooked and run restaurants, here and in Ireland. It suits me . . . perhaps more than that other world ever would have. And I still have the training. It's affected the menu here and there. I get to play a little with things that interest me. So I think I am having my cake."

She nodded, then fell silent again, apparently lost in thought.

"You know," he said, at length, "you didn't follow in your parents' footsteps, in terms of being a shopkeeper, or even in the antiques business, right? Your mom said you are an artist."

"I'm in advertising."

Sean knew that, but he also knew that, according to her mom, anyway, it was just what paid the bills. Art was her passion. "No one is going to fault you if you decide this isn't for you. Your mom—"

"Says she'd be fine with whatever my decision is."

"Well, then . . . ?"

Holly sighed lightly. "That's what she says. But it's not how I feel. Now that I'm here. I know what this meant to her. If she was truly okay with dismantling it, she'd have done so."

"There's a difference between being okay with it no longer being here . . . and quite another to be the one in charge of taking a beloved possession apart, piece by piece. Maybe she simply didn't have it in her, and knew that you being not so emotionally attached, might find that easier. I'm not trying to overstep here, but . . . it's your legacy to do with as you please, right? Maybe you should just think of it that way. It could be something you find you enjoy . . . or the sale of it could provide you with the nest egg to pursue your own dreams. Don't you think your parents would be happy with either outcome?"

She held his gaze for the longest time. "What I think is that I wish I could have this conversation as easily with them as I'm having it with you."

He smiled. "I know they're your parents, and nobody knows them better than you do. But if you want an outside friend's opinion—"

"I think I already have it." She smiled then. "And it's appreciated. More than you know."

"Anytime."

Time spun out and neither of them moved. Or stoppped smiling.

Maybe it was the late hour, maybe it was the sense of intimacy created by standing in the darkened shop, or the connection he felt they shared, lives being abruptly changed, or simply a childhood of separate, but shared memories of growing up in the same town, surrounded by the same things, the same people. Whatever it was, he found himself shifting a step closer. She didn't move away. And all he could think as he slowly dipped his head toward hers, was why had it taken half of his life to finally work up the nerve to kiss Holly Bennett.

Be on the lookout for
THE MANE SQUEEZE from Shelly Laurenston,
coming next month from Brava . . .

The salmon were everywhere, leaping from the water and right into the open maws of bears. But he ruled this piece of territory and those salmon were for him and him alone. He opened his mouth and a ten-pound one leaped right into it. Closing his jaws, he sighed in pleasure. Honey-covered. He loved honey-covered salmon!

This was his perfect world. A cold river, happy-to-die-for-his-survival salmon, and honey. Lots and lots of honey . . .

What could ever be better? What could ever live up to this? Nothing. Absolutely nothing.

A salmon swam up to him. He had no interest, he was still working on the honey-covered one. The salmon stared at him intently . . . almost glaring.

"Hey!" it called out. "Hey! Can you hear me?"

Why was this salmon ruining his meal? He should kill it and save it for later. Or toss it to one of the females with cubs. Anything to get this obviously Philadelphia salmon to shut the hell up!

"Answer me!" the salmon ordered loudly. "Open your eyes and answer me! *Now!*"

His eyes were open, weren't they?

Apparently not because someone pried his lids apart and stared into his face. And wow, was she gorgeous?

"Can you hear me? He didn't answer, he was too busy staring at her. So pretty!

"Come on, Paddington. Answer me."

He instinctively snarled at the nickname and she smiled in relief. "What's the matter?" she teased. "You don't like Paddington? Such a cute, cuddily, widdle bear."

"Nothing's wrong with cute pet names . . . Mr. Mittens."

She straightened, her hands on her hips and those long, expertly manicured nails drumming restlessly against those narrow hips.

"Mister?" she snapped.

"Paddington?" he shot back.

She gave a little snort. "Okay. Fair enough. But call me Gwen. I never did get a chance to tell you my name at the wedding."

Oh! He remembered her now. The feline he'd found himself day dreaming about on more than one occasion in the two months since Jess's wedding. And . . . wow. She was naked. She looked really good naked . . .

He blinked, knowing that he was staring at that beautiful, strong body. *Focus on something else! Anything else! You're going to creep her out!*

"You have tattoos," he blurted. Bracelet tatts surrounded both her biceps. A combination of black shamrocks and a dark-green Chinese symbol he didn't know the meaning of. And on her right hip she had a black Chinese dragon holding a Celtic cross in its mouth. It was beautiful work. Intricate. "Are they new?"

"Nah. I just covered up the ones on my arms with makeup, for the wedding. With my mother, I'd be noticed enough. Didn't want to add to that." She gestured at him with her hand. "Now we know I'm Gwen and I have tattoos . . . so do you have a name?"

"Yeah, sure. I'm . . ." He glanced off, racking his brain.

"You don't remember your name?" she asked, her eyes wide.

"I know it has something to do with security." He stared at her thoughtfully, then snapped his fingers. "Lock."

"Lock? Your name is Lock?"

"I think. Lock. Lock . . . Lachlan! MacRyrie!" He glanced off again. "I think."

"Christ."

"No need to get snippy. It's *my* name I can't remember." He nodded. "I'm pretty positive it's Lock . . . something."

"MacRyrie."

"Okay."

She gave a small, frustrated growl and placed the palms of her hands against her eyes. He stared at her painted nails. "Are those the team colors of the Philadelphia Flyers?"

"Don't start," she snapped.

"Again with the snippy? I was only asking."

Lock slowly push himself up a bit, noticing for the first time that they'd traveled to a much more shallow part of the river. The water barely came to his waist. She started to say something, but shook her head and looked away. He didn't mind. He didn't need conversation at the moment, he needed to figure out where he was.

A river, that's where he was. Unfortunately, not his dream river. The one with the honey-covered salmon that willingly leaped into his mouth. A disappointing realization—it always felt so real until he woke up—but he was still happy that he'd survived the fall.

Lock used his arms to push himself up all the way so he could sit.

"Be careful," she finally said. "We fell from up there."

He looked at where she pointed, ignoring how much pain the slight move caused, and flinched when he saw how far down they were.

"Although we were farther up river, I think."

"Damn," he muttered, rubbing the back of his neck.

"How bad is it?"

"It'll be fine." Closing his eyes, Lock bent his head to one side, then the other. The sound of cracking bones echoed and when he opened his eyes, he saw that pretty face cringing.

"See?" he said. "Better already."

"If you say so."

She took several awkward steps back so she could sit down on a large boulder.

"You're hurt," he informed her.

"Yeah. I am." She extended her leg, resting it on a small-boulder in front of her and let out a breath, her eyes shutting. "I know it's healing, but, fuck, it hurts."

"Let me see." Lock got to his feet, ignoring the aches and pains he felt throughout his body. By the time he made it over to her, she opened her eyes and blinked wide, leaning back.

"Hey, hey! Get that thing out of my face!"

His cock was right *there*, now wasn't it? He knelt down on one knee in front of her and said, "This is the best I can manage at the moment. I don't exactly have the time to run off and kill an animal for its hide."

"Fine," she muttered. "Just watch where you're swinging that thing. You're liable to break my nose."

Focusing on her leg to keep from appearing way too

proud at that statement, he grasped her foot and lifted, keeping his movements slow and his fingers gentle. He didn't allow himself to wince when he saw the damage. It was bad, and she was losing blood. Probably more blood than she realized. "I didn't do this, did I?"

"No. I got this from that she-bitch." She leaned over, trying to get a better look. "Do I have any calf muscle left?"

He wasn't going to answer that. At least not honestly. Instead he gave her his best "reassuring" expression and calmly said, "Let's get you to a hospital."

Her body jerked straight and those pretty eyes blinked rapidly. "No."

That wasn't the response he expected. Panic, perhaps. Or, "My God. Is it that bad?" But instead she said "no." And she said it with some serious finality. In the same way he'd imagine she would respond to the suggestion of cutting off her leg with a steak knife.

"It's not a big deal. But you don't want an infection. I'll take you up the embankment, get us some clothes—" if she didn't pass out from blood loss first "—and then get you to the Macon River Health Center. It's equipped for us."

"No."

"I've had to go there a couple of times. It's really clean, the staff is great, and the doctors are always the best."

"No."

She wasn't being difficult to simply be difficult, was she?

Resting his forearm on his knee, Lock stared at her. "You're not kidding, are you?"

"No."

"Is there a reason you don't want to go to the hospital?" And he really hoped it wasn't something ridiculous like she used to date one of the doctors and didn't want to see him, or something equally as lame.

"Of course there is. People go there to die."

Oh, boy. Ridiculous but hardly lame. "Or . . . people go there to get better."

"No."

"Look, Mr. Mittens—"

"Don't call me that."

"—I'm trying to help you here. So you can do this the easy way, or you can do this the hard way. Your choice."

She shrugged and brought her good foot down right on his nuts.